Beloved LADY MISTRESS

D Jordan Redhawk

Bella
BOOKS
2012

Copyright © 2012 by D Jordan Redhawk

Bella Books, Inc.
P.O. Box 10543
Tallahassee, FL 32302

All rights reserved. No part of this book may be reproduced or transmitted in any form or by any means, electronic or mechanical, including photocopying, without permission in writing from the publisher.

Printed in the United States of America on acid-free paper
First published 2012

Editor: Katherine V. Forrest
Cover Designer: Linda Callaghan

ISBN 13: 978-1-59493-294-6

PUBLISHER'S NOTE
The scanning, uploading, and distribution of this book via the Internet or via any other means without the permission of the publisher is illegal and punishable by law. Please purchase only authorized electronic editions, and do not participate in or encourage electronic piracy of copyrighted materials. Your support of the author's rights is appreciated.

Other Bella Books by D Jordan Redhawk

The Strange Path

Dedication

Anna Trinity Redhawk—First you helped me find myself. Then you helped me love myself.

Thank you.

Acknowledgments

Roll call for all the individuals who helped me get this book into the world cannot be complete without the following names:

Janet Redhawk, Agatha Tutko, Carol Dickerson, Teresa Crittenden, Jean Rosestar and Jaq Hills—thanks for being sounding boards and giving me your unadulterated critiques. I might not have enjoyed some of them, but it wasn't because they were wrong. (Grin.)

Anita Pawlowski, Shawn Cady and Anna Redhawk—I appreciate your sticking it out through multiple versions that came into being over the years. I couldn't have done it without the in-depth discussions we had.

Karin Kallmaker, Katherine V. Forrest, Jessica and Linda Callaghan—Bella Books puts out a wonderful product, and I think it's because of the winning team you women have created. Thanks for taking a chance on me.

CHAPTER ONE

"What do you mean she's not here?" Margaurethe O'Toole glared at the Human woman who'd had the misfortune of answering the door. Around the two of them stood Margaurethe's personal guard, a half dozen tense Sanguire in dark suits, bristling with potential danger.

The young security guard swallowed, the sound audible to the visitors' advanced senses. "I'm sorry, ma'am. We weren't informed of your arrival today, so she and her friends went out for the evening."

Margaurethe had to give the woman credit. Despite the number of menacing Sanguire and the obvious anger directed at her, the hapless Human displayed no fear though the small foyer reeked of the scent. *But a Human security company? Whatever is Dorst thinking? How can he possibly believe that a Human can protect the future* Ninsumgal? "Where has she gone?"

Another swallow. "For security reasons I'm not allowed to say."

Margaurethe loomed closer to the woman. "You very much can say," she advised in a voice rich with threat. "And if you do not, I'll see you terminated." She left open for speculation whether she meant the security officer's job or life.

They locked stares for a moment before the woman broke away. "Excuse me. I need to contact my supervisor."

Smiling, Margaurethe became the epitome of grace. "Of course." She watched the woman move into the living area, and pull a cell phone from her pocket. Turning slightly, Margaurethe ordered one of her guards to have her belongings brought in from the car. As he relayed the order via a discreet radio, she glanced around the foyer, finding nothing to attract her interest. When the Human returned, she gave the woman her polite attention.

"Father Castillo wishes to convey his regret that he wasn't here to greet you, ma'am. He and Whiskey are at Club Express downtown. I'm to give you directions."

Margaurethe dipped her head, refusing to display her distaste for the young woman's use of Ms. Davis's nickname. "Thank you."

A commotion at the door distracted her. She turned to see her driver setting several pieces of luggage on the floor. "Give the directions to Phineas, and see that my things are taken to my room." She left the woman no avenue to naysay her commands. Something Margaurethe had learned early in her days as *Ki'an Gasan* was how imperative it was to act like one expected all servants to follow one's orders. Confidence was key to political power.

As proof, the woman opened her mouth, and then snapped it closed. No doubt, she had decided to call this Castillo person back once they were away. "Of course, ma'am. I'll take care of it."

While Phineas received instructions, Margaurethe pulled aside the captain of her guard. "I want you to remain here. See that my things are settled, and have a look around. Do you want anyone to remain with you?"

"I'll keep one, *Ki'an Gasan*," he said, indicating a burly guard. "Do you want me to call in reinforcements?"

"Not yet, I think. Let's see the lay of the land first."

He nodded, and stepped away to speak to his lieutenant.

Phineas, a lanky young man who looked barely seventeen, came to her side. "Begging your ladyship's pardon," he said, a puckish grin on his face. "If you're ready to go, I've got the way to our destination."

Despite her concern, Margaurethe grinned at him. "When are you going to move past your backcountry upbringing, and address me with my proper title?"

He held the door open for her, and two guards slipped out first. "Aw, cuz, what would be the fun in that? You'll get airs, you will. This way you'll forever be reminded of your lowborn roots."

Margaurethe shook her head at his impertinent tone, and preceded him out of the house.

***

It had been four months since the secretive assassin, Reynhard Dorst, had shown up in Margaurethe's private office with news of Elisibet's return, four months of cautious logistical and financial planning on Margaurethe's part. He'd reported that the traitorous Valmont had been sniffing around in Seattle, so the *Agrun Nam* must have heard rumors. This Jenna Davis needed to be protected at all costs until her position was secured. To that end, Margaurethe had demanded Dorst remove Ms. Davis to a safer location. Valmont had been the cause of Elisibet's demise; history could not repeat itself. She'd been sorely disappointed. Rather than cart Davis across country, Dorst had settled her a mere four hours away in Portland, Oregon. Since then, he'd refused to answer Margaurethe's missives demanding explanation, frustrating her no end.

Margaurethe had used her vexation to create several dummy corporations, and funneled money into their coffers. That money then created a trust fund for one Jenna Davis, the reins of which were in Margaurethe's capable hands. After the distributing corporations had been dismantled, several limited liability companies had been created, each one "owning" various pieces of property—the house Margaurethe had just left, for one, and several vehicles of assorted makes and models. Those companies belonged to a single holding company under the control of the trust fund. Margaurethe felt certain that the convoluted business path would keep the *Agrun Nam* and their lackeys from discovering anything of vital importance for a long while yet.

Margaurethe stared out the water-streaked window of the Town Car as Phineas traversed the rainy Portland streets. A lump of nerves churned her stomach, almost making her regret the *kizarus* she had refused to feed from on board the private jet. She had been too agitated then, she recalled ruefully. Had she partaken of a little fresh blood, she would not be out of sorts now.

In an attempt to keep her mind off the pending meeting, she ticked off the tasks that needed doing over the coming days. The first was to sack the security company Dorst had hired. She had brought enough of her personal guard to take over that particular duty, and more personnel would be arriving from Europe within the week. Once she had the chance to assess the household staff here, she would know who else to bring over the pond. Additionally, she wanted to begin scouring the city for a likely building. The Pacific Northwest of the United States was as good an area as any to set up a permanent base for the fledgling *ninsumgal*, despite the dangers, international politics be damned.

In that instant, Margaurethe saw Elisibet in her mind. The sight brought her a mixture of emotion that threatened to drown her—love and adoration, deep regret, and the long familiar sorrow that had colored her world for almost four centuries.

They had been together for over two hundred years when Elisibet had been murdered by her closest friend and confidant, Valmont. Two hundred tumultuous years of bloody war with those Humans who had tried to stamp the Sanguire race out of existence, two hundred years of barbarisms on both sides. Elisibet had been known as a tyrant by her own people, her merciless rule equaling that of Vlad Dracule, and lasting five times as long.

Most could not fathom the root of Margaurethe's love for Elisibet. It was assumed Margaurethe's naiveté was the sole cause. She had been a mere twenty years old to Elisibet's two centuries when they had met. Perhaps naiveté had been the initial case. Sanguire rarely left the confines of their homes until they were in their fifties. Margaurethe had pestered her parents incessantly to be brought to court for the Harvest Ball to celebrate her newfound adulthood. They eventually succumbed to her wheedling, suffering eternal horror when their supreme ruler debauched their daughter. The O'Tooles had demanded satisfaction for Elisibet's scurrilous actions, possibly assuming they would receive lands or monetary value in return for ruining the poor girl. No one was more surprised than Margaurethe when Elisibet offered her a place in court, lands, and the title *Ki'an Gasan*.

Naiveté could not explain the deepening emotion Margaurethe had held for her lover. She had been drawn to Elisibet from the beginning, yes. Beautiful, cold, powerful—the woman was the epitome of magnetism, appearing casual and calm even as she ordered others to their deaths. Once past the first blush of romance, Elisibet had shown a vulnerable side of herself to Margaurethe that she had revealed to no one else. In conversations with others who had graced the tyrant's bed over the years, Margaurethe discovered she had been the only one who had experienced such trust. It was an astounding gift that Margaurethe vowed never to abuse, even if it meant turning her back on a multitude of reprehensible activities in which Elisibet was involved. With the clarity of hindsight four centuries past, Margaurethe knew that this had been her fatal error.

One she was not going to repeat.

CHAPTER TWO

Margaurethe took Phineas's hand as he helped her out of the vehicle. The rain had stopped, leaving a clean scent in the air. The seedy street held few cars, testament to the fact that it was a Sunday night. Apparently the club in question did not do much business on a day when one's soul gained precedence over one's baser instincts. A large oval of etched steel held the street number but no name, and every window was blacked out. The only indication she was in the correct location was the throbbing bass music rumbling under her feet.

"Doesn't look like much, cuz, does it?"

Scanning up and down the street, Margaurethe noted two vagrants sleeping in a doorway across the way. The business next door had shoved two rolling bins of trash and recycling onto the curb, some of which had spilled over. A rat darted down the gutter, the presence of people interrupting its late night foraging. "No, it doesn't." She avoided a puddle on her way to the entrance, and Phineas opened the door for her.

A beefy Human filled the small alcove inside, low overhead lights reflecting dimly against his bald pate. His voice suited his size as he rumbled, "This is a private party."

Margaurethe raised an eyebrow. "We're invited. Please check with—" She slightly turned to Phineas, feigning ignorance. "What did that woman say his name was?"

"Father Castillo," he supplied.

"Of course." She returned her attention to the giant. "Father Castillo."

The bouncer observed them with suspicion as he stepped back to the inner door. When he poked his head inside, the music swelled louder, the seductive beat rattling Margaurethe's heart. He had to yell to be heard by whomever he spoke with, but she did not catch the words. The door widened, and a small, swarthy priest bustled toward them.

"*Ki'an Gasan* Margaurethe!" He bowed deeply, tilting his head to one side to expose his neck in the proper manner. He was young, maybe half Margaurethe's age, with no lines gracing his face. "I'm so sorry I wasn't at the house to receive you."

She waved away his apology, urging him to rise. "Hardly necessary, Father. We did descend upon you without warning." She gestured toward the now closed inner door. "Shall we?"

Castillo appeared taken aback at her abruptness, but nodded. "Of course. You must be anxious to meet Whiskey. Please come in."

The bouncer held the door open for them, and they walked into a sea of sound. All told there were about two dozen guests and security here. A bar stood along one wall, and a number of people filled the dance floor and tables beyond. The establishment was small with stairs leading to a second level above. Halfway up the steps, a Sanguire man with a blue mohawk was partaking of a *kizarus*, the copper smell spiking over the aroma of alcohol and musk as he drew fresh blood from his Human's throat.

Margaurethe wrinkled her nose, and looked away. It was considered rude in modern society to feed in public, but that didn't seem to be a problem here. She scanned the area with both eyes and mind, noting the sprinkling of both Sanguire and Humans, searching for light blond hair. A large sign at the top of the stairs discussed the rules for the "Mattress Room," rules that included nudity as a requirement. On a hunch, she turned to Castillo. "What sort of club is this?"

He had the sense to blush. "During normal business hours, it's an adult sex club, *Ki'an Gasan*."

She did not quite grind her teeth. *Leave it to Elisibet's heir to find the most scandalous place in the city to have her little soiree.* "And you could find no other place for your charge to enjoy herself? Exactly what religion do you profess to follow?"

Castillo raised his chin, a gesture of capitulation in Sanguire society. "It's one of the few places that will allow private rentals that also include bartender and DJ services, *Ki'an Gasan*." He glanced around the room at the servers. "And considering the nature of our people, it seemed best to be somewhere that the staff doesn't ask questions."

He had Margaurethe there, so she didn't pursue the subject. She clicked her tongue at the number of Sanguire younglings in evidence. So much for discretion; it looked like half the youngsters in the Colonies had found their way here. She even noted what looked like a native Indian among the crowd. *I'll have to attempt contact with the* We Wacipi Wakan *sooner than planned it seems.* "Have you informed her of my arrival?"

"Not yet. I wasn't sure if you were coming here, or awaiting our return."

Her next sound was a forcibly expelled grunt of surprise as the crowd on the dance floor parted.

Elisibet came into view, an Elisibet she had never before seen—young, vivacious, smiling as she danced enticingly with another young blond woman. She wore leather pants and a tight tank top, and was writhing against her partner, the slow beat a counterpoint to her seduction, oblivious to her spectator. The same height, the same build, the same light blond hair, the same mannerisms—the only visible differences were the burgundy dye coloring the last six inches of her hair, and the black dragon tattoo snaking up one arm. The song ended, melding into another with a faster beat. Elisibet initiated a searing kiss that ended the dance, an obvious familiarity burning between the two participants. Margaurethe felt a sharp pang of jealousy, the well-worn stab breaking through her reverie.

Without thought, she reached out with her mind. She easily dominated the young woman in Elisibet's arms, blocking the cheeky girl from retaliating. Extending herself to Elisibet, her heart physically ached as the familiar essence washed over her. The scent of roses wafting through her soul after so long an absence made her swoon. She barely felt the firm grip of the priest at her elbow when she faltered, or heard his questioning voice.

Whiskey turned, startled black eyes meeting Margaurethe's. The shock of not seeing Elisibet's ice-blue gaze confused Margaurethe, the catalyst allowing her to examine the young woman's mental touch. Margaurethe noted the scent of blood beneath the roses, the taste of water, neither of which Elisibet had ever held. *She's not Elisibet! She's not!* The impostor attempted to strengthen the connection, physically setting her dance partner aside and stepping closer. Margaurethe fought it off, turning away and into Phineas's arms. *My gods! She's so powerful!*

"Get me out of here!"

Without a question, Phineas wrapped his arms around her, bustling her back out the door. In mere seconds she was hunched over in the backseat of the car, fingers at her temples as she fought off the joining of souls that she had begun. Phineas pulled away with some speed, and distance finally accomplished what she could not. Panting, she slumped in the backseat, staring at the ceiling.

"Are you all right, cuz?"

Margaurethe lifted her head, seeing Phineas's worried scrutiny in the rearview mirror. "I'll be...fine."

He nodded, but did not appear convinced. "It was her, wasn't it?"

Her throat tightened, and she clamped down on the sob that wanted to express itself. "Yes." She laid her head back on the seat, turning it to stare out the window. "Yes, it was."

***

Cora hissed in Whiskey's arms, sagging.

Alarmed, Whiskey tightened her grip. "What's wrong?" She ducked her head to look at Cora, seeing the not-quite-beautiful face twisted in pain. "What is it?"

The answer came from elsewhere before Cora could speak. A sensation of heat washed over Whiskey, the faint smell of woodsmoke and mulled wine made her breathe deep though she knew the aroma was in her mind. An acute pain stabbed once within her chest. She recognized it as the yearning she'd had all her life finally meeting what it had been missing. Mouth dropping open, she spun around.

Margaurethe O'Toole. She stood near the door with Castillo. *She's real.*

Cora was forgotten. Whiskey's stare locked with Margaurethe's as she reveled in the remembered sensations. Elisibet's memories did them no justice, the reality so much more satisfying than the secondhand versions to which Whiskey had had access. All the flashes of memory, the sudden insights into Elisibet's thoughts and the nightmare of Elisibet's death that had plagued Whiskey for months were nothing compared to the smell of woodsmoke and mulled wine that now filled Whiskey's soul. Accepting the connection, she extended her own senses in an effort to strengthen it. Margaurethe sagged into a man's arms. She said something to him, and he turned and escorted her out of the club.

"Wait!" Whiskey moved forward with mind and body. "Don't leave!" The crowd ebbed around her as she pushed through them, swearing in frustration. By the time she made it to the outer door, Margaurethe was in a car rapidly speeding away, the connection fading with the growing distance. "Wait!"

Curious bystanders spilled onto the street behind her— Castillo, her current crowd of sycophants, and the ever-present security guards hired by Dorst. Those not there in an official capacity whispered among themselves, their words easy to overhear with her heightened senses. It reminded her of her memory of Elisibet sitting in the throne room, and the buzzing gossips of court discussing her latest activities. She felt a petulant anger race quicksilver through her blood, a reminder that Elisibet was always close by in her head and heart.

"Where is she going, Padre?"

Castillo held up his hands in a placating gesture. "Calm down. She's probably going back to the house."

Of course. Whiskey shook her head, looking around at the people gathered out in the cold. Cora had remained inside. The rain had begun again, sprinkles of chill ice bringing her to her senses. *Get a grip, Whiskey.* She ran a hand through her hair, turning back toward the club.

"Show's over, folks," Castillo called. "The party's not finished yet, so let's get back to it, shall we?"

The crowd accepted the priest's words, and began to migrate back inside. When only the security guards remained with them, he turned to her. "Are you okay?"

Whiskey swallowed and nodded, once more running her hand through her hair. "Yeah. I just—I wasn't expecting—"

Castillo chuckled. "I don't think she was, either."

It eased her mind knowing she wasn't the only one surprised. "It was her, wasn't it, Padre? She was here, right?" she asked in a small voice.

"It was her, Whiskey." He put an arm around her shoulder, and squeezed. "That was Margaurethe O'Toole."

With confirmation that she was not going crazy, she glanced down the now empty street. "What happened?"

"I don't know. You tell me."

Whiskey rolled her eyes at his non answer. "She forged a connection with me." She bit her lower lip, holding the memory of Margaurethe's essence to her as she stared down the empty street. "It was—It was just like I remembered, like *she* remembered," she added, not saying Elisibet's name. Despite having a firm grasp on what had driven the former *ninsumgal*'s actions, Whiskey was disgusted by the atrocities her predecessor had instigated. She rarely spoke the name.

"I recall you telling me that *Sañur Gasum* Dorst had felt the same when you first met him, as well."

"Yeah." She took a deep breath, wanting to re-experience the woodsmoke and mulled wine that had so quickly fled her mind. Turning to him, she gave him a self-deprecating smile. "I guess it was to be expected, huh?"

He mirrored her grin, bowing once. "Maybe. But neither of you were prepared for what you'd meet."

"No," she whispered.

Castillo moved away, and held the club's door open. "Let's get back inside."

Whiskey frowned, the urge to get out and have a good time no longer imperative. "I think I'll go back to the house."

He allowed the door to close. Stepping closer, he lowered his voice so the Human spectators would not catch his words. "She's had a frightful shock, Whiskey. She fled because she needs time alone. I'm not a gambling man, but I'd wager she wasn't expecting you to be so much like the Elisibet she remembers. Let's give her a little time to collect herself."

She considered his words, not wanting to concede. The yearning for Margaurethe superseded everything. *What if she leaves before I get there?*

Sensing she was on the edge of acceptance, Castillo added, "She came at your summons. She won't leave now with so much undone. She'll be there when we return."

Whiskey grimaced as he named her fear. Reluctant, she looked at the doors of the club, feeling the music beneath her feet. Whether she liked it or not, she had guests. It would not be polite to bail on them. As she took the first grudging step back inside, she realized she had not once thought of Cora. A wash of distaste flowed through her for being so callous. *I'm not her.*

CHAPTER THREE

Lights splashed across the windows, heralding the return of the partygoers. Margaurethe rose from the desk, and braced herself. She stepped out of the room that Americans called a "den," and waited in the entryway, hands clasped before her to control their shaking.

The sound of them approached, garrulous voices discussing music and fights and something called Mass Effect. Then the door flew open, spilling the chatterers into the house. Young Human and Sanguire together rolled like the incoming tide into the living room across the entryway from Margaurethe. A television came on, and a gaming console started as they bickered over who would kick whose ass. Two others separated from them, heading for the kitchen at the back of the house, taking orders for beer and chips from their comrades. Not a one paid Margaurethe any mind, their arrogance both amusing and annoying her.

Last to enter were the two girls she had seen on the dance floor. They held each other's hands. Keeping a tight rein on her emotions, Margaurethe quashed the spike of jealousy. She appraised the stranger; a too heavy facial bone structure, tilted eyes, and streaked blond hair made her more handsome than pretty. The youngling refused to look her in the eye. Margaurethe did not recognize the features, and so could not place the woman though her coloring made her European heritage evident. Still, it was possible she had been American-born; one never knew these days.

Castillo and one of the security guards came in behind them, closing the front door. A small circle of quiet developed in the hall, an odd counterpoint to the catcalls and jeers and simulated gunfire from the other room. Castillo dismissed the guard.

Margaurethe addressed him. "Father Castillo, if you'd be so kind."

"Of course." The priest indicated the young women. "Cora Kalnenieks and Jenna Davis."

Margaurethe caught a faint movement from Whiskey at the use of her given name rather than the ludicrous nickname for which she was known, and smiled. The smile faltered as Cora gave a slight curtsy. *Trained in courtly manners. Kalnenieks... Perhaps not American. I'll have Dorst do a little research on her family.*

Castillo gestured toward her. "This is *Ki'an Gasan* Margaurethe O'Toole."

She closed the gap between them, reaching out to shake Whiskey's hand. That it forced the younglings to release their grip on one another only sweetened the situation. "It's a pleasure to meet you, *Gasan.*"

Whiskey swallowed, hesitant as she took the offered hand. "You, too."

Margaurethe felt a tendril of roses caress her mental barriers, and blocked it with an iron will. She was glad when Whiskey did not force the issue; she didn't think she could emotionally survive a joining, not after the way it had affected her at the club. "I'd like to speak with you a moment, if I may."

"Uh—" Whiskey shifted awkwardly. "Sure. I guess."

Seeing the mirror image of her cool and calculating lover full of adolescent uncertainty sparked a wash of affection. Margaurethe pushed it away; now was not the time. Should the time ever come at all. She had spent the last hour coming to terms with the fact that though the holder of her heart was prophesied to return, the gods had been cruel in their follow-through. This replicant was not her Elisibet, not the woman she'd loved so deeply, not the woman she'd mourned for decades. After centuries of waiting for their reunion, Margaurethe found only the reflection of her past staring back at her.

She turned, gesturing toward the den. "If you please."

Whiskey nibbled her lower lip, glancing once at the priest before leading the way into the next room.

"I'll wish to speak with you, Father Castillo, when we're finished."

The priest gave her a deep bow. "Of course, *Ki'an Gasan*. I await your pleasure."

Following Whiskey, Margaurethe felt the flow of the connection between her new charge and the clergyman. She made note to separate the two as soon as possible. This Castillo fellow had done an adequate job of keeping Whiskey safe, but he was young, inexperienced and had made more than enough mistakes. According to Dorst, Castillo was responsible for alerting the *Agrun Nam* to Whiskey's existence to begin with. While that may have been the catalyst to bringing Margaurethe to this time and place, she couldn't forgive the man's misguided attempt at "doing the right thing." The threat of Valmont was a direct result of Castillo's foolishness. His choice of establishments for Whiskey's entertainment didn't help his cause.

Whiskey needed elders, influential Sanguire who could protect her from the political arena within which she was destined to compete. Whiskey was rumored to be mentally powerful, something Margaurethe had already received a glimpse of at their first meeting, but it would behoove everyone involved to have a number of stronger personalities in house to contain her. The priest didn't have a position of strength so much as a confidant and peer to an uneducated youngling who needed extensive lessons in order to take her place in the world. Dorst had reported that Castillo was also a Human-lover—an obvious conclusion considering his line of work in the Human religious sector. While Margaurethe did not hold with the racist Sanguire view of Humans as cattle, it was preferable that their kind mixed as little as possible with Humans. Mistakes in the distant past had caused too much violence between the races.

Margaurethe closed the door, passing silently by Whiskey to sit behind the desk. "Please, be seated."

After a moment's hesitation, Whiskey perched on the edge of a chair.

Giving the young woman a smile, Margaurethe leaned back in her chair. "How have you been holding up?"

Whiskey blinked. "I'm—I'm okay." She leaned closer. "What about you? Are you all right? You left so quickly."

"I'm fine. It was a bit of a surprise." Margaurethe raised a placating hand. "As I'm sure you know."

"Yeah. It was that." Whiskey squirmed a bit. "I'm sorry I pushed myself on you."

It was Margaurethe's turn to feel astonishment, though she chastised herself immediately. Elisibet had never been one for apologies, even when she knew she was in the wrong. Hearing the words come from the same honeyed voice that had sent thousands to their grisly deaths startled her. "I should be the one to apologize," she finally said. "It was the ultimate in bad manners to interrupt your…you."

The admission apparently eased Whiskey's nerves. She scooted back a bit on the chair, and her shoulders relaxed. "It's good to see you." Her fair skin reddened, and she looked away.

Margaurethe's mouth quirked, though sadness smothered her heart. The eye color wasn't the only difference between Elisibet and Whiskey. With each passing moment, she saw the divergence that she hadn't had time to discover at the club. Dorst had said Whiskey remembered things from Elisibet's point of view. *At least you're not the only one finding this strange, lass.* She refused to echo the sentiment. "Thank you."

She busied herself with the paperwork she had arranged on the desk, segueing away from the personal and into business. "I'd like to meet with you tomorrow regarding some papers that need signatures. I've set up everything you need at the moment, but it's time to move on."

"Move on?" Whiskey frowned.

"Yes. I've created a private corporation called The Davis Group that will be under your primary control." Margaurethe scanned the room. "This residence is fine for the interim, but we need to find a secure building from which to do business as well as keep you protected."

"Wouldn't that bring me to the attention of the *Agrun Nam*?"

"One would hope so." Seeing Whiskey's raised eyebrow, she leaned toward her, her elbows on the desk. "If they were to find you now, they could have you murdered, and no one would be the wiser. The sooner we get you into a fortified environment, and announce your return, the sooner we can begin the process of putting you into power."

Whiskey's eyes widened, and she pushed back in her chair. "I don't want to be in power."

Puzzled, Margaurethe frowned. *Yet another difference between them.* "Unfortunately, what you want may not be what you receive, Jenna. The fact is that you're the *Ninsumgal* reborn, and there are a lot of people who wish you harm. This is the best way I can see to protect you."

"My name's Whiskey."

Margaurethe scrutinized the jutting jaw and narrowed eyes. *That, at least, is the same. Why couldn't she have returned without the stubborn streak?* "Your name is Jenna Davis. Your nickname is Whiskey."

She received a blank stare in answer.

Nettled, Margaurethe cocked her head. "Wherever did you receive such a crude moniker?"

The direct question unsettled Whiskey. She answered reluctantly with vague surprise on her face, as if the information was startled out of her. "My initials, J.D. Jack Daniels is a brand of whiskey."

"Ah." Covering the awkward atmosphere, Margaurethe returned to her paperwork. "I think it best that you remain in seclusion until we've completed this stage of our plan."

"Seclusion?"

Margaurethe looked up. "Yes, seclusion. Valmont," she said, referring to their common enemy, "is no longer in Seattle. He remained for a time after you moved to Portland, but has been seen in British Columbia for a time, and then in northern California. We assume he received information from some of your former Human companions of possible locations and was scouting those areas. He hasn't been observed in two weeks, however. There's a good chance he's finally received intelligence that you're here. At the very least, you need to remain in the house until we can ascertain his location." Seeing the youngling balk, Margaurethe lowered her chin. "It's for your own safety."

Whiskey jerked her thumb over her shoulder at the door. "What about my friends?"

"Ah, your friends." Margaurethe braced herself for a battle. "I'll have my people begin thorough background checks on all of them. Once they've received clearance, they can return. Until then, I have to ask that they leave."

"No!" Whiskey shot to her feet. "Some of them don't have anyplace to go. They're here because of me, and I'm not going to toss them into the streets."

Standing as well, Margaurethe spoke in a calm voice. "I'm not asking you to throw them into the streets, Jenna. I'll have an apartment set up for those that are indigent—"

"The name's Whiskey! Don't forget it."

Margaurethe ignored the finger waving under her nose, drawing herself up to her full height. "And I'll ask you not to forget with whom you're speaking." She fought for control of her temper. "I'll make certain that those without a home be given someplace to stay in the interim, but this is necessary for your—"

"Bullshit! If these people wanted to have me killed, I'd already be dead." Whiskey turned and strode toward the door. "You do your security checks, Margaurethe, but you're not getting rid of the people who were here before you."

She pushed the door open with such force that it slammed against the wall. Entering the foyer, she marched up the stairs, towing Cora by the hand.

With exquisite control, Margaurethe ignored the multiple

stares from the living room. She crossed the den, and carefully closed the door. Leaning against it, her hands balled into fists, she stared up at the ceiling. Through the wood, she heard the younglings begin talking again, and she tuned them out. Hearing their speculations about the row accomplished nothing. Moving to the desk, she paused at the chair Whiskey had occupied. She sat in it, perched on the edge as Whiskey had been. The position offered her little insight.

She had considered many things over the past months as she set up Whiskey's power base—methods to finance the new regime, security measures to implement to ensure her safety, locations for her headquarters and place of residence, the proper way to introduce her to the world at large. She had even had the occasional adolescent daydream of reuniting with her lover, though the cruel light of reality reared up to smash those fantasies. After centuries of waiting, it had been a pleasure to actually be doing something. She had spent the majority of the last four hundred years in true Limbo, neither here nor there. For a change Margaurethe felt alive.

She was not prepared for a *Ninsumgal* who refused the position.

Margaurethe pushed up from the chair, and drifted behind the desk to look out the window.

What am I going to do?

CHAPTER FOUR

Margaurethe opened the door to find the priest leaning in the living room doorway, watching the antics of his charges. "Father Castillo?"

He quickly turned. "Yes, *Ki'an Gasan*. Are you ready to see me?"

"Yes, please." She moved back into the room, leaving him to enter behind her and close the door. "I'm assuming this is your office?" she asked, waving him to the chair that Whiskey had so recently fled.

Castillo sat down, adjusting his cassock. "Yes, it was. It's yours now, of course."

Happy there would be no territorial spat for resources,

she gave him a nod of acceptance. "Thank you. It will only be temporary until we can find somewhere more accommodating." She pulled a legal pad toward her, and leaned back in her chair. "Tell me about the people here."

If he was put off by her direct manner, he did not show it. He had to have heard the explosive squabble between her and Whiskey. One hand went to his trimmed beard, stroking as he thought a moment. "What would you like to know?"

Margaurethe smiled. "You have a collection of youngling misfits in the other room, Father. I'm sure it hasn't been easy to 'ride herd' upon them. Our charge is in significant danger, and I want to know who they are and why they're here."

He gave a slight lift of his chin. "A handful of them are with us from Seattle. Four in total. The pack leader they ran with attempted to interfere with Whiskey, hoping to use her likeness to gain power, and was killed in a legal duel."

She frowned, shuffling through her files. "I wasn't told of that." Admittedly, Dorst hadn't informed her of much, just that Margaurethe had been summoned. It was her desire to create the backbone of the new *Ninsumgal's* base that had kept her from coming with any haste. That and pure terror at what she would find upon her arrival. As a result, she would have to spend the next few days playing a game of catch-up. "Who was their leader?"

"Fiona Bodwrda."

Startled, Margaurethe looked up. "Bodwrda? I know her family. They were firm supporters of Elisibet. You say she's dead? Who did she duel with?"

"Whiskey."

Her mouth dropped open of its own accord. *I knew she was powerful, but...*"Fiona had to be close to sixty or seventy years of age, Father. You must be mistaken."

He grimaced in commiseration. "No, I'm not mistaken. Whiskey challenged her to a duel in order to gain the release of Cora, Daniel, Alphonse and Zebediah." He sighed. "I'm told she ripped Fiona's throat out. *Sañur Gasum* Dorst was her second."

Margaurethe snapped her mouth closed, and sat back in her chair to consider. She had assumed that Whiskey's apparent mental power in the club had been more Margaurethe's own unpreparedness than actual strength. "Elisibet was formidable in her time, more so than most. It was thought that the decision to send her through the *Ñíri Kurám* at such a young age was the cause." The *Ñíri Kurám*—a series of meditations all young Sanguire participated in to awaken their Sanguire natures and talents—had also been reproached as the cause of her tyrannical spirit.

"It seems that Whiskey has inherited that gift. Whiskey's held me to a standstill. Perhaps had *Ninsumgal* Elisibet waited until her majority, she'd have been just as powerful, just as quickly."

His soft voice reminded her she was with someone she didn't know. Blathering her thoughts to a stranger was not her wont. She pushed away the speculation for later perusal. "And the four you mentioned...those are the ones who have nowhere to go?"

"Yes, *Ki'an Gasan*."

She could see how Whiskey would develop a sense of responsibility if she had braved an adult Sanguire to save them. It did not make her job any easier. "Tell me about them."

He pursed his lips. "Daniel is our physician. He monitored Whiskey during her *Ñíri Kurám*. His family is European, but not well-to-do. I believe they suffered during the Purge, and were driven underground. Alphonse and Zebediah are mere children—not yet in their thirties." He nodded at her scowl. "Yes, it's criminal that they're on their own. They don't talk much about their past, so I'm not sure whether they've run away or their parents were killed prematurely. From their speech, I'm certain they're American-bred. Chances are good that they grew up like Whiskey."

"Meaning they had no idea they were Sanguire until someone came to them with the Book of meditations?"

"Exactly. They have little knowledge of our ways except for what they picked up in Fiona's care. *Sañur Gasum* Dorst is impressed with their technological expertise, and has been working with them."

Margaurethe raised an eyebrow. "Training his new cadre?"

A faint grin crossed Castillo's handsome face. "I believe so, yes."

Bracing herself, she attempted a casual tone as she asked, "And this Cora?"

He answered in kind. "Again, born here in America, though she's had a proper upbringing."

She did not ask what Cora's strengths were; that had been obvious at the club. She warmed her *ninsumgal's* bed, nothing more. "I noticed that she at least made an attempt at the proper courtesies."

"She's fairly smitten with Whiskey, though I don't believe the feelings are returned."

Margaurethe shot him a stern look. "Jenna's romantic entanglements are not my concern unless they threaten her welfare, Father."

Chastised, he bared his throat, wisely keeping his own counsel.

She cursed inwardly at her waspishness. "And the others?"

"Four Humans. Rufus Barrett is an aspiring artist of the Gothic persuasion. He and his friends have been hanging out here for two or three weeks. There are about fifteen *kizarusi* that are in and out depending on the day."

That made sense considering the number of Sanguire on the premises. Yet another item on Margaurethe's ever-growing checklist was to secure enough *kizarusi* to keep all the Sanguire in fresh blood. They might eventually need to open a blood bank if their population increased overmuch. "Do we know why Mr. Barrett is here? Is he aware of us?"

Castillo shifted in his chair. "You know, I'm not sure. He's never been told outright what we are, so I think he's under the assumption that we're...vampires." He grinned as she rolled her eyes. "I know. I imagine the others have fostered his belief, spinning yarns about the curse of the 'living dead.'" He used air quotes.

"Really," she murmured under her breath, shaking her head as she jotted down a note. "The gullibility of some Humans simply amazes me."

"He's been trying to get Whiskey to sit for him. He has in mind a life-sized portrait of her."

Margaurethe nodded, writing more. "I'll have a look at his work. If he passes a security check and is good enough, perhaps we'll hire him for that." Movement brought her gaze up from the pad, and she raised an eyebrow at the priest's apparent amusement.

"I'm sorry, *Ki'an Gasan*." Castillo muffled a chuckle, shifting in his chair. "I've seen Rufus's work. He's photorealistic, but tends toward the dark fantastical in his representations."

"You don't think he'll accept a commission from us?"

"I'm not sure a state portrait would be what we received from any commission for which we hired him."

She gave a light snort, her attention back on her pad. "Then we'll go somewhere else. There are a number of Sanguire artists who would be interested." *But that must wait until she's as safe as we can make her.* "Did I not see a member of the *We Wacipi Wakan* amongst your number?"

"That would be Nupa Olowan. I'm not positive that he's actually with them." At her look of askance, he continued, "He's made no mention of them in any conversation I'm aware of, and acts as wild as the others. I've wondered if he's turned his back on them."

Other than their existence, Margaurethe knew little else of the American Indian Sanguire governing body. They held dominion over the entirety of North America, and only allowed other Sanguire upon their sovereign ground with permission. "I can't imagine them ignoring the European *Ninsumgal* showing up on their soil. Have you attempted to contact them?"

"They haven't bothered to respond."

Either they did not care that Elisibet's doppleganger had shown up in their territory, or they were waiting to see what would happen. Even by Sanguire standards, the *We Wacipi Wakan* saw things from the long view, following the adage of allowing things to mature in their own time. Margaurethe hoped to get through to them before Whiskey's presence was publicly announced. It would be nice to know whether or not she would have to face deportation charges in the midst of the political fracas such an announcement would create.

Having learned all she currently required, she contemplated the priest. "I have an assignment for you. I'd like you to start tomorrow. We need to locate temporary housing for Jenna's guests until they've been through a background check. Mr. Barrett and his friends will need to find somewhere else to occupy their time for the same reason."

He gave her a concerned look. "Is that wise?"

Not caring to be questioned by a soft-hearted Sanguire who followed a ridiculous Human religion, Margaurethe lowered her chin and glared at him.

Castillo saw the error of his ways. "Not that I'm questioning your judgment, *Ki'an Gasan*." He raised his hands in supplication. "I just meant that if any of them had designs on Whiskey's life, wouldn't throwing them out tip them off?"

"Since they won't be allowed back until they've been checked, it hardly matters, does it?" She tossed the pad onto the desk, leaning her elbows on it. "There will be no more nonstop party, no more foolish risks with personnel, and no more calling awareness to ourselves until we've secured a base of operations. There are political and legal ramifications that must be taken into account. We are on hostile ground with an assassin searching for us, and I will do anything to protect Jenna." She projected her mind, pushing brusquely against his though not enough to intrude.

He blinked at her, and swallowed. "Of course, *Ki'an Gasan*. As you wish."

"I believe we're done here. Thank you, Father." For a moment, she thought he would argue; he appeared to debate whether or not to speak before rising to his feet. Bowing, he murmured a proper goodbye, and let himself out of the den, closing the door behind him.

Slumping, Margaurethe fell back in her chair. "Can this night get any longer?"

CHAPTER FIVE

The following morning found Margaurethe in the dining room having breakfast. She had yet to go to bed, having spent the night conducting business online. It helped that the majority of her contacts were in Europe, and she was still on European time. It had been a long night, just the same. When not answering emails, transferring funds, or finalizing her search for likely places to headquarter The Davis Group, she went over her meetings with Castillo and Whiskey. As the sun broke through the trees outside to play across the table, she rubbed at her tired eyes.

"*Ki'an Gasan?*"

With a sigh, Margaurethe looked up to see a punk caricature smiling back at her.

Reynhard Dorst gave her a deep bow, his three spiked mohawks bristling at her along his otherwise bald pate. He wore all the trappings of Whiskey's friends complete with silver spikes, chains and zippers on his boots and pants. His leather overcoat creaked and jingled as he stood. "What kept you?" A wide grin split his gaunt face, a countenance made even more ludicrous by the total lack of eyebrows.

Despite his youthful appearance, he was older than Margaurethe, older even than Elisibet was when she was in power. He was a shape shifter, a *Gúnnumu Bargún*, so his true age was unknown. It was this skill that made him so formidable in his occupation. For all she knew, he had been young when the world was made. She made a mental note to see which of the special Sanguire gifts Whiskey had manifested. "I had some things to attend to." She gestured toward one of the chairs.

With a dramatic flourish, Dorst seated himself. "It's so good to see you again."

Reaching for the tea set on the table, Margaurethe raised her eyebrow at his gush. She poured him a cup and slid the sugar container toward him, knowing he would want it.

He clapped his hands in joy. "You remembered!"

As he added two lumps of sugar to his cup, she picked hers up for a sip. "Where have you been?"

"Oh, here and there," came his evasive response. The room filled with the gentle *tink* of silver against china as he stirred his tea. "You know how it is."

"Spying on the *Agrun Nam*?"

He did not pretend shock at her accusation, instead giving her a sly wink before drinking from his cup.

Despite herself, she laughed, and sat back. "It's good to see you again, too, Reynhard." If she were honest with herself, she was glad to see anyone familiar at this rate, even if it was the most farcical and dangerous Sanguire ever to have existed.

"How was your trip here?"

"Long and dreadful."

"A pity you arrived at night. For a major city, Portland certainly has its beauty."

It did not surprise her that he knew when she had arrived. He would be slipping otherwise. "I'll have a chance to look at it over the next few days." She set her cup down. "Tell me what you know about the people here."

He displayed exaggerated innocence. "You mean Portlanders in general? Or are you referring to Americans overall?"

Margaurethe scowled. "You know what I mean." Something Castillo had said came to mind. "Tell me about Jenna's duel."

Both of Dorst's hairless eyebrows rose. "Someone's been talking, I see," he murmured. He cocked his head at her. "I haven't been sworn to secrecy. What would you like to know?"

"Everything."

"Only that?" He grinned. When she did not rise to the bait, he conceded with a subtle raise of his chin. "We were there to rescue Daniel and Cora. Fiona had reservations about the matter, but Whiskey showed her the error of her ways."

"Only Daniel and Cora? I thought the other two were involved, as well."

He shook his head. "Their only involvement was Fiona's sword hanging over their heads. They skipped away to join up with Whiskey a day earlier."

Margaurethe thought about the political and familial dynamics of a modern Sanguire pack. Unlike the traditional family unit, disenfranchised younglings tended to band together, following the strongest among them. "Why would they go against their leader like that? Did Whiskey convince them somehow? Or did they believe the prophecy, and want to support her?"

Dorst helped himself to a piece of toast. A knife manifested in his hand, and he flicked it open, availing himself of a bit of jam. "She overcame them when they attacked her. Being but children, they threw their lot in with her since she was the more powerful."

This was the second time she had heard specifics of Whiskey's legendary power. "Castillo said she's strong enough to hold him to a standstill. Do you agree with his assessment?"

He neatly cleaned the blade before putting it away. "The priest hasn't had much in the way of training as far as battle goes, and I believe that should be taken into consideration. Still, an untrained child shouldn't have been able to overcome him." He shrugged, and looked at her. "In any case, her ability to duel an adult fifty years her senior is unprecedented."

Lips pursed, she watched him eat his toast. "So she did do it."

"Oh, yes! Succeeded quite handily, as a matter of fact."

Margaurethe lifted her napkin to her lips. Elisibet had enjoyed the killing, often going out of her way to set up circumstances in order to duel or mete out punishments. Accepting that dark part of her had been the hardest thing Margaurethe had ever done. She imagined the scene between Whiskey and Fiona, imagined the bloodshed and Elisibet's feral joy as she wallowed in the gore. *No. Not Eisibet. Jenna.* Setting her napkin beside her half-eaten meal, she studied Dorst. "How did she react?"

He feigned somberness. "Not well, I'm afraid. The *Ñíri Kurám* was taking its toll at the time, and she collapsed."

She twitched, startled. Displeasure flickered through as she realized what he had implied. "What do you mean?"

A dodgy grin quirked his thin lips. "She hadn't finished her walk upon the Strange Path. The priest tried to talk her into allowing the two of us to deal with the issue, but she refused."

"Refused?" Margaurethe stood so quickly that her chair toppled over. "Are you telling me that you allowed a mere child, one who hadn't even completed the *Ñíri Kurám* to engage in a duel with an adult Sanguire?"

For the first time since their reunion, Dorst's face became deadly serious. His eyes were as black as Whiskey's, and held none of their normal sardonic humor. "I did as my *Ninsumgal* ordered."

His tone splashed across Margaurethe, cooling her rancor, reminding her. Dorst had been Elisibet's most loyal lapdog, ever adoring, ever fierce in his protection of her from the day of her investiture. The only reason Valmont had succeeded in his assassination of her was because Dorst had been away and unable to intercede. He had mourned Elisibet as deeply and thoroughly as Margaurethe herself had. He had spirited Margaurethe away from the palace hours before the Purge began, saving her pitiful life only because his *Ninsumgal* would not have wanted her to die.

Obviously, his loyalties had already been transferred to Whiskey. Restraining the urge to shout, she took a deep breath. There was nothing to be done for it. *Past is past. Look to the future now.* "I understand." She loosened her hands from the fists they had made. "I assume you've already sworn fealty then?"

A faint echo of his humor glimmered across his features, and he bowed his head. "I have."

"Of course," she muttered. It would make working with him all the more difficult. "Has anyone else?"

He rose to collect her chair, setting it back on its legs. "I do not believe so."

That was a relief. Margaurethe could at least control the upcoming ceremony that would entail such matters. Ideally, the *Agrun Nam* would be first to kneel before their new ruler. She murmured her thanks, and reseated herself. *Back to business.* "Tell me about the security company you've hired."

"My *Gasan* wasn't certain who she could trust. She thought a Human contingent would be beneficial in keeping her whereabouts unknown." Dorst sat down, and picked up the remains of his toast. "This particular company comes highly recommended. I researched their facilities and training manuals; they've been quite professional and competent."

"An intelligent move," she acknowledged, "but I've brought my own people to replace them. More will be coming over the next few days. Once we have enough to take over all security duties, I want the Humans' contract canceled."

"Providing our *Ninsumgal* has no problems with that, I'll see to it."

Margaurethe suppressed the urge to growl. With every meeting she found obstacles in her path. "Have we any information on the location of Valmont?"

"We do," he said, his natural ebullience returning. "He flew into town three days ago, and is currently staying at the Kierney Hotel."

Her heart seemed to drop into her stomach, then leap back to its place to pound hard and fast. "He's here? In Portland?"

"Most certainly, *Ki'an Gasan*." Ignoring her shock, Dorst chuckled. "I can only imagine that he's recently received intelligence about your interests in the area from the *Agrun Nam*."

She had hoped for at least a little more time before Valmont would show himself, time that she could have used to secure Whiskey's future. She would have to move much faster now.

It was imperative that the unknown Sanguire and Humans be removed from the household today. "Have you been able to ascertain where he's searching?"

He primly wiped his mouth with a napkin, and then slouched in his chair. "He's still focusing on the homeless youth. I'm assuming he found a lead in Seattle regarding an unsolved murder my *Gasan* was involved in, and has been looking down possible avenues she could have fled to avoid prosecution."

Margaurethe frowned. "Fiona?"

"Oh, no, *Ki'an Gasan!*" He chortled at her mistake. "This was the Human runaway that my *Gasan* killed while she was cavorting with Fiona's pack."

Again the world flew out from under her feet. *Another surprise. I suppose I should get used to them when discussing Elisibet's heir.* "She's killed a Human, too?"

He waved dismissal of her question. "Quite by accident, or so I've been assured. She told me her goal had been to knock the hapless fool unconscious before one of the others did the deed. It was simply bad luck that her blow killed him." Seeing Margaurethe's apparent dismay, he hurried to ease her mind. "She was quite distraught over the matter."

Margaurethe reached up to rub her temples in an effort to massage away the headache threatening her. "So our young charge has killed a Human, overcome the joined forces of two Sanguire, killed another in a legal duel, and held a four-hundred-year-old Sanguire to a standstill?"

Dorst pretended to think over her statement before nodding cheerfully. "Yes, *Ki'an Gasan*, that about covers it."

Good gods, can I do this alone?

CHAPTER SIX

Whiskey drifted down the stairs, cautious as she scanned the first floor. It was too early for the other denizens of the house to be up, and quiet permeated the atmosphere. A subdued Cora followed, fingers hooked into Whiskey's back pocket. Whiskey's stomach gurgled in anticipation at the smell of fresh coffee and bacon. She stretched out her mind, and noted the majority of her Sanguire friends crashed in the bedrooms above. A couple had sacked out on the couch. There were others also, strangers interspersed throughout the house and yard, Margaurethe's security and servants. Whiskey didn't attempt to connect with any of them, just brushed across their senses to note their locations.

At the scent of mulled wine and woodsmoke, she paused at

the bottom step, Cora almost running into her from behind. Whiskey heard the faint sound of a keyboard from the open den. She took the final step to the ground floor, and looked through the door.

Margaurethe sat at the desk, looking as if she had not slept. Wisps of her perfectly coifed hair had escaped their binding, and she absently brushed a lock aside as she concentrated on what she was typing. She paused, rubbing her eyes, before returning to her task.

Whiskey could not help the smile on her lips. The previous night's unpleasantness faded away, replaced with the ever-familiar longing. *She's beautiful.* She had a vision of going to Margaurethe, running her fingers through that mahogany hair, releasing it from its prison as she massaged and caressed—

"*Aga ninna?*"

She gasped at the interruption, glancing sharply behind her at Cora. The typing sound halted, and she risked a hurried glance into the den to find Margaurethe staring at them. Whiskey swallowed. Turning to Cora, she said, "Go get some breakfast. I'll be there in a minute."

Cora's glance flickered between Whiskey and Margaurethe. Chewing her lower lip, she raised her chin in consent, and slipped past and away.

Whiskey waited until she was gone before turning toward the den. Margaurethe had not moved. *It would be so easy to walk in there and kiss her.* Instead, she walked into the room, and placed her hands on the back of the chair she had sat in the night before. "Good morning."

"Good morning." Margaurethe's shoulders relaxed a little, as if expecting a less pleasant greeting. "Did you sleep well?"

"Yeah." Whiskey studied her, noting darkness circling the emerald green eyes. "Did you sleep at all?"

The ghost of a smile quirked Margaurethe's lips. "Not yet. I'm afraid I'm still on Eire time." She pushed the laptop away from her. "It may take a few days before I'm firmly entrenched in this time zone."

Whiskey nodded. The Irish accent was still there, though not as strong as she remembered it. *As she remembers.* Margaurethe looked older than those memories. Not by much, to be sure, but she appeared to be nearing thirty rather than enjoying the full bloom of her early twenties. "I'm—" She paused. "I'm sorry about last night."

A flash of something indefinable crossed Margaurethe's demeanor. "I'm sorry, as well."

Uncertainty flooded through Whiskey. In her daydreams of Margaurethe's return, she had never considered this awkwardness between them. She had always assumed they would return to a closeness somewhat akin to what was shared between Elisibet and Margaurethe. The reality created quicksand under her intentions, sending everything into instability. She loved this woman with her life, but didn't know her. "I just—" With an annoyed sigh, she looked away. "You're different than I expected, that's all."

"As are you."

The soft words brought Whiskey's attention back to Margaurethe. "I bet I am." They stared at one another for a moment before she gave a thoughtful nod. "What are you working on?"

Margaurethe took a deep breath, then turned the computer around. "Quarterly earnings for a number of corporations I own." She craned her neck to see the screen, scrolling through the current document. "This spreadsheet indicates earnings, profits, taxes paid, and royalties on several patents under my control. Some of the corporations are public, and I have to report to the shareholders. The majority are private, however."

Mystified, Whiskey peered at the columns of numbers.

"You are a very rich young woman, Jenna."

A spark of bitterness warred with confusion. "It's Whiskey," she reminded Margaurethe, voice low.

Exasperation crossed Margaurethe's face, and she almost rolled her eyes before she lifted her chin in concession.

Whiskey grinned, recalling multiple times when Margaurethe had rolled her eyes at Elisibet over the decades. She received a small smile in return.

"You're a rich young woman, *Whiskey*," Margaurethe repeated. Businesslike, she turned the laptop back around.

"When I'm finished, you'll have a very hefty treasury to draw from during your reign."

Sobering, Whiskey frowned. "I don't want to rule."

"I'm aware of that, Je—Whiskey." Margaurethe had also become serious. She rested her elbows on the desk, propping her chin in her clasped hands. "However, in order to keep you safe, we must put you into a position of power. If you are too strong to be taken down, your detractors won't attempt it. The cost will be too much."

Whiskey had to admit that was logical. More so than being thrust into a leadership role because of some silly prophecy made four hundred years ago. Grudgingly, she gave a nod. "So how are we going to do that? The *Agrun Nam* won't want me taking over from them."

Relief eased the lines of Margaurethe's face, and she sat back. "First we get you into a secured facility. Then we present you to the local authorities, and arrange for your *Baruñal* ceremony. From there, we begin to petition the various governments regarding your political status."

"You mean, like the Asians or the *We Wacipi Wakan*?" Whiskey rubbed a hand across her forehead. *God, this is getting complicated.*

"Yes. You know of them?"

She nodded. "I've heard of them in conversation."

Margaurethe raised an eyebrow. "If you're to be recognized as *Ninsumgal*, there is a concern regarding you being on North American soil. Treaties must be made here, as well as abroad. The *Agrun Nam* will be the most difficult to persuade, so it behooves us to have ourselves organized with the other nations. They cannot ignore you if you've taken over in all but name."

The tactic made sense. The easiest way to bypass any authority was to sneak in the back window. Whiskey had had plenty of experience in that area during her homelessness. She felt a thrill of joy as she contemplated thumbing her nose at the ruling Sanguire council in the process.

"I wanted to talk to you about the Human security company you've hired."

Whiskey frowned. "What about them?"

"After tomorrow they'll no longer be needed. I have a number of my household and security en route to take over. Reynhard told me the Humans were hired on your word, and he won't release them until you order him to do so."

"Wouldn't more security be better?" Whiskey nibbled her lower lip.

Margaurethe gave her a patient look. "They're Human, Whiskey."

As if that explains everything. She'd run into this racism many times over the last few months, the Sanguire in her presence treating their Human companions like second-class citizens. Like cattle. "I never expected to hear racial discrimination from you."

"Racial—" Margaurethe shook her head. "You misunderstand me. Sanguire are physically superior to Humans. It's proven fact. And there are Sanguire assassins searching for you. A Human cannot scan a room to locate which of the people in it are Sanguire, nor could a Human intercede quickly enough on your behalf to save you from an attack."

Whiskey blinked. "I hadn't thought of that."

"Nor should you have to," Margaurethe answered. "That's my job, as well as Reynhard's and Father Castillo's. We're here to help."

The essence of ashes lightly touched Whiskey. Cora had been placid since Margaurethe's appearance, and this was the first time she had made an attempt since their encounter at the club. Whiskey just as gently blocked the questing tendril. The moment took her away from the conversation, and she refocused on Margaurethe's words.

"—the task I've set him. He'll be looking for a suitable place to house your friends until their background checks can be completed."

"Wait. What?"

Margaurethe raised an eyebrow. "I've asked Father Castillo to research temporary housing for your friends."

The frustrated indignation she had felt at their last meeting triggered a return of her acrimony. "I told you no last night. I'm not kicking them out."

"I'm not asking you to 'kick them out,' Jenna. I'm simply

moving them to another place until their intentions can be investigated." Margaurethe growled in frustration, throwing her hands up into the air. "*Whiskey.*"

Her self-correction would have been funny if not for the outrage coursing through Whiskey. "You're not getting rid of them, and that's final. I'm responsible for them."

Margaurethe dropped her head in her hands. When she looked up, a line had developed between her eyebrows. "Your familial obligation to them is laudable, Whiskey. You're completely correct that some of them are yours now, as they'd been Fiona Bodwrda's before you. I understand that. What you must understand is that Valmont is here—in Portland— searching for you."

Whiskey's fiery righteousness changed to icy hostility. "He's here?"

"Arrived three days ago according to Reynhard."

"All the more reason to keep my friends close."

Silence grew between them, broken only by sounds of people in the distant kitchen. When Margaurethe spoke again, her voice was soft, forcing Whiskey to strain to hear.

"Do you really think your youngling friends can stand up to a six-hundred-year-old Sanguire?"

The question surprised Whiskey. Everything she knew of Valmont came from Elisibet's memories, including her arrogant opinion of him. He had dueled Elisibet to the death with conventional weapons because he would never have succeeded with his mind. Elisibet's failure had been the conceited belief that she could take him on at a physical level. If it came down to a face-to-face confrontation, Whiskey knew she could take Valmont; she had already controlled the padre before finishing the *Ñíri Kurám*. The thought of her pack attempting the same objective alarmed her. Even Fiona's old pack combined couldn't take on Castillo. Valmont would tear through their minds with ease, leaving them dead or just as good as.

"You understand now?"

Whiskey focused once more on Margaurethe. "I do."

Margaurethe's countenance held a mixture of regret and acceptance. "One of them may already be compromised. We must be sure before allowing them back."

Her hands gripped the back of the chair so hard, she heard the crackle of the wood compressing beneath her fingers. "None of them have been compromised. I've been with them the last three days that Valmont has been here. I *know*."

"Whiskey—"

"No! What I said last night stands. They stay." She watched a defeated and hurt look cross Margaurethe's face. It shocked her out of her anger. She had never seen it before, not in all the foreign memories she held of the woman sitting before her. Whiskey lightened her grip on the chair, wishing she could withdraw her words, wipe the defeat from Margaurethe's face. She could not let her people be put into danger, however, no matter how "safe" it would make her.

"And the Human security company?" Margaurethe asked, her voice toneless.

"As soon as you have enough people, I'll release them." Whiskey tried to catch Margaurethe's eye to no avail. "The others—"

"Yes?"

Whiskey felt a rush of annoyance, knowing her next words would sabotage her remaining control of her life. "Rufus, his friends. You can have them leave." She watched Margaurethe's eyes raise from their concentrated perusal of her computer screen. Whiskey shook her head, and looked away, finding the wall decoration fascinating. "Until they've passed your inspection or whatever."

"Thank you."

Risking a quick glance, Whiskey saw the line bisecting Margaurethe's brow ease. Margaurethe looked more like the young woman Whiskey remembered. She even recognized a shy smile curling the corner of those full lips. She longed to circle around the desk, and kiss the consternation away.

Daniel thumped down the stairs trailing a Sanguire sensation of flowering plums and vanilla, interrupting Whiskey's reverie. She looked over her shoulder at the open door, catching sight of the blond man passing on his way to the kitchen. Turning back to Margaurethe, she hooked a thumb behind her. "I should...go get some breakfast."

Businesslike, Margaurethe straightened files on the desk, keeping her hands busy. "Of course."

Whiskey stepped backward once, twice. "You really should get to bed anyway. You need the rest."

Margaurethe glanced up at her, smiling. "I shall. Thank you."

Unable to think of anything else to say, Whiskey gave her an uneasy wave, and escaped for the kitchen. *Will there ever be a time we'll be in the same room without arguing?*

CHAPTER SEVEN

Margaurethe stepped lightly out of the car, emerging to duck under an umbrella held by her driver. Despite the dreary weather, the street bustled with activity. An assortment of pedestrians sported hooded jackets and umbrellas, the majority wearing casual clothes though they worked in the city's business district. A light rail train rolled past, its electric engine whizzing along. The air smelled clean, an anomaly despite the rain and considering the number of people who made Portland their home. Rain spattered the sidewalk, and Margaurethe stepped through the puddles toward the main entrance of the tallest building in downtown Portland. She had been told the building glowed pink when struck by the sun, though she had yet to see anything beyond gray clouds in her two days here.

At the covered entrance, Phineas shook out the umbrella. "Do you want to keep this with you?"

She peered up at the sodden sky. "I think not. I'll call the minute the meeting is over."

"Right." He held the nearest door open for her. "See you in a bit, cuz."

Margaurethe gave him an exasperated smile, but said nothing as she entered the building.

Several minutes later, she found herself in the law offices of Bastion & Burke on the twenty-second floor. Her financial reputation saw her immediately welcomed by the receptionist, and ensconced in an office a with coffee carafe. She barely had time to enjoy the magnificent view of the misty northwestern hills when one of the senior partners entered the room.

"Ms. O'Toole, it's a pleasure to meet you at last!"

Margaurethe turned to see James Bastion coming toward her. She returned his smile with a gracious one of her own. "And you, as well, Mr. Bastion. Thank you for making room in your schedule to see me."

He took her hand. "You're one of my newest clients. I couldn't shuffle you off to a paralegal now, could I?" Both of them knew that she was also one of his most lucrative, the real reason for the excellent treatment she had received thus far. He gestured toward the desk and chairs. "Please, sit. I see Frannie has offered you coffee. Would you like something to eat?"

"I'm fine, thank you." She opened her briefcase, and extracted several file folders.

"Have you been in town long?" He availed himself of the coffeepot, adding creamer to his cup.

"A few days." She set the briefcase aside. "Were you able to draw up those papers I requested?"

After a healthy slurp of coffee, he said, "Of course." It was his turn to rummage for files, extracting one from his desk and handing it to her. "Business incorporation of The Davis Group, financial accounts ready to go, and a rudimentary business plan drawn up, insurance and business licenses in place. I'll need your signature and that of Ms. Davis on these, and have the documents notarized. Once they're filed with the court, the corporation exists and it fully accords with federal and state law." He fished out a pair of Ben Franklin half-spectacles, and perched them on the end of his bulbous nose.

"Brilliant." Margaurethe looked over the paperwork, noting where signatures and initials needed to be added. "I'll see these taken care of and returned by the end of the day." She handed over three folders in return. "And The Davis Group is interested in acquiring these properties. I trust you can make the proper inquiries?"

Bastion took the paperwork, curiously flipping through them. "I can." An eyebrow rose in surprise. "Prime downtown property? That'll definitely cost, you know."

"I'm aware of the cost, Mr. Bastion." She accepted his embarrassed, apologetic wave. "There are three I'm interested in, though the building on the waterfront is the most imperative. Anything you can do to speed up the process of purchasing that one will be handsomely rewarded."

His eyes were the only thing to move as they peered over the top of his glasses at her. They studied her long enough for him to understand the underlying implication. "Of course, Ms. O'Toole. I'll see what I can do."

"Thank you."

"In fact, if you could wait here a moment, I'll assign someone to look into it now."

Margaurethe smiled. "I would be most appreciative, Mr. Bastion."

Once he was gone, the smile left her face. She perused the paperwork once more, observing the differences between international and local law. She could have generated the paperwork, saving herself the time and trouble, but having a local attorney on hand to expedite matters was worth its weight in any currency of the day. If things went well, The Davis Group would have a headquarters by spring.

With a sigh she closed the folder, and placed it inside her briefcase. She'd had the priest authorized as a notary public in the state of Oregon, knowing one would be necessary for the unending documents a corporation could generate. This way Whiskey would not endanger herself en route to legal offices for signatures.

The thought of Whiskey preoccupied Margaurethe. Their last discussion had signaled a truce. Rufus Barrett and his acquaintances had left, as well as the American Indian Sanguire who had taken to following Whiskey around, without complaint from their young benefactor. Whiskey's responsibility stopped at the "Fiona Four," as Margaurethe coined them, the Sanguire that had joined her after Fiona's defeat and death. That was fine by Margaurethe as it afforded less of a security risk, though not much of one.

Nevertheless, a subtle tension remained. Margaurethe's initial meeting had thoroughly intimidated the little blonde warming Whiskey's bed. Cora stared at her shoes or lap whenever Margaurethe entered a room, fleeing at the first opportunity. Margaurethe had no problem with that.

The eldest, Daniel Gleirscher, seemed the most mature. Introverted by nature, almost bookish, he had no trouble ignoring everyone around him as he surfed the Internet or read medical journals. The colorful younglings, Alphonse and Zebediah, chafed the most at the enforced restrictions, their grumbles echoed by their mistress, Whiskey. The ongoing awkwardness between Margaurethe and Whiskey hadn't quite turned the environment into a battlefield, but she knew opening shots would be fired soon. With the background checks completed and a larger building purchased everyone could breathe easier.

Margaurethe heard Bastion at the door. Woolgathering could wait.

***

Margaurethe entered the house with little fanfare. The Four were ensconced in the living room, the current video game loud and obnoxious enough to suggest she stood in the center of a war zone. Only one of them noted her arrival; Cora's eyes flickered once in Margaurethe's direction before again staring at the action on the large flat–screen television. Preferring to be ignored, Margaurethe looked away from their play.

"Daydreaming?" she heard Castillo ask.

Turning toward the den, Margaurethe discovered the priest

and Whiskey. He sat in one of the armchairs, and Whiskey stood at the window. They hadn't observed her return. Drifting closer, Margaurethe paused at one side of the doorway, listening.

"Of course not. You were discussing the different branches of Sanguire and the abilities inherent in each."

"*Rúmun Unkin*," Castillo said. "And family lines are...?"

"*Im Rigu Libi*." Whiskey's voice sounded as if she had turned away.

"Very good. Can you list the *Rúmun Unkin* abilities?"

With a sigh, Whiskey left the window. She sat in the armchair beside Castillo. "The Sanguire have developed five different *Rúmun Unkin*, or talents, each with their own strengths and weaknesses. The *Gúnnumu Bargún* are shape shifters. They can alter their appearance depending on their ability." Whiskey paused. "Reynhard said you're one."

"I am. It's been quite helpful in staying with the Church over the decades. I never worry about running into older priests who knew me years earlier."

"Show me?"

Castillo laughed. "Certainly." He shifted in his chair.

Margaurethe peeked around the corner. Whiskey had leaned forward for an improved view, propping her elbows on her knees. She smiled at Whiskey's fascinated curiosity as the priest's eyes gently drifted wider apart, their shape becoming more almond. His nose altered, thickening as it hooked into a near beak. Hair, once curly and somewhat wild, straightened of its own accord.

"That is so cool," Whiskey said when the transformation finally ceased.

The unfamiliar visage smiled. "It's very useful." After another short period of concentration the face Margaurethe knew returned.

"How long do you keep a...I don't know. A look?"

"As long as necessary. Usually twenty or thirty years, depending on where I'm placed in the Church."

"How extensive is your ability? I mean, how much can you actually change of yourself?"

Castillo drew a deep breath, and frowned. "I can change my general appearance. On good days I can affect eye and hair color, too. As with any of the gifts, some are stronger than others. I know of one or two who can even change their height and build." He winked at her. "But this is not answering the question. The next *Rúmun Unkin*?"

"Slave driver." Whiskey leaned back in her chair, resting a booted foot on one knee. "*Tál Izisíg* are pyrotechs. They start fires with their minds. Do I know any of them?"

Castillo considered the question. "I believe Councilor Cassadie of the *Agrun Nam* is one."

Whiskey frowned in distant thought. "Aiden Cassadie. He taught *her*."

Margaurethe brought a hand to her chest in an attempt to still her thundering heart. She had known that Whiskey held Elisibet's memories, but this was the first time she had heard her speak it.

"Yes," Castillo agreed. "Are the memories coming faster?"

Whiskey rubbed her temple with one hand. "Yeah. And somewhat confusing."

"I can't say I understand, but I can certainly imagine. What *Rúmun Unkin* is next?"

Margaurethe took a slow, deep breath to calm herself as the lesson continued.

"*Tál dile Imramun Tu*, storm singers." Whiskey paused. "You know, I've read some things. It was rumored that Merlin was a Sanguire and *Tál dile Imramun Tu*. Is that true?"

"I couldn't say. All I've heard are rumors, as well. Though you might ask *Ki'an Gasan* Margaurethe. It's said her mother learned her skills at Merlin's knee. She's one of the strongest *Tál dile Imramun Tu* among us."

"You're kidding!"

Castillo shook his head. "Serious."

"Wow."

"Next?"

"*Dilída Ru'oníñ á Sudśe*, they can move objects with their minds. And last are the ghost walkers, the *Gidimam Kissane Lá*, rumored to be able to walk through solid objects. It's also said they're extinct since no one has seen or heard from one in several hundred years."

"Correct. They withdrew from court not long after Elisibet came to power."

"Small wonder." Whiskey snorted. "If she'd been able to use their ability, things would have been a lot worse."

Margaurethe quelled an automatic rise of choler at the criticism. *What's past is past. And who but Elisibet's heir has the right?* Still, it rankled to hear this youngling upstart with a thimbleful of experience in life pillory her predecessor.

Castillo made no comment, instead forging onward. "Five talents of the Sanguire, four of which are accounted for. Do talents run true to family lines?"

Whiskey smiled. "Too easy. No. Due to intermarriage between different *Rúmun Unkin*, abilities show up among all family lines. Take Margaurethe; her mother is a storm singer but her father is something else entirely. She takes after her mother."

Castillo closed the small book in his lap. "You've passed with flying colors."

"Cool. What's next in the lesson plan?"

"Politics." He chuckled at her groan. "I know it's not your favorite, but circumstances being what they are..."

"Yeah."

He tilted his head. "Do you have any questions of me before I go?"

Margaurethe frowned at the sudden silence. Whiskey scrutinized her booted foot as she fiddled with the laces. Castillo didn't press, waiting for her to speak her mind. Her voice, when it came, was soft enough that Margaurethe had to strain to hear the words.

"When do you know what ability you have?"

The priest moved to the edge of his seat, his hand stilling Whiskey's. "Normally, it would be assumed you had one of your parents' *Rúmun Unkin*. You would have been raised in their presence, and known to some vague degree how to use whichever talent is yours by the time you completed the *Ñíri Kurám*."

Whiskey scoffed, but didn't pull away or look up.

"In your case, we can only hope you'll stumble across it as you become acquainted with other Sanguire. You've had a minor demonstration of *Gúnnumu Bargún*. We can have *Sañur Gasum*

Dorst give you a more extensive one. I'm fairly certain that Cora is a pyrotech, though I'd have to ask. *Ki'an Gasan* Margaurethe can show you *Tál dile Imramun Tu.*"

"Valmont's telekinetic," Whiskey stated flatly.

Margaurethe felt a chill down her spine at the name, her heart once more pounding. She doubted Dorst had made mention of such a fact, which meant this was another memory.

"I wouldn't know."

Whiskey looked up at Castillo. "No, he was. I remember." She pursed her lips. "*She* was a pyrotech, too, I think."

"She was." Margaurethe entered the den. "Elisibet's strength after the *Ñíri Kurám* was extensive, but her abilities as a *Tál Izisíg* were limited. That's why you remember Aiden Cassadie teaching her."

Castillo promptly stood at Margaurethe's entrance, murmuring a greeting.

A frown crossed Whiskey's face before she looked away.

Margaurethe wondered at Whiskey's unreceptive attitude. Other than keeping the children in house, Margaurethe had done nothing to incur her rancor. *Can she be upset about my eavesdropping?* "I apologize. I just returned from a meeting, and wanted to look in on you."

"We were just finished." Castillo made a bow to both of them. "I'll see you tomorrow then? Same bat channel, same bat time?"

A reluctant smile crossed Whiskey's face. "Is that a lame vampire reference or a superhero one?"

Castillo bobbed again, grinning. "Whatever works for you, Whiskey."

"I'll see you later." She chuckled, and waved him away.

He bowed a third time, backing away as was proper for vassals of a ruler. Margaurethe gave a significant look toward the door, and he nodded, closing it behind him.

"I hate it when he does that. It reminds me of Reynhard."

Margaurethe turned back to Whiskey. The smile still quirked her lips, though the displeasure at the priest's display of manners shadowed her tone. "Unfortunately, you'll need to get used to it. Proper etiquette demands such things." She set her briefcase atop the desk, walking around to sit in the chair as she ignored a rude gesture from Whiskey's vicinity. "I'm glad you're here. I have some business to discuss, and will need your signature on some legal documents before the end of the night."

"What kind of legal documents?"

Margaurethe retrieved the folder from her case, looking at Whiskey's suspicious bearing. It hurt to see this lack of trust, something she had never seen on that very same face over the years regardless of the circumstances. She automatically lashed out. "I know you've had a rough time with the legal establishment, but not everyone is out to incarcerate you." The minute the words were out of her mouth, she wanted them back.

Whiskey became sullen, not responding as she glared at Margaurethe.

Closing her eyes, Margaurethe raised her chin in supplication. She sighed. "I'm sorry. I shouldn't have said that."

"No shit," Whiskey growled.

Margaurethe looked at Whiskey, seeing no change in her countenance. *Why is it that I can never put my foot right with her? What does she remember about me? Can this get any more difficult?* Schooling her appearance, she leaned forward. "Truly, Whiskey. I am sorry. I'm having as much difficulty with this as you—who you were, who you are. I've made a mistake. You have my utmost apologies."

Mollified, Whiskey's face changed into one of grudging commiseration. "Okay."

Feeling as if she had just forged a storm-swollen river without a boat, Margaurethe took a deep breath.

Whiskey jutted a chin at the file folder still in Margaurethe's hand. "So, what's it about?"

Margaurethe accepted the olive branch, and stood. She laid the folder on the desk, opening it so that Whiskey could see the contents. Spreading the documents out, she began explaining each facet of the paperwork that would be the basic building blocks of Whiskey's new regime. How she managed it without reaching out to run her hand over the light blond head bent before her, she never knew.

CHAPTER EIGHT

Whiskey scowled at the television, not seeing the car chase depicted on the screen as Daniel and Zebediah played a video game. Cora sat at her feet, content to remain quiet in her presence, no doubt sensing the building explosion growing in Whiskey's chest. Alphonse was playing mumblety-peg with a large butterfly knife. He had done it often enough that the spot of carpet he used as a target had long since been chewed up to reveal the sub-flooring. Castillo had noticed the damage a few days ago, but had said nothing.

It had been three weeks since Margaurethe's arrival. Three weeks since the boom had dropped, forcing everyone to stay indoors and silent. Three weeks of sheer boredom that was slowly killing Whiskey and her friends. Bad enough she couldn't go out when she wanted, but the others chafed under a restriction that had nothing to do with them. A renewed anger washed over her, aimed at both causes—Margaurethe for ordering it, and Valmont for making it necessary. Had Valmont not been in the city, the others would not be suffering. Even if Whiskey had to remain behind, it was better than all of them having to tolerate the tedium.

There had been little to report this morning when Whiskey had asked Margaurethe about the background checks on people still banned from the residence. Checking up on Whiskey's friends held a low priority. Since then, Whiskey had been withdrawn and sullen, not responding to those who spoke to her. *You'd think with the amount of money she throws around, she could grease a few wheels on this.*

Margaurethe's argument held true, though. None of them were capable of standing up to an elder. Even Alphonse and Zebediah linked had held Castillo off for no more than a quarter hour. All four together couldn't stand against Valmont, and they held the knowledge regarding Whiskey's existence and whereabouts.

Zebediah whooped at scoring against Daniel, drawing Whiskey's attention.

When he and his brother had attacked her all those months ago, she had defeated them. They had immediately switched sides, becoming her unwanted protectors as she fled Fiona's grasping fingers. Their defection had always worried Whiskey. If Valmont got hold of them, would they just as quickly help him take her down? Or had her treatment of them been more satisfying than Fiona's, thereby creating a sense of loyalty that the other woman had never enjoyed? Whiskey would never know until their allegiance was put to the test, a test that could have devastating consequences.

She watched Daniel's subdued reaction to the digital thrashing he received, his eyes narrowing with a familiar intensity as he proceeded to win back what he had lost. He had been the first to turn against Fiona, the first to support Whiskey in her *Ñíri Kurám*. He had done so because he cared—not for Whiskey personally, but for her as his patient. He had paid for that with the torture his pack leader had put him through. She still noted patches of smooth scarred flesh where Fiona had skinned him in her effort to break him. Whiskey had an obligation to keep him safe, but did that mean she had to pen him up like a tiger in a zoo?

Cora shifted on the floor, and Whiskey's fingers ran through the dirty blond hair, more out of habit than desire. Her feelings for the lone woman were ambiguous at best. Cora was genuinely attracted to Whiskey, but she had been set to play Fiona's whore with Whiskey from the beginning. How much of it had been real affection, and how much completing the task to which she had been ordered? It was easy to continue such a scam and reap the benefits. Whiskey recalled her occasional sense of revulsion regarding Cora. It tied into the disgust Whiskey felt for herself, always bringing her back to that night several months ago when Fiona's pack had targeted an arrogant but inexperienced teenager who'd been intent on teaching Whiskey a lesson. If she closed her eyes, she recalled the dead look in his bruised eyes, the broken nose gushing blood. She recalled the sights and sounds and smells, the impact of her fist as she hit him in her misguided attempt to finish the beating before things got even more out of hand. Worse, she remembered the visceral joy that had risen within her. It had been Cora who had given Whiskey a knife, and urged her to kill their prey; Cora who had assumed Whiskey's accidental murder of Spot had been because Whiskey had wanted to do it by hand rather than with a weapon; Cora whose main concern had always been that Whiskey remembered who helped her in the early days. Still, it had been less complicated to keep Cora in her bed, allowing herself the physical pleasures of a familiar, warm body while everything around her changed so dramatically.

One of the security guards wandered through the living room from the kitchen, a glass of milk in hand. The Human company had long since been released from their contract. This one was Sanguire, one that Margaurethe had brought over from Europe. Her personal guard. Whiskey watched him pause behind the couch, observing the television for a moment before his eyes slid over to her. He gave her a respectful lift of his chin.

Whiskey raised an eyebrow, and returned the greeting with a slight nod.

The niceties met, the guard left the room for parts unknown. Margaurethe had found a place nearby that she rented to house the off-duty security. This one had just completed his shift a few minutes ago. With nothing else to do, Whiskey had begun watching the comings and goings of the people set to keep her imprisoned. There were always six on duty—one supervisor overseeing the others, one in the foyer, one just outside the front door, and three performing random patrols of the property. They worked twelve-hour shifts, and the supervisor was responsible for covering the others during meal breaks. Within the next ten minutes, shift change would be complete, and the morning crew would return to the other residence.

Twenty minutes drifted past. Daniel championed his cause, resulting in a spectacular car crash and a string of swearing from Zebediah. He demanded satisfaction, and Daniel made a move to toss the game controller aside.

"Keep playing," Whiskey said in a whisper loud enough that only they could hear.

The two contestants glanced at her, and Daniel queued up the game for another round.

Whiskey's mind expanded across the property, noting locations of everyone. The security supervisor was speaking to the door guard in the foyer, three others patrolled outside, and the exterior guard idled by the door. Castillo was in the den with the door closed, having no interest in listening to explosions and gunfire from the living room. Margaurethe had left an hour ago with her driver for some meeting.

She touched Alphonse's essence, the sensation as good as tapping him on the shoulder. "Garage. Check the car. Let me know when you're in place—don't start it until I tell you."

A grin crossed his face. With a smooth motion, he rose to his feet, flipping the butterfly knife until it safely closed. By the time he reached the kitchen and the door to the garage, it was tucked inside his jacket.

The sense of anticipation became palpable in the living room. Whiskey kept to the whisper, knowing it would not carry to the two security officers in the foyer. "Is there a demo on that game?"

Zebediah's red mohawk ducked in a nod. He exited out of the new round they had started, and found the demonstration mode. At Whiskey's curt gesture, he started it. The splash screen of *Auto Destruction* played across the screen, followed by an explosion as it began its display. He and Daniel remained on the couch, waiting.

Tugging gently on Cora's hair, Whiskey said aloud, "Can you get me a soda?"

"Of course, *aga ninna*."

As Cora stood, Whiskey pulled her down for a kiss. "Go to the garage, get in the car, wait for us." She received a thoroughly lascivious smile, and a kiss to match before Cora left the room.

Again Whiskey scanned the property. The supervisor had finished his discussion in the foyer, and had stepped into the den to talk to Castillo. Daniel was closest to the kitchen, and Whiskey whispered, "Daniel, go."

Daniel tossed the controller onto the couch, and sauntered from the room.

Whiskey wondered what was taking so long with Alphonse. Just as she began to think something had impeded her spur-of-the-moment plan, she felt a sense of smothering. She forced herself to not fight for breath as the feeling was Alphonse's essence stroking against hers. "Go. Tell him to start the car as soon as I get into the garage. You be ready to open the door."

Whiskey almost laughed at Zebediah. It was taking all his self-control to not whoop in joy at their jailbreak. He jumped up and left the room. Once more she checked the house. The guard in the foyer was a secondary line of defense should someone get through the door, not there to make certain everyone remained inside. There were no failsafes in place for Whiskey making a break for it, which suited her fine.

Standing, she glanced into the empty foyer, and at the closed den door. With a nod of satisfaction, she strolled through the living room, and into the kitchen. Through a window she saw two of the guards in the backyard, pleased to see that neither of them were near the garage. She was fairly certain that they would assume Castillo was off to run an errand, buying her a few precious seconds.

Heart pounding in anticipation, she stepped into the garage. The minute she did so, Alphonse started the car. The front passenger door stood open for her. Zebediah threw open the overhead door, and piled into the backseat on the driver's side. Whiskey jumped in, slamming her door closed. "Everybody down! Let's get out of here."

Alphonse hit the gas, and the car flew down the drive. Whiskey heard someone yell, then felt one of the security guards questing. She blocked his attempt at controlling Alphonse, Daniel and Cora linking with her to bar other attempts. The attack lessened with distance, and within five minutes, they reached the highway. Zebediah and Cora yelled in delight, Zeb pounding the back of the driver's seat as he hollered.

Grinning, Whiskey turned to Alphonse. "What the hell took you so long?"

"They had a tracking device on the car. *Sañur Gasum* Dorst told me about it last week." He merged with traffic heading north. "I had to find it, or they'd be on our ass."

Whiskey rolled down her window, letting the crisp air flow through her hair. "I'm going to have to give Reynhard a raise."

***

"You can't track her?" Margaurethe's voice was little more than a growl. She had wrapped up a meeting about the new building, feeling all was right with the world. The phone call she had received from Castillo had wiped away her good spirits. She had sped home, demanding Phineas break every known traffic law in the process. It had been a wonder they had made it without being pulled over. Not that it had done the least amount of good. Whiskey had been gone for thirty minutes before Margaurethe's arrival. "I thought Reynhard had put measures in place."

The priest held up a small black box. "He did. They removed them."

Margaurethe swore, snatching the tracking device from him. She squeezed it hard in her hand, battling the urge to throw it across the room. "Where's Reynhard?"

Castillo paled, taking a step back from her outburst. "I've already called him. He said he'd be here soon."

"Not soon enough!"

His joyful tones rang over the tableau. "Oh, I *do* love a good brawl! It appears I've arrived just in time."

Margaurethe whirled to see Dorst standing in the open front doorway. Succumbing to impulse, she threw the tracker at him, catching him in the chest. "She's gone!"

Unperturbed, Dorst closed the door behind him, stooping to retrieve the surveillance equipment. "So I've heard. She waited much longer than I imagined. Apparently I haven't given her patience enough credit."

"You must have some way to track them. That can't be your only method. Find her."

Dorst gave one his ludicrous genuflections, sweeping the length of his jacket in the process. "Of course, *Ki'an Gasan*. And when I do, what shall I tell her is your message?"

"Message?" Margaurethe closed on him, teeth extended and bared. "You'll take me to her."

He appeared forlorn, his twinkling eyes belying his expression. "I'm afraid not, *Ki'an Gasan*. Had my *Ninsumgal* wanted you to join her, she'd have requested your presence. I can only assume she prefers to...sow her wild oats, as it were, without all the prying." He gave a general wave, and looked about the foyer.

Margaurethe's fury was such that she lost all composure at his flippancy. Forgetting that Dorst was ancient and powerful when she had been a mere child, she reached out with her mind in an attempt to compel him to do her bidding. Amber and steel met her, blocked her with ease, and pushed back. She staggered, and supporting hands grasped her upper arms. Lashing out, she attacked whoever held her, flaying dark, bitter chocolate until the hands retreated.

Dorst clicked his tongue. "Has it come to that so soon, Margaurethe?"

She took a shaky step back, reeling in her lightly bruised mind, and focused on her immediate surroundings. Castillo sat on the floor nearby, holding his head as if he thought it would explode.

Dorst did not appear concerned, gazing at her with a calm, unruffled demeanor. He strode past her, and helped the priest to his feet. "Really, how juvenile," he admonished, dusting and straightening Castillo's cassock. "I didn't recall you having such a temper before."

Perhaps because Elisibet didn't try me near as much as does Whiskey. After considerable effort, Margaurethe controlled her temper. She approached Castillo, ignoring his subtle flinch as she took his hand. "My apologies, Father. I had no intention of using you as a punching bag."

"Of course, *Ki'an Gasan.*" He accepted her apology with grace, his voice as faded as his reflection, removing himself from her touch as soon as politely possible.

Margaurethe could not find it in her heart to be upset about this distance between her and Castillo. Like Whiskey, he had been raised Human and had Human sensibilities, even becoming involved in their petty little religion. He and Whiskey held a close friendship. The sooner she could get the priest out of the picture, the better. Still, it would behoove her to make such changes slowly. She still needed the *puru um.*

Dorst lightly clapped his gloved hands together. "Ah, how special. Now that we've kissed and made up, shall we return to the topic at hand?"

Unwilling to put up with his sardonic ways, Margaurethe turned to glare at him. "Locate her."

He screwed his gaunt face into a parody of deep thought. He crossed his arms, and held one finger to his chin as he considered a moment. "I do believe we've already covered that ground, dear Margaurethe. We became rather sidetracked when it came to the message you wished me to deliver."

Margaurethe felt her canines elongate, but did not threaten him again. "Ask her to return home where she's safe."

"Gladly, *Ki'an Gasan*! It will be my pleasure."

She forced her teeth to sheathe, grinding her molars at his apparent joy.

Dorst spun around, his trench coat gusting out like a billowing cloak, and opened the front door. He revealed two security guards on the porch, flanking it. "She can't have gotten far, and there are only so many places for her to entertain herself. I'll be in touch soon."

The door closed, and Margaurethe drew a deep breath. Her

bodyguard and Phineas had both miraculously disappeared as soon as she had stepped inside. Castillo still cowered near the living room entryway. She turned toward the den. "Come with me, please, Father. I need you to tell me what happened."

She did not look to see if he followed.

CHAPTER NINE

They drove around town for a few hours, the drizzly gray sky darkening to the gentle golden glow of streetlights. The radio volume was jacked up to not-quite-intolerable levels. They had stopped once at a liquor store for snacks and drinks. Whiskey spent the time glued to the passenger window, looking out at the city. It had been years since her last visit, having headed to Seattle at fourteen. Since her return, her activities had been curtailed, leaving no time to roam. There had been a lot of changes in the last four and a half years. Every so often, she regaled her companions with memories of hanging out at the Square, fights she had seen under the bridges, or the oddities of the people she had known. Every time they passed a knot of homeless teenagers,

Whiskey scanned their faces, searching for anyone she knew. Even that had changed too much in the intervening years, for she recognized no one.

As the hours dragged by her mood worsened. Busting out of the house had seemed like a great idea. With nothing to do and nowhere to go it had lost its mystique. Had she been alone, she would know where to go to have fun, but her companions had different ideas of what constituted entertainment. She had to take those opinions into consideration. The last thing she wanted was to have the cops come down on them.

It was Cora who saw the all-ages club. "Look! Shall we go there, *aga ninna?*"

Whiskey, slouched in the passenger's seat, feet on the dashboard, studied the building. Perking up, she brought her feet to the floor. "Yeah, that looks good."

Lights flashed in the windows, and the bass was loud enough for her to feel despite their blaring radio. A dozen people lounged outside, smoking cigarettes. Reaching out with her mind, she felt no other Sanguire in the area.

"Let's find a parking spot." Whiskey glanced over her shoulder at the three in the backseat. "No fighting. At least not until we're ready to go, okay? I don't want to get kicked out before we've had a chance to enjoy ourselves."

Zebediah looked a little put out, but promptly raised his chin in acceptance of her order.

Whiskey grinned at him. "Don't worry. We'll find somebody who needs his ass kicked. I promise." *Hell, all I need to do is make out with Cora in public. That ought to draw some homophobic asshole.* "Anybody got a cell phone?"

"I do." Daniel held up one.

"Call Rufus, and tell him where we are." Whiskey thought a moment. "Aleya, too. Maybe some *kizarusi* will want to party."

In less than fifteen minutes, Whiskey sat at a conglomeration of tall cabaret tables cobbled together for their use. Half-empty drinks littered its surface, and a number of girls had gravitated toward Daniel's somber good looks. The music was more pop than Whiskey preferred, but it didn't matter. Being surrounded by an exciting crowd of teenagers more than made up for the lack of musical taste. Not allowed to start fights, Alphonse and Zebediah had stepped outside to smoke cigarettes and impress the other troublemakers.

"Ah, here she is!"

Whiskey looked over from the dance floor to see Rufus Barrett standing at the table nearest her. His shoulder-length blond curls were as unruly as ever. "Hey, Rufus! Glad you could make it!" She glanced around him. "Just you?"

"Yeah, just me." He sat uninvited on a stool, and poked among the available glasses. Finding one to his liking, he raised it. "Cora," he said by way of greeting before taking a sip. "The party kind of ended when we had to leave your place. The others wandered off to find something else to do."

Whiskey shrugged, and smirked. "Sorry about that. It was out of my control."

He grimaced at the glass, and pushed it away. Waving down a roving waitress, he gave her an order. "I'm surprised you haven't spiked these, yet."

"Give it time. I think we ran out. Zeb will probably be the first to hit the liquor store before they close." She frowned. "When do they close?"

"Dunno. But they probably are by now." He glanced at his watch. "It's almost eight."

Whiskey blinked. "Already?" It suddenly occurred to her that Margaurethe was probably becoming concerned.

Rufus snorted. "Don't worry. It's not past your vampiric bedtime, yet. You've got hours until sunrise." He was interrupted from further comment by the arrival of his drink.

She rolled her eyes at him. One of Rufus's most annoying traits was the belief that they were all mythical vampires. Whiskey knew he socialized with them only because he was under the delusion they could make him a vampire. The others supported his assumption. She hadn't had the heart to tell him the truth, unwillingly finding it funny.

Cora distracted her with a caress along her jawline. "Dance with me, *aga ninna*?"

Whiskey scanned the crowd, checking for potential trouble. This club was relatively mainstream, with a number of high school jocks in attendance. She didn't want to get into a brawl quite yet. There were many girls-only tables, and a group of four had laid claim to a corner of the dance floor, shunning all masculine interest. Chances were good no one would get bent out of shape this early. It would be later—after the older attendees had had time to get drunk from the beers they had stashed in their cars— that the potential for a fight would rise. "Okay." Leaning across the table, she patted Rufus's arm. "We'll be back in a bit."

"Whatever floats your boat, *Ninsumgal*."

She grimaced at his adoption of the title, but didn't have time to argue as Cora dragged her away.

Upon her return twenty minutes later, another table and several chairs had been added to the mix. Zebediah had a plump Human on his arm, and was nibbling at her neck as she laughed. Three other Humans had pulled up stools, and were talking animatedly with Rufus and Daniel.

"Aleya!"

The woman with Zebediah pulled away, a smile on her heart-shaped face. "Hey, Whiskey! Thanks for putting the word out."

Whiskey released Cora to give the new arrival a welcoming hug. Aleya had been her first vessel, the first *kizarus* from whom Whiskey had drank blood. She didn't know if other Sanguire remembered or even cared about their first, but Aleya had eased what had been a potentially traumatic experience for Whiskey. It had created a special bond between them, strong enough that when the pack left Seattle Aleya had followed.

Cora frowned, but said nothing as she returned to her seat.

"Did *Ki'an Gasan* Margaurethe finally see the light?" Aleya continued.

Whiskey released her, looking away. "Not...exactly."

Aleya gave a slight gasp. "You ditched her? You ditched the house?"

Zebediah guffawed, and pulled Aleya back into his arms. "We sure did! They're still looking for us."

Whiskey grinned, slipping back into Cora's embrace. She shook a finger at Aleya's recriminating face. "We were dying there, *lamma*. We need a little excitement and action."

A rousing chorus of agreement erupted around the tables.

"Don't worry. We'll be good little boys and girls, and behave ourselves."

"I must say, *that's* a relief," said a musical voice. "Though how you behave yourselves is the true question, is it not?"

Whiskey felt her heart drop into her stomach as Dorst materialized at their table. If she didn't know he was a shape shifter, she could almost conclude he was a ghost walker with his ability to show up unannounced the way he often did.

"How'd you find us?" Alphonse stared at him, the woman he'd been flirting with completely forgotten. "I checked out that car with a fine-tooth comb. There's no way you could have tracked us."

Dorst smiled at his protégé. "Me to know, you to find out," he said in a singsong voice.

"We're not going back right now, Reynhard. So you can tell Margaurethe—"

He gave Whiskey a slight dip of respect, interrupting her. "I most humbly beg your pardon, my *Gasan*. Have no concern that I'm here to retrieve you like an errant puppy gone off her leash."

Whiskey scowled at his choice of words. Beside her Rufus chuckled briefly, her sharp glance stifling his humor. "Are you supposed to play bodyguard then?"

"No, no, no, though I'm at your disposal for such a thing if you wish." He grinned at her. "*Ki'an Gasan* Margaurethe is most displeased at your absence. Most displeased. She wishes you to return forthwith to the safety of your home."

"Isn't that sweet?" Rufus snickered.

Dorst raised a hairless brow at the Human's interjection. No one would dare to speak in such a manner about Margaurethe, not even Whiskey. Margaurethe's strength surpassed that of every youngling there, and the *kizarusi* came from long lines of Human families indebted to her kind. Her political and financial clout didn't even come into the equation.

"Shut up," Whiskey said.

Rufus shrugged, still smirking as he stirred his drink with his straw. He remained silent.

Whiskey studied Dorst's impish grin. *Most displeased* coming from him meant Margaurethe was in a towering rage. She felt a stab of guilt, but pushed it away. Margaurethe had to understand that Whiskey wasn't a fragile porcelain doll to be locked up in a glass cabinet, and trotted out for the occasional government function. That was what Fiona had wanted to do with her; and though Margaurethe's reasons were benevolent, it didn't appeal. "We'll be home when we're home."

"Of course." Dorst gave his little bow once more. "Is that the message you'd like me to relay?"

"No." Whiskey had already bucked authority; there was no need to exacerbate matters more than necessary by acting rude. "Tell her we'll be fine, and I'll come home…later." As an afterthought, she added, "And you aren't to tell her where you found us."

"I wouldn't dare!" Dorst said with mock outrage, a hand over his heart.

Whiskey grinned at him. "Thank you, Reynhard."

He stepped back, and gave her his patented obeisance. "It is my undying pleasure, my *Gasan*." He spun around, and disappeared into the crowd.

Slowly, the group at the table returned to laughter and talk. It was in continual flux as people came and went—dancing, ordering drinks at the bar, smoking cigarettes outside, and visiting the restrooms. The only other Sanguire to join them was the American Indian, Nupa Olawan, who arrived after Daniel called him on the phone about an hour later. Regardless of the exciting party atmosphere, a center of calm enveloped Whiskey, unbroken by the chaos and noise.

Now that she had gotten out of the house, all she could think about was Margaurethe.

CHAPTER TEN

The tapping should have distracted her. It went on and on, only pausing when headlights splashed across the foyer, beginning anew when the wayward younglings didn't burst through the door in a wild mass of exhilaration from their adventure.

Margaurethe forced her hand into her lap, silencing the tap of her nails against the desktop.

Castillo had called everyone he knew in Portland, every business he had arranged private parties with, all the people who might offer assistance to the runaways. No one had seen or heard from them. Not surprisingly, Rufus Barrett did not answer his phone. Neither did a number of young *kizarusi*, the ones who had acted less the meal ticket and more the groupies with

Whiskey's pack. Dorst had returned triumphant, his *Ninsumgal* found, and message delivered. He feigned sorrow at the return message he gave her, and left with her curses ringing in his ears, refusing to give her the location of her charge. Castillo had long since disappeared, as had the security detail, all staying out of her sight for fear of reprisals.

She didn't know what to do.

Elisibet had always been willful, stubborn to the point of parody at times. It looked like Whiskey had inherited that trait in abundance. Margaurethe wanted to call Castillo to her office to quiz him, determine what type of person Whiskey had been before the *Ñíri Kurám*, compare his responses to her memories of Elisibet. But to do so would mean appearing unconfident, something she had learned early in her political career was a death sentence.

Margaurethe went to the window, staring out at the side yard and the neighboring house. She could just see the street from here. It remained utterly devoid of traffic. Feeling out of control, portents and omens appearing everywhere, she had felt this helplessness only once, when Elisibet had died in her arms. Before that, though, she had sensed the beginnings of the downfall, the niggling little doubts that perhaps Elisibet was losing control, that Margaurethe had lost her long before.

"I am not positive this is the best way, m'cara." Margaurethe studied Elisibet from across the room. She sat before the crackling fire of their private sitting room, her needlework forgotten in her lap.

Elisibet wore her riding trews as was her wont when not attending official functions. A scowl creased her pretty face, giving her a petulant appearance. "Then what am I supposed to do, Margaurethe?" She slapped her hand onto the desktop, upsetting the missives there. "He has made a formal announcement to the Agrun Nam against me. Me, the Ninsumgal! I cannot let this challenge pass unanswered, else I will hear it from all of my subjects."

Margaurethe shook her head, her attempt to respond interrupted.

"I cannot! If the Nam Lugal of the Agrun Nam can insult me in a public statement, others will do the same. Nahib has announced that my actions are evil, that I am no better than a devil." Elisibet pushed away from the desk to prowl the room, her anger a living thing shadowing her every step. "It cannot go unchallenged."

"*Then counteract with your own statement,* m'cara. *Let the people know your only concern is their welfare. Truth will always outshine lies.*"

"*But whose truth?*" *Elisibet stopped pacing to look at her, an expression of love and aggravation on her face.*

Margaurethe recognized it, having seen it too many times to count over the course of their relationship. The look spoke of undying love, but also the belief that Margaurethe knew nothing of politics or the world, that her view did not touch reality. Lately such beliefs annoyed her. Too often she suffered patronization from members of court as they reacted in the manner their ruler had shown by such example. Again she wondered at the whisperings she had overheard, the ones that always stopped when her presence was noted. They worried her, those whispers.

Elisibet smiled, came forward and kissed her temple. "Thank you, minn'ast. *As ever, you have shown me wisdom."*

Margaurethe accepted the words and touch, knowing deep in her heart that they were not real.

Headlights pulled Margaurethe out of her memories, her heart quickening as a car drew close. It was not the pack, and she pushed away from the window in disappointment.

***

There came a light knock on the door. "*Ki'an Gasan?*"

Margaurethe looked up from the computer screen at which she stared, emails unread, reports unremarked upon. Dawn had come and gone with no word from Whiskey. Margaurethe felt thin and dry, her ceaseless worry draining her of all other emotion. "Yes, Father?"

Castillo stepped hesitantly into the room. He held up his cell phone. "I've word."

Adrenaline crashed through her, and she shot to her feet. "Is she all right?"

"She's fine." He swallowed, not coming nearer. "She wants me to go to her, but she doesn't want me to tell you."

Her knees gave way, her supporting strings cut as she flopped down into her chair. Should she be pleased that Whiskey was alive and well, glad of Castillo's report, or angry that Whiskey had not come home? The emotional miasma, coupled with the hours of anxiety, left a hollow in her chest.

"What do you want me to do?" His voice was a whisper.

Margaurethe gazed at him, saw herself reflected in his eyes, not caring for the fragility she witnessed. They both knew she could take over his mind, bitterly plunder it for the information she wished; that she could compel him, have him lead her to where Whiskey waited; that he had no real defense against her. She debated doing all those things, considered the fierce joy her fury would experience at finally having a target. She remembered Dorst's words from the day before. *Really, how juvenile.*

She looked away from the priest. "Go to her. Give her what she needs. Keep her safe."

Castillo took an uncertain step into the room. "Are you sure?"

The decision made, Margaurethe gathered about herself an implacable, resolute air. "Of course, Father." She rummaged in a drawer of the desk, pulling out a folder. Opening it, she glanced at the banking information. "In fact, if you'd be so kind as to sign this document." She turned it around, and pushed it across the desk at him. "I can give you a credit card."

He approached the desk, and picked up the form. "The Davis Group?"

"Yes." Margaurethe held out a pen. "I have several cards attached to the account. The money's there to keep her healthy and safe. No reason why it shouldn't be put to proper use now." She pointed the pen at the document. "That's a standard contract, basically stating you won't use the card to your personal advantage, that you're responsible for all funds you remove, and that you'll file monthly statements with the executor of the company, me. Save the receipts."

"Of course." He took the pen, careful to not touch her fingers, and signed the document.

Margaurethe handed over a card. "Sign the back." When he'd done so, she gave him a false smile. "Congratulations, you're the first new hire. I hope you don't mind, there aren't much in the way of benefits."

He gave her a kind smile. "Thank you. It's a good thing I'm relatively healthy."

She nodded. "Go, then. Keep her safe."

Castillo bowed his way back to the door, something he had only done with Whiskey before. "I'll keep you informed as much as possible, *Ki'an Gasan*."

Something flickered through her heart, whether it be offense at his presumption or a pitying relief at his offer, she didn't know. "Thank you, Father."

He kowtowed once more and left.

With him went her last vestige of strength. She dropped her head to the desk, leaning her forehead against her arm.

If she did not think, did not feel, she could almost convince herself that she had returned to that empty husk she had become just after Elisibet's death. The sensations felt similar. Not knowing what the next day would bring, not caring, for that matter. Margaurethe had remained poised between life and death in her abysmal grief for months. Catatonic had been the word that described her, though it had not come into usage until centuries later. She had subsisted on weak porridge and tea, hand-fed to her by her mother, had suffered bedsores and skin rashes as servants changed her soiled diapers and sweaty sheets. Only when Margaurethe had overheard others talking about Mahar's prophecy did she rouse herself; only when she had discovered a sliver of chance that her Elisibet, her heart, would return from death did she struggle from the dark deathbed to which she had succumbed.

She had relearned how to walk, how to be gracious, play the courtly games, protect herself. She had refused all suitors—not that there were many who wanted to take on the Sweet Butcher's leavings. She had developed a wicked sense of business, and built a corporate empire to rival Elisibet's monarchal one, all because she knew her lover would return one day.

But Elisibet wasn't here.

***

Margaurethe looked up at the knock, slightly guilty. She stood in Whiskey's bedroom, surrounded by clothes and personal belongings, not sure for what she was searching. She set down Whiskey's hairbrush, and turned toward the sound. "What is it?"

Phineas cracked the door open, peering cautiously in at her. "Hey, cuz."

She felt even more foolish at a family member catching her. Crossing her arms over her chest, she attempted to look like she belonged there. "What is it?"

He stepped further into the room, curiously scanning it. "How are you holding up?"

Margaurethe sighed, wishing that for once he would at least make an attempt to follow proper protocol. But a faint smile crossed her face, knowing he only acted this way because he cared. "Fairly well, under the circumstances. Father Castillo tells me they've holed up in a local hotel for a few days. So far, the financial damage has been minimal."

Scratching his closely cropped hair, he nodded. "That's good then, innit?"

"It is, yes." Turning away, she reached out to adjust the placement of the hairbrush. The room wasn't lavishly decorated. Whiskey's backpack sat on the unmade bed, the detritus of her life spilling out onto the sheets.

"Is that hotel anywhere near SW Park Avenue downtown?"

She frowned at her cousin, looking at him. "No, it's on the east side of the river. Why do you ask?"

Again Phineas scratched his head, rubbing the back of his ear. "Valmont was seen going into the Ronston Hotel. Might want to have *Sañur Gasum* have a look-see."

Her frowned deepened. "Where did you hear this?"

"From one of the guards. He said he'd seen Valmont leaving Tribulations last night when he was driving past. Followed him to the Ronston."

That particular hotel was located uncomfortably close to the youth club that Whiskey and her pack had taken to frequenting. If Valmont so much as strolled past on the sidewalk, the number of young Sanguire in the vicinity would make the club shine like a veritable beacon, drawing him right to her.

Margaurethe stepped forward, ushering him out of Whiskey's room. No one had told her that he had changed hotels. "Thank you for telling me, Phineas." She closed the door behind her, and set off down the stairs. "Has anyone reported this to Reynhard?"

He trotted after her. "He's not answering his phone."

She made a noise of aggravation. "Fine time for that." At the bottom of the stairs, she made her way into her office. "Has anyone attempted to contact Father Castillo?"

"I don't think so."

Margaurethe nodded, and picked up the phone. "I'll see to it."

Summarily dismissed, Phineas gave her a slight wave, and left.

Her call to Castillo resulted in being sent straight to voice mail. Vexed, Margaurethe left a message for him to call her as soon as possible. She stared at the phone in thought. It had been four days since Whiskey's flight. Margaurethe was of the opinion she remained away out of sheer spite. Positive there would be no answer, she dialed Whiskey's number. As expected, no one picked up, and again she left a voice message. For all she knew, Whiskey's phone was upstairs in her backpack.

Growling under her breath, she took a steadying breath, counted to ten, and picked up the receiver once more, this time calling Dorst.

"'Allo?"

A flutter of nerves rose in Margaurethe's stomach. The sensation annoyed her. She ground her teeth, and forged onward. "Reynhard, I've recent word of Valmont. I can't seem to reach Father Castillo or Whiskey. We need to talk."

"Most indubitably, *Ki'an Gasan*. When and where should we meet?"

Though it would be easier for him to come to her, she had the sudden urge to get out of the house. It felt abandoned without the younglings here, and asking him here flaunted her inability to control Whiskey. "Where would you suggest?" She almost saw his mind working, the vagueness of his countenance as he considered her question, perhaps a long finger tapping at his chin in the process.

"There's a nice little coffee shop in Pioneer Square downtown," he drawled, chuckling. "Nothing more than a brand-name chain, of course, but plenty of people will be present to distract any unwanted eyes and ears."

"That will be fine. When can you be there?"

"Within the hour, *Ki'an Gasan*."

She made note of the location, and said her farewell. Rising, she brushed against her cousin's mind, calling him to her. "Phineas, we're going for a ride downtown."

CHAPTER ELEVEN

Phineas pulled over to allow Margaurethe out of the black Town Car, ignoring the honks of irate drivers as they protested his double parking. He stepped out, and opened her door. "I'll find a parking space up ahead. Give me a buzz when you're ready to go, cuz."

Margaurethe nodded absently. Bricks covered the ground beneath her feet, the majority with names etched onto them. She wondered how it had been determined whose names to use as she glanced about Pioneer Square. A midsized amphitheater had been created by rows of steps, leading down to a central circle. It currently held a stage and overhead awning. Whatever had been scheduled was finished for the day; a large truck had pulled in, and workmen swarmed over the area, dismantling things. A handful of people sat along the steps, enjoying the rare lack of precipitation and their coffee. Here on the upper level, food carts clustered together, and a light rail train pulled into its stop to disgorge its stale passengers for fresh ones.

She turned toward the coffee shop, a good-sized business on the northwest corner of the plaza. Dorst stood out, a beacon of gothic drama in a sea of casual sensibility. An unwelcome sense of relief flooded through Margaurethe at the sight of him.

"*Ki'an Gasan!*" he exclaimed making a formal bow, a paper cup in each hand. "It is good to see you once again."

Annoyance chased away her relief as people veered out of his way, staring at his conduct. "Stop that, Reynhard. Quit playing with the Humans."

He gave her a mock pout, but straightened. "But it's most entertaining, you can't deny that."

Despite herself, she smirked. "To business."

"Ah, to business then."

He handed her one of the cups, and led the way down some steps to an outdoor table. The sky remained gray, but no rain was in the forecast, for which Margaurethe was pleased. This place was worse than her homeland for its dank, overcast days. They sat down, and she leaned close. "I've word of Valmont being seen at the Ronston Hotel."

"Yes, I've heard that." He sipped at his drink. "Do be careful. The coffee is most hot."

Does no one else see the danger here? Her anger rose to a low simmer, and she felt a growl rumbling within her chest. "Is that all you have to say? You've heard that?"

Dorst gifted her with an astonished look. "You expect more?" Not waiting for an answer, he sat back and tilted his head. "Very well then. Valmont checked out of the Kierney Hotel two days ago, and checked into the Ronston, though it is unknown why. Perhaps their maid service left much to be desired. Perhaps he simply wanted to be closer to the downtown area where the majority of homeless Human children reside. He spends most of his time roaming the streets at all hours of the night, and goes to Tribulations when he wants a break from it all. He's been seen in the company of a number of Humans there, all of which are *kizarusi*, so it's assumed he's only there to partake of a light snack upon occasion. He's made no contact with any of the politically inclined Sanguire living in the region.

"I've already spoken with Father Castillo regarding the issue, and he's moved my *Gasan* to another location for her impromptu parties. She no longer frequents the downtown area in any way. She has not been in contact with any of her former acquaintances on the street. I'm given to believe that too much time has passed, and all the Humans she knew have moved on to greener pastures."

Margaurethe let out the breath she did not know she had been holding. Knowing that Whiskey was in less danger eased her mind, though not entirely. "Do you have any idea why he came to Portland?"

Dorst gave a light shrug, mouth pursed in thought. "The *Agrun Nam* has been quite close-mouthed and elusive these days. It's been difficult keeping tabs on all of them. I assume that Whiskey's old Human friends in Seattle may have been a deciding factor. That and the sudden influx of O'Toole wealth and influence into the area have given them cause to consider Portland a likely place to search."

She scowled, sitting back with a *harrumph*. "Valmont was here days before I was, Reynhard. That can't be why."

"Perhaps, but your money preceded you by several months. It's also possible Valmont found someone in Seattle who revealed that Whiskey was raised in Oregon. If anyone would come running to her aid, it would be you, *Ki'an Gasan*. You can't deny that. It would have been an easy thing for someone to get the information that you planned to come to Portland. What's that crass American saying? 'Loose lips sink ships'?"

"You think they know I'm here?"

"I do."

Margaurethe considered his words. She did not think that any of her people was a spy for the *Agrun Nam*. They had all been with her for far too long. She trusted them. Anyone with an ounce of intelligence would have had her under scrutiny, especially once word had reached them that Elisibet's possible reincarnation had been spotted. "In that case, I'll need to check in with the local *Saggina*."

"It is only polite."

She grimaced at him. "And you have nothing else to report about the *Agrun Nam*?"

"No. They're sitting pretty in their council chairs, acting blissfully ignorant of the entire matter." He leaned close, lowering his voice. "Though rumors are beginning to circulate. Father Castillo's contacts have been chattering, and it's been several months since his initial report. I sincerely doubt the *Agrun Nam* are not aware, nor do I believe *Sublugal Sañar* Valmont is here without their backing."

Margaurethe didn't need the reminder of the priest's ineptitude. *And he's the one on whom you've entrusted the hope of the entire European Sanguire people.* "How is she?"

Dorst smiled. "She's doing well. She's keeping her pack close to hand, allowing them just enough freedom to combat the doldrums. Father Castillo has found them a house in what is termed 'Felony Flats.'" At her raised eyebrow, he chuckled. "It's a low-income neighborhood, one where the majority of Humans don't pay much attention to what their neighbors are up to as a simple act of self-preservation."

"It sounds dreadful."

"Perhaps. While it's not upscale, it at least affords her a place to relax that doesn't raise many questions. People can come and go at all hours with little repercussion. In fact, considering the location, three a.m. parties are the norm rather than the exception."

"Is she—" Margaurethe felt the sudden lump in her throat, and shook her head, looking away.

"She's well, *Ki'an Gasan*, as well as to be expected. I can't say she's happy, but she needed the time away to think."

Margaurethe didn't like the sympathetic tone in his voice, but would look a fool if she argued. She inhaled deeply, smelling a hint of rain on the air. Apparently the weather professionals were fallible the world over. "Has that American Indian turned back up…the one that's been socializing with her?"

"Nupa Olowan? He has indeed."

"The *We Wacipi Wakan* has yet to answer my missives. Father Castillo is of the opinion that this Nupa isn't affiliated with them. What say you?"

"I say Father Castillo has a naive streak that's quite detrimental to his political acumen." Dorst smiled at her sudden bristle. "Nupa is no doubt a spy for the *We Wacipi Wakan*. I've already notified our *Ninsumgal* of my suspicions. She saw no reason for him to discontinue his association with her."

"No reason?" Patrons at other tables glanced their way at her outburst, reminding Margaurethe that they were not alone. She lowered her voice to a bare whisper, not able to contain the outrage. "Does she not understand the political disaster in the making? She's the leader of a people who, for all intents and purposes, are setting up her government in the sovereign territory of another!"

He cocked his head at her. "Of course, she's aware of the ramifications, *Ki'an Gasan*. I made certain to explain them in exquisite detail when I made my report to her."

Margaurethe glowered, but had no rebuttal. *The eunuch is at least as old as Mahar was when she made her prophecy. He, of all the people I know, would understand the ins and outs of this powder keg.* The thought did not ease her asperity.

"Were you aware that my *Gasan's* mother was a half-blood American Indian?"

She blinked, her fury vaporizing, mind scrambling to catch up. "Yes, I'm aware of that."

"Then you must also be aware that by the very laws of the *We Wacipi Wakan*, she is a member of their people…probably more so than she is European. We've yet to find a genealogical connection for her father."

Margaurethe slumped slightly in her chair, lips pursed as she considered his words. She had been prepared to bring Whiskey to power, to overthrow the *Agrun Nam*, and scourge those that so richly deserved punishing for their involvement in Elisibet's assassination, to bring her back to Europe as the leader of her people. The right to ascend Europe's throne didn't come from bloodline, though a debate could have been made as such when Elisibet had taken over at her father's death. The *Agrun Nam* had backed her claim in an effort to forestall a civil war when the European Sanguire were at their weakest against Human attacks, nothing more. It would be simple for Margaurethe to use

Mahar's prophecy to force the Euro Sanguire to accept Whiskey as their new *Ninsumgal*.

Gareth Davis had yet to be located in any genealogical database connected with the European Sanguire. Either he and his family were unclaimed bastards from the Dark Ages, or he belonged to another genetic line altogether. Whiskey's pale complexion and hair had to have come from someplace, but unless they could find Gareth or his parents, there was nothing indicating his daughter was European. Without that tenuous connection, Whiskey could never ascend to the throne of the Euro Sanguire.

Dorst said, "It's only natural that they be curious, and send someone along to learn more about her."

She stared at Dorst blankly for a moment, bringing her mind back to their conversation. "You don't believe he's there to cause trouble, or report her weaknesses to his people?"

Dorst smiled. "Oh, he's there to report any weaknesses. They'd be fools not to look for them." He held his hands up in a "who knows" gesture. "But is he finding any? He sees a very powerful young woman who doesn't use her strength to subvert or cause pain, one whose primary concern is keeping her friends safe from harm, yet is happy and content. I daresay our *Ninsumgal* inherited quite a bit of her leadership abilities from her mother's people. Her only failings are her age and Human upbringing."

Curiously, though none of Dorst's news was good, Margaurethe felt better for having met with him. She quashed a sense of hesitancy. "Do you think there's the chance she'll return to the house soon?"

"Of that I'm not certain."

She hadn't expected much else. "I've purchased a building for The Davis Group. The final paperwork was signed yesterday. In another month, the penthouse will be ready for her occupancy."

Dorst raised his paper cup in toast. "In only a month? My, you've certainly lit a fire beneath their buttocks, haven't you, *Ki'an Gasan*?"

Her lip curled, but she did not take the bait. "Can you please let her know? As interior renovations are completed, she and her friends will have a safe haven to enjoy themselves."

"Of course."

Ignoring the look of sympathy on his face, she lowered her chin. "Then I believe that's all I had for you, Reynhard."

He accepted her dismissal. Standing, he gave her a flagrant bow, drawing the regard of everyone in the small seating area. He smiled at her discomfiture. "Please call me at your leisure, *Ki'an Gasan*. I'm ever your servant."

Margaurethe waved him off without answering, watching him turn and trot away, up some steps and around the corner. As the other patrons returned to their conversations, she rummaged for her cell phone to call Phineas around with the car.

CHAPTER TWELVE

"Sweet! Check it out!"

Whiskey paused the video game to glance at the text message Zebediah had just received. "A rave?"

"Rave?" Daniel sat at the dining room table, looking up from his book. He gave one of his rare smiles, setting the book aside. "When and where?"

"Southeast, in the warehouse district." Zebediah turned to stare at Whiskey. "We're going to go, aren't we? We have to!"

"We don't *have* to," she started, interrupted by the chorus of groans and complaints around her. "What?"

Cora stroked Whiskey's upper arm. "It would be so much fun, *aga ninna*. We haven't had much of that lately."

It had been three weeks since they had run away. Because of reports of Valmont's increased activities, the pack had changed residences once already. While they enjoyed more freedom than they would have had they stayed at Margaurethe's, they were still leashed by the danger imposed by Valmont's presence. It was similar to staying at Margaurethe's with the exception of having the freedom to allow people to come and go. They had been unable to pull off a private party anywhere, though. All the places they had rented from in the past were downtown. Whiskey wasn't sure Castillo was even looking all that hard for alternatives, preferring to keep her safe at home.

Whiskey held her hand out for the phone again. Zebediah passed it over without comment. She accessed the message, and studied it a moment. The address was indeed across the river from where Valmont lurked. There would be loud music, and hundreds of teenagers and young adults. It promised to be wild and entertaining, hours of blissful chaos in which she could lose herself and her past. Most importantly, there would be no well-meaning chaperones or bodyguards hanging about.

She handed the phone back to Zeb. "Guess we're going." The resultant celebration caused her to smile. She accepted Zebediah's thanks, taking the rough buffeting as he pounded on her arm and shoulders. Other than her, he was the youngest of all of them, and Whiskey had begun to think of him as her little brother.

Nupa and a *kizarus* sauntered in from the kitchen, arms laden with popcorn and bottles of beer. "What's up?"

"Rave!" Zebediah whooped.

"That's fantastic." The *kizarus*, a lithe little redhead, smiled and came directly to Whiskey, handing her a beer. "Can I have the first dance, *ninna*?"

Whiskey smiled flirtatiously, accepting the bottle, the Human's fingers caressing hers in the exchange.

Cora pushed forward, between them. She bared her teeth at the woman, and growled.

The Human blanched, hastily stepping back from the threat.

"Hey!" Whiskey reached out with her mind, and grabbed Cora's. She wrapped the sensation of ashes, and gave it a light jerk. "Back off."

It got Cora's attention more than hurt her. She spun around, looking abruptly contrite, fangs sheathed, chin raised.

Whiskey glanced around at the others. Most of them ignored the interchange, though Zebediah's mouth held a faint grin. Nupa looked blank, and Daniel held a faint commiserating air about him. "Are you all right?"

The Human answered with a fast nod, though she looked no less frightened.

Whiskey could think of nothing else to do, but—"Go to our room. I'll talk to you later."

Cora whispered, "Yes, *Ninsumgal*," and padded away, vanishing down the hall.

Once she was gone, Whiskey turned back to the others. "The rave starts in a few hours. We can start the pre-party party here. Make the phone calls, have someone pick up some booze and food on the way."

Zebediah gave an excited yell, drawing Alphonse from outside where he had been smoking.

Whiskey raised her beer in toast, and took a long swallow of it. She collapsed back onto the couch, the video game forgotten.

The *kizarus* had found her way back to Nupa's arm, and all evidence of the tense moment had disappeared. Daniel and Zebediah both had cell phones in their hands, texting and calling the growing network of young Sanguire and Human hangers-on that surrounded Whiskey. Castillo had begun referring to them as Whiskey's new court. Alphonse went in search of Castillo. The priest's credit card and vehicle would be needed for the upcoming libations.

She drank her beer in peace, wondering what the hell to do about Cora.

At night, Whiskey dreamed of Margaurethe—Elisibet's memories mingling with her own, until she couldn't tell one from the other upon waking. She thought she spoke in her sleep because Cora had become more and more desperate to keep her occupied, jealously guarding her against any woman that dared show Whiskey attention. Cora's behavior coupled with the poignant dreams had made it more difficult for Whiskey to connect with her.

Somehow, she had to break away from Cora without causing the other woman to feel abandoned. She had made a promise to Cora months ago, and planned to keep it. Whiskey would never forget who had helped her in the beginning; Cora would never need to worry about being taken advantage of again.

How to get that through to her, though?

Whiskey listened to her pack as they plotted and planned their evening of fun, wondering how it was possible that she could be so much the center of their world, but so far removed from their lives.

***

Whiskey danced on a crowded floor with Cora, Rufus and Nupa, given no room to do more than jump up and down to the electronic music blaring throughout the abandoned warehouse. Daniel, Aleya and a number of *kizarusi* guarded their belongings and table—an overturned wooden crate—and Zebediah and Alphonse were somewhere outside with a handful of others, probably getting into one of their beloved brawls. She had no idea where the padre was. He disliked the music. So did she, for that matter; she was attracted more to the wild atmosphere than the tunes.

Cora acted subdued. She knew which way things were going, and didn't care for it. She had been remorseful when Whiskey had returned to their room, apologizing for her infraction, even offering to apologize to the *kizarus* she had threatened. That alone let Whiskey know how repentant Cora was. Sanguire thought of Humans as prey or servants, hardly equals to be treated with concern.

Whiskey's mood soured at the memory. A callous part of her had enjoyed causing the emotional pain, had reveled in the tears she had caused, and she felt a wave of disgust. No longer wanting to dance, she backed off the floor, shoving her way through the unruly crowd. Cora attempted to follow, but Whiskey shook her head, waving for her to remain, following it up with a mental command. The last sight she had of Cora was one of tremulous chin and resignation.

At the crate turned table, Whiskey chased everyone else away, moving drinks aside to give her room to sit upon the splintering wood. She gulped from a cup of what turned out to be tequila, and leaned back against the wall behind her.

She was getting too old to run away. Living on the streets, dodging the authorities and living hand-to-mouth had far surpassed the foster homes where she had been placed as a child. It had even been fun, a risky challenge to skate through life without responsibilities. That circumstance no longer applied. Whether she liked it or not, she had enormous obligations these days, the least of which were her pack. She had inherited them, and could not turn them away to drift along on their own. They would be fresh meat for any older Sanguire who had the strength to control them, any Sanguire who might not be as kindhearted as she.

Leaving the house Margaurethe had set up had been another situation where Whiskey knew she had reacted in a juvenile manner. It was all childish bullshit. There was no denying she had Elisibet's memories, so her squirming to avoid the duty so neatly placed upon her shoulders was stupid. Despite this, she couldn't bring herself to return. Not yet. The Margaurethe of her memories had held no true political advantage over Elisibet. The current-day Margaurethe seemed to have decided to rectify that issue. Whiskey had no trouble comprehending the need for it, and even agreed that part of Elisibet's downfall had been the lack of allowing Margaurethe to soothe those rough, violent urges. There was no way Whiskey would be a simple figurehead, however, and Margaurethe had to understand that she did not hold all the power.

Whiskey drained the cup, leaning her head back against the grimy wall as the alcohol burned its way down her throat. Rufus arrived at her side, searching through the litter of cups to find his drink.

"So, when can I get you to come to my studio?"

She looked up at the Human with a raised eyebrow. He always harped about painting a portrait of her. "Sooner or later," she yelled so he heard her over the music.

He scoffed, grinning. "C'mon! It'll only be a few hours, I promise."

If she had not had the welfare of her people to worry about, she would have shown up on his doorstep weeks ago. She waved his plea away with a snort, and peered at the cups surrounding her for something else to drink.

She felt Alphonse before she saw him, shivering at the sudden sensation of smothering that swept over her. Looking up, she saw him push his way through the crowd, his skin pale. "What is it?"

"Valmont."

Swearing, she jerked to her feet, mind automatically searching the warehouse. Zebediah stood near one of the closest doors, probably set to guard it from Valmont's approach. Cora and Nupa remained on the dance floor, now accompanied by Daniel and the *kizarusi*. The Humans would be fine; unless Valmont knew who to look for in the mass of humanity, he would never pick them out of the crowd. It was the Sanguire that were in danger. She dared not extend her senses beyond the warehouse. Dorst had told her that she felt similar to Elisibet. If she brushed against Valmont's mind, he would be certain he had located her.

Rufus had frozen, cup halfway to his lips at her abrupt movement. He had not heard Alphonse's voice. "What's going on?"

She ignored him. "Where's he coming from?"

"Down Second Street, about a block away. Zeb was on the way to a store, saw him, and doubled back." A frown of confusion crossed his face. "He has a camera."

Whiskey clutched Alphonse's shoulder, pointing to the dance floor with the other. "Get them and Zeb out of here. Call the padre, get back to the house only if you're not followed."

"What about you?"

She glanced back at Rufus. "I'm going with Rufus. Valmont is looking for a group of younglings. He won't think to follow me if he doesn't see me."

Alphonse looked unconvinced, looking the Human over with a jaundiced eye.

Asserting mental pressure upon him, Whiskey bared her teeth. "That's an order. Go!"

Unhappy with the command, Alphonse nevertheless turned toward the dance floor.

Whiskey turned back to Rufus. "C'mon," she yelled, grabbing his arm, and hustling him toward another door. "Let's get out of here. I'll sit for a portrait right now."

Rufus's bearded face cracked into a smile. "You're on!"

CHAPTER THIRTEEN

Rufus's apartment was across the river from the rave. The once abandoned northwest warehouse district stood on the edge of downtown, and had recently experienced a popularity boom as old buildings were refinished and new businesses and residences added. After a short walk from the Old Town light rail station, they came to a squat two-story building, dwarfed by those on surrounding blocks. Two picture windows flanked the door, displaying several paintings.

Still freaked out about Valmont's appearance at the rave, Whiskey dithered at the windows. She studied the paintings as Rufus unlocked the door. "Your work?"

He grinned. "Yeah. That's mine." He stepped closer. "What do you think?"

With a frown, she examined the artwork. He was liberal with the deep blues and black, his subjects all thin and pale and haunting, each with exaggerated features or otherworldly characteristics; red eyes, leathery wings, fangs. They resonated with a mourning, soulful quality. "I like."

"Good!" He returned to the door, and held it open. "Come on in."

She gave him a calculating examination, reminding herself that he had had ample opportunity to hurt her over the last several months. Valmont and other Sanguire were a known danger, but Rufus was a Human who wanted to become a vampire. He wouldn't jeopardize that potential, ridiculous as it was, by harming her. Reaching out with her mind, she found no other Sanguire within the building. Going with her gut instinct, she smiled, and sauntered inside.

More loft than apartment, the residence was a converted storefront. The lower level was long and narrow, the back transformed into a kitchen and dining nook. Just inside the door to the right were a couch, love seat and small television. The rest of the area held easels, worktables, canvases in various states of color, and assorted junk the use for which she couldn't imagine. Stairs led the way to an upper level over the kitchen, and Whiskey saw a rumpled bed and a dresser through the railing.

"Make yourself at home." Rufus closed and locked the door. "You want something to drink?"

She sat on the couch. "Yeah, that'd be good. You mind if I smoke?"

"No. Go ahead." He rummaged in the refrigerator. "There's an ashtray on the TV."

Leaning forward, Whiskey collected the ashtray before pulling out her cigarettes and lighting one. As smoke drifted above her head, she scanned her surroundings.

The paintings here were as interesting as those in the windows, maybe more so. Setting her cigarette in the ashtray, she stood. Upon closer inspection, she noted that the subject was of one nude with an intricate tattoo of a winged angel that sparkled iridescently in the dim light of the portrait.

"Here you go." Rufus handed her a bottle of beer. Gazing at

the painting, he asked, "What do you think? I'm almost finished with it."

"Interesting." Whiskey watched him study his work. "When do we start?"

He looked at her in eagerness. "Now would be good, if that's all right."

She knew she should call Castillo or Dorst to let them know she was all right. Cora would be worried sick, as would the others. It had been so long since she had been out on her own, however, she was loathe to return too quickly. She had not been the true mistress of her fate since the night Fiona Bodwrda had shown up to save her from a beating and rape. It was nice not to have everyone hovering about her. "Okay. Where do you want me?"

Chewing his lower lip thoughtfully, Rufus moved chairs and clutter around. A black velvet backdrop hung along one wall, and it was here he set up a stool. He glanced at Whiskey, who had finished her cigarette. "If you'd have a seat here whenever you're ready?"

She sauntered over, and slid onto the stool. "How do you want me to sit?"

Rufus fussed around, turning her this way and that until she was positioned as he wished, giving her a pair of dark sunglasses to wear. He took more time turning on lights, and adjusting a white screen to create different shadows. Once everything was in place, he grinned. "Perfect."

Whiskey was glad for the sunglasses with all the light directed at her. "Glad you think so." She gave him a droll grin. "Now what?"

"Now, with your permission." He held up a camera.

"Picture? I thought you painted."

"I prefer working with live models, but you can't sit there for the twenty or thirty hours it'll take for me to finish." He set the camera on a tripod. "This way, while you sleep, eat, and have a life, I can continue working."

Sighing, Whiskey nodded. "Go for it." Vampires hated mirrors because they cast no reflection, and it was said photos couldn't be taken of them. She wondered how this sat with his belief regarding what she was.

Rufus took a handful of photos before he was satisfied he had captured what he wanted. He moved the tripod to one side, and arranged an easel and canvas in its place. "You ready?"

Whiskey shrugged. "As I'll ever be."

***

The cell phone woke Margaurethe. She peered at the bedside clock, noting it was not yet two thirty in the morning. Ringing phones at this hour boded ill, and her heart did a fine job of waking her as she sat up to answer the call. "Yes?"

"*Ki'an Gasan?*"

She recognized Castillo's voice, which did nothing to ease her trepidation. Scooting to the edge of the bed, she threw her legs over, feet blindly searching for her slippers. "Father? What is it?" She heard chaos on the other end as a number of excited voices spoke over each other, none audible enough for her to catch.

"Valmont was spotted near the place where the younglings had been partying. They split up to evade him."

Margaurethe's heart jumped into her throat, beating hard and fast. "Where's Whiskey?"

There was a long pause. "We don't know. She left with Rufus."

Her mouth dropped open.

"*Ki'an Gasan?* Are you still there?"

"You left her with a *Human?*" Margaurethe demanded.

"I—" Another pause, this one muffled as he covered the phone with one hand, and bellowed for silence. "I didn't leave her anywhere. When Valmont was seen, she had the younglings gather their friends and leave. She went with Rufus of her own volition."

Forgetting she was on the phone, she asked herself aloud, "Why would she do that?"

"I don't know, *Ki'an Gasan*, but that's what Alphonse said she ordered him to do."

Startled from her confusion, her rage once more flared forth. "You will tell me where this house you've set up is, and you'll tell me now, priest."

Her tone was enough to dissuade him from contention. He gave her the address. "What do you want me to do?"

"Calm the children. Get rid of the Humans there. Call Reynhard at once. Perhaps he can locate her before Valmont does." She had already stripped out of her nightgown, slippers long forgotten as she dragged clothes from her drawers and closet. "And stay put. You and I are going to have a chat."

She tossed the cell phone onto the rumpled bed as she hastily dressed.

***

Whatever had possessed her to leave Whiskey in the care of a priest and a eunuch? Phineas had awakened quite speedily at her abrupt mental prod, and they were now almost to the house that Castillo had rented for the young pack. The neighborhood was exactly as Dorst had described—run-down, neglected, a third of the residences boarded up or giving the appearance of being abandoned. Graffiti decorated every open expanse of peeling house paint or concrete wall. The occasional trash can resided on the curb, though the weed-strewn yards looked to be able to fill a hundred more rubbish bins if given half a chance.

"We're here."

The Town Car pulled into the driveway of a beaten down ranch house. Not waiting for him to assist, Margaurethe climbed out of the car and proceeded into the darkened carport. Even at three in the morning, a party was in progress a block away. She felt as well as heard the music in the distance, giving grudging credit to Castillo for finding the proper location to avoid observation. Not bothering to knock, she opened the front door and stepped inside.

The house had seen its last renovation in the mid-eighties. Lemon colored Formica countertops graced the kitchen, and the appliances were an olive green. Reaching forth with her mind, she found Castillo ahead and in the living area. The living room carpet was old-style shag, colored in random patches of oranges and browns. Yellow velvet furnishings cinched the deal, and Margaurethe grimaced at the atrocious decor.

Castillo stood before the unlit white stone fireplace. "*Ki'an Gasan.*"

"Has she returned?" Margaurethe scanned the rest of the house, not finding the familiar essence of roses.

"No, she hasn't. I've left messages for Rufus on his phone, but he hasn't answered, either."

Margaurethe quelled the urge to pick him up and shake him. He was Sanguire, not an errant animal that had piddled on the ghastly colored carpet regardless of his stupidity. "And Reynhard?"

He raised his chin. "I've notified him. He's searching the warehouse and surrounding areas now."

"Do we not even have the address of this Human?"

"No, *Ki'an Gasan*, we do not."

"Do we know if he would have brought her to his home, or another hideout?"

"No, we do not."

She stepped forward, fangs unsheathing. "Do you know *anything*, Father Castillo?"

He trembled, but did not back away. Nor did he answer.

At his lack of defense, she glared. "This is entirely your fault. First you notified the *Agrun Nam* of her presence in Seattle. You allowed her free rein as she partied her way around the city there and here. You let her go to a public function with hundreds of others in attendance, not even thinking that Valmont would also consider this 'rave' a likely gathering place for homeless children."

Castillo remained silent.

"If she is in danger, if Valmont finds and hurts her, you can be very certain that I will flay every inch of flesh from your worthless carcass, priest." When he again did not respond, she spun around, looking at the empty living room. Casting her mind forth, she realized that they were alone in the house. "Where are the others?"

He took a deep breath, and she turned to glare at him. "I did as you requested and sent home the Humans and *kizarusi*. The younglings are at a hotel on the outskirts of town."

Margaurethe had held hopes of interviewing them, perhaps forcing them to return with her. Perhaps without her lackeys in attendance, Whiskey would decide to tuck tail and come home where she belonged. Castillo's actions had aborted that half-formed idea, and it infuriated her. She had promised herself she would not physically attack him, but that did not preclude a verbal lashing. "You imbecile, you *ñalga súp*! Who are you to disobey me, you gelded Human-lover?"

Watching him flush, she patted herself on the back. Only when he countered did she realize that her words had had a completely different effect upon him.

"I am Whiskey's friend, *Ki'an Gasan*, and her teacher. I'm not her jailer, nor will I ever aspire to that position."

Margaurethe gaped at him as he continued.

"Furthermore, Whiskey isn't ready to return. I have urged it on many occasions, but it's not an option she feels she should take at this time. I cannot allow her pack to be taken into custody while she's away. To do so would be a betrayal of her wishes."

"You overstep your bounds, priest."

"No, *Ki'an Gasan*. You do. You are attempting to hold her too tight, and that will only strangle her. I don't believe that's your intention, but that will be the result of this power struggle between the two of you."

Margaurethe stared, flabbergasted. This wasn't a power struggle; she was trying to keep Whiskey safe from harm. Why couldn't he see that? Defending her actions to him, however, was abhorrent. He was young in the scheme of Sanguire life, sworn to celibacy in his misguided adoption of the Human religion, and did not understand the need to keep children safe, to keep Whiskey safe.

What if he's right?

Castillo paid homage, tilting his head slightly to reveal his neck. "If you'll excuse me, *Ki'an Gasan*. I must get to the hotel, and make certain everyone is settled in."

Again he unsettled her. Somehow he had gained mastery of the conversation, and now had ended it. She wanted to argue, yearned to allow her fury an avenue of escape, but something stopped her. Instead, she watched him pass her, and leave the room.

The front door closed softly behind him, leaving a dismayed Margaurethe in the gauche living room, wondering what had happened, what she should do.

CHAPTER FOURTEEN

The bouncer gave Margaurethe a raised chin, sussing out her nature as he courteously held the door for her. She slipped into the upscale club. The wash of Sanguire essences that touched her drowned out the music.

Taking up an entire city block and two floors, Tribulations was cavernous, comprised of light gray stone walls. Double bars mirrored each other from across the room, and a stage took up space at the far end between them. It currently bore a DJ and his equipment spinning ambient trance. A modest dance floor held a number of Humans and the Sanguire seducing them for an early morning snack. Tables held multiples of both races as they enjoyed each other's company. The faint smell of blood drifted to Margaurethe from her right where a series of decorative tapestries hid access to a number of doors—the private rooms for her kind to partake of the life blood needed to survive without alarming the uneducated Human unfortunate enough to wander into their territory.

It did not seem to make an impression on anyone that it was nearly four in the morning. That suited Margaurethe. She offered her rain jacket at coat check, took her claim ticket, and stepped deeper into the establishment. Skimming her mind across the multitude, she searched for a specific sensation, not finding it among the crowd. Her scan sparked the interest of the others, however, and glittering eyes regarded her from the low ambient light. The majority of them were nowhere near her age, so she felt no threat. None would band together against her. Sanguire preferred a solitary approach to feeding. Only children gathered in packs to hunt, and no youngling would come here; they would be too vulnerable to the whims of their elders. Margaurethe ignored the audience, and approached the nearest bar.

The barkeep sidled over. "What can I get for you, *gasan?*"

Margaurethe studied him. "A snifter of brandy should suffice, the more expensive the better."

If he was impressed with her request, he showed no sign. A few moments later, he delivered the requested libation.

Throwing caution to the winds, she handed a credit card to him to pay for the drink. Her presence here in Portland was no longer a secret, at least not to the people who mattered.

His eyes widened as he read the name on the card. Setting it on the counter, he slid it back toward her. "My pardon, *Ki'an Gasan.* Accept this drink as a gift."

A whisper flowed from the nearest tables to the farthest reaches of the room as her rank, and therefore her identity, passed among the Sanguire. The music continued to play, but a number of people on the floor paused in place at the news, halfheartedly returning to the dance after a moment's surprise.

She bowed her head. "Thank you."

He raised his chin to her, and stepped away, nervously wiping down the counter. Behind her, people moved past their shock, and returned to their conversations and entertainment, though the sound was more muted than before.

There was a slight hiccup in the noise levels as she turned around on the barstool to survey the room. From their appearance and the sounds of their accents, the majority of the Sanguire here were American born. She detected a handful of European and African dialects, as well. Margaurethe frowned in the direction of a table full of Japanese businessmen. She had no doubt that Tairo-no-Mitsuko would be notified of her location before the hour was over. One could always count on Asian Sanguire's obedience to their Empress.

She did not have long to wait.

Three men rose from a table and approached her, one with drink in hand. When he was within polite distance, he gave her a low obeisance. "*Ki'an Gasan* Margaurethe O'Toole, it is such a pleasure to meet you."

She took the trouble to step off her stool, and curtsy in return. "Thank you."

He held a hand to his chest. "I am Alfred Bescoe."

"Ah, of course!" Margaurethe held out her hand to clasp his. The lack of introduction of his companions told her they were servants rather than equals. "The Portland *Saggina*. I've been meaning to contact the embassy, but business has gotten in the way."

Pleased that she knew him, at least by reputation, he smiled. "I can certainly understand that. It is fortuitous that we've run into each other tonight then, isn't it?"

"Indeed. Would you join me in a drink?" She half turned back toward the bar, and her brandy waiting there.

He dithered a moment. Had she been lower ranking, he would have insisted they return to his table. The fact that she was one step removed from the *Agrun Nam* stayed his invitation. "Certainly, I'd be honored."

They settled together, his two men staying unobtrusively a few feet away as they turned to observe the rest of the patrons. The barkeep returned, and freshened both their drinks.

"What brings you to our fair city, *Ki'an Gasan*?"

"Business, for the most part." She turned on her stool to face him. "I've long considered exploring this area of the Americas, and now seemed as good a time as any."

His chest puffed out in pride, as if he had had something to do with the potential draw toward the city and state. "It's most pleasant here. Mild climate—though we have our occasional harsh winters—clean air and streets, low crime in the majority of the neighborhoods. What business were you looking to expand here, if I may be so bold? Perhaps I can point you in the right direction."

Settling into the small talk, she discussed a number of things that had no real bearing on The Davis Group, or its future headquarters and purpose. They passed the time this way for half an hour before she got down to her true purpose for coming to Tribulations. "Perhaps you can help me, Alfred." She reached out, placing her hand on his forearm.

"Anything, *Ki'an Gasan*. Anything." Hesitant, he lightly patted the back of her hand.

"There's but one deciding factor regarding my decision to opening a branch office here. I've heard some disturbing rumors that Valmont Strauss himself has been seen here. Is this true?"

His obsequious manner vanished, replaced with nervousness. He not-so-subtly pulled away from her touch. "Why do you ask, *Ki'an Gasan*?"

Not quite discarding the gracious businesswoman act, Margaurethe cocked her head. "As you're no doubt aware, we've had some major…differences in the past." She paused, waiting for his nod of response. "If he's here, and planning to stay, then I'd much rather find somewhere else to locate my business."

His anxiety faded, though not by much. He darted glances around them, no doubt scanning for Valmont himself. That he did so indicated he had been in contact, else how would he know for what to search? Not finding the individual in question, Bescoe blew out a breath. He leaned forward, lowering his voice to a fraction of a whisper. "I must admit, *Ki'an Gasan*, he is in the vicinity, and has been for a number of weeks."

Margaurethe affected a wounded demeanor, letting her companion be inclined to think she held concern for her own safety. "Do you know for how long?"

"*Sublugal Sañar* Valmont has not given me a time for his departure. In fact, he hasn't given me reason for his presence, at all." Bescoe gave the appearance of being put out, assuming he had a sympathetic audience.

She pulled back from him, debating how to drive the conversation.

"Please, *Ki'an Gasan!*" This time he placed his hand on her forearm. "Have no worries. *Sublugal Sañar* Valmont has assured me he won't be in town for long."

"Are you certain?" she asked. "I'd much rather open a branch office in some other area of the country if he will be a steady visitor to this region."

He gave her arm a gentle squeeze. "He's only here to locate something; he told me so. Once he finds what he's looking for, he plans to return home."

I just bet he will. Margaurethe continued to play the scared dame, wondering how the pompous official could fall for her act. She glanced quickly about the room, as if expecting Valmont to pop out from under a table. "Does he come here often?"

"He has upon occasion, yes. But have no fear." Bescoe gave her a supportive smile. "You are surrounded by my friends and countrymen."

Which did not answer her primary question—was he expected in tonight after searching for Whiskey, or would he return to his hotel room? Margaurethe did not bother gracing Bescoe's comment about her safety with a response. Half the people in the room would help eviscerate her for her relationship with Elisibet. Of that she had no doubt.

"If you'd like, I can get you a list of *kizarusi* in the city and outlying areas. There's no need for a woman of your rank to resort to trolling for food when it can be so easily delivered."

Margaurethe debated tossing aside the damsel-in-distress routine, but decided against the idea. If she did as she planned, there was no reason to alienate the local European Sanguire political structure in the city. "Oh! That would be most kind of you. Let me give you my business card."

Once they traded contact information, she made her excuses. Bescoe made a half-hearted attempt to bring her to his table, which she declined with just the right amount of reminder that she outranked him.

While she waited for her jacket, she went over the new knowledge she had gained. Unlike younglings, who needed to feed on Human blood every three or four days, Valmont was of an age that it was no longer necessary. At the most, he would be there every seven days, providing Tribulations was the main source of his nourishment. Margaurethe could find out from Dorst what Valmont's feeding schedule had been over the last few weeks, and make plans.

She felt him only moments before she heard his voice.

CHAPTER FIFTEEN

"Why, Margaurethe. What a pleasant surprise."

She spun around, fighting the urge to attack him with every ounce of her being. "Get away from me, you *san kurra!*"

Valmont raised an eyebrow at her slur. "Really? A foreign slave? Is that the best you can come up with after four hundred years?"

She refused to respond to the jibe, glaring at him. He no longer wore the dapper clothes he had enjoyed at court, descending from the bright reds and blues and yellows he had so adored into dusty browns and blacks. His black skin blended so well with his clothing, that she knew he would be difficult to visually track at night. Perhaps that was why he had effected the change.

"I'd have thought you'd have found much more creative abuses to revile me with."

His sardonic words reminded her of Dorst. That startled her, as Valmont had never spoken so disdainfully of himself in the past. "Why are you here?" She kept her voice quiet despite the venom, not wanting that idiot of a *saggina* to come rushing to her rescue.

Valmont shrugged, a faint grin on his handsome face. "The same reason you are, Margaurethe, yes? Attempting to verify the identity of a young woman, to ascertain if she is Elisibet reborn."

"You stay away from her."

"Ah, so she is here." He glanced around the vestibule. "Thank you for the confirmation."

Margaurethe swore at revealing such information, and wrestled with a tremendous urge to rip the triumphant smile from his face.

"Ma'am? Your jacket?"

The Human at coat check held out her rain jacket. She did not want to turn her back on Valmont to retrieve it.

"Ma'am?"

"Allow me." Valmont stepped past her, taking the coat from the hapless man. He handed over a substantial tip. "Thank you so much."

Margaurethe turned, snatching the jacket from his fingers. "Come with me." She marched out of the building into the cool, rainy street. Behind her, she heard his footsteps follow.

"I'm assuming that your being here indicates our goal is somewhat mutual. It's her?"

Margaurethe continued walking, heading toward the Town Car. She saw Phineas hastily jump out, his naturally light complexion paling even more as he realized who escorted her. Giving him a slight shake of the head, he stood silently by as they passed. "I don't know what you're talking about."

"Please, Margaurethe, we may both have our frailties, but stupidity isn't one of mine."

"So you say."

He ignored her insult. "I know this girl bears a striking resemblance, but mistaken identity has happened before."

Margaurethe forced her jaw to relax, not wanting the sound of her grinding teeth to give her unwanted companion any pleasure. She could see that further denials would do no good; she had already spilled the beans about Whiskey's existence. "Yes, it's her."

The sound of his footsteps stopped, and she strode onward a moment before realizing she walked alone. Spinning around, she felt a perverse glee at his expression. "You heard me well enough, Valmont. It's her." She paused. "But it's not."

He stared at her, previous good humor smothered by agitation as he paced in front of a store window. "What's that supposed to mean? Either the prophecy is true, and Elisibet has returned, or she hasn't. There's no room for prevarication here."

Margaurethe smiled sweetly.

Valmont growled, and stepped closer, lowering his voice to a whisper. "Where is she?"

"Someplace safe." Steel rang in Margaurethe's tone. "Any advantage I can give Whiskey over you, I'll give. Are we understood?"

They studied one another, the bubble of turmoil surrounding them nearly tangible. "You have my word, Margaurethe," Valmont finally said. "Elisibet is in no danger from me."

She scoffed loudly and stepped back. "Sure, and I'm to believe you're an honorable man? Your honor was forfeit when you murdered her." She crossed her arms over her chest. "Did you find it again? Where does a dishonorable man find a replacement?"

"God, you are impossible!" Valmont jammed his fists into his pockets. "I didn't want to do what I did! I was convinced it was the proper course of action!"

"Oh, aye, and been pining away ever since with guilt."

Valmont took an ominous step forward. Then he turned, and stalked away.

Margaurethe watched him go, a feral smile on her face. Deep in her heart, she felt a spark of sympathy, a remnant of their old friendship surfacing and then saddening at his predicament. Quashing the sensation, she muttered to herself, "No more than he deserves. Less even." Her Irish brogue had thickened in her anger, now noticeable even to her. With a sigh, she shook off the emotion, knowing that to dwell on it would do her no good. Besides, she hated when her accent got the better of her; it made her sound like a serving wench in a backwater pub.

"Cuz?"

Phineas had followed, and she turned toward him. "Is the car ready?"

"Yeah." His eyes darted into the darkness where Valmont had vanished. "Are you all right?"

She sighed, feeling suddenly exhausted. "I'm fine." Moving to him, she put a hand on his arm as she made her way back to the car. "It's been a long night. Let's go home."

"Aye, cuz. I'll get you there safe and sound, guaranteed."

If only I could say the same about Whiskey.

***

The phone rang, and he checked the caller ID. With a curse, he dashed back around his desk to answer it. He had been expecting this call for over two months.

"It's me."

He waved to his aide waiting in the doorway. "I'll be a minute. Close the door."

The woman curtsied. "Of course, sir. Shall I inform them of your delay?"

"Yes, yes! I can't miss this call." Once he was alone, he sank into the leather chair behind his desk. "You're late, and now so am I. This had better be good."

"It is, sir!" the voice assured him.

"Well?"

"It's been difficult, but I've got photographic evidence. It's her."

He was glad to already be seated as he felt his knees turn to water. He stared at the mahogany destkop, unseeing. "There's no doubt?" A part of him was amazed his voice didn't reflect the turmoil in his mind, instead sounding rational and calm to his ears.

"None, sir. She's the spitting image. I'll email the JPEGs to you."

It's her. The implications of those two little words would have drastic repercussions throughout Sanguire society, especially with the *Agrun Nam.* He sighed and closed his eyes, propping his elbow on the chair arm, and covering his face with a hand. What would happen when they received this information?

"Sir?"

Jolted from his thoughts, he realized he was still on the phone. "Yes. I'm here. Do you have anything else to report?"

"No, sir."

"Thank you. You'll be well rewarded. Keep an eye on her. Report when you have something."

"Yes, sir."

"And be quick, damn it!" He hardly heard the acquiescent response as he slammed the phone into its cradle.

The prophecy was coming true. Elisibet had returned, and was in the process of gathering her power. He wasn't ready. He had a sudden desire to clear his desk in one violent swipe, letting phone, computer and desk accoutrements slam to the floor in a resounding, satisfying crash. Instead, he gripped the arms of his chair, knuckles white, fingernails digging into the padded leather.

Several moments passed before he had his emotions under control once more. Rising, inwardly cursing at his still shaky knees, he went to the door and opened it. He passed his aide waiting in the hall. "See that another desk chair is brought up while I'm in chambers."

"Yes, sir." She glanced inside the office, eyebrows rising in surprise as she saw shredded leather and stuffing sprouting from either arm of the chair in question. "Right away, sir."

***

The smell of steak tickled her nose, dragging her from sleep. Opening a bleary eye, Whiskey stared up at a gray ceiling. She yawned and stretched, hearing cooking noises somewhere behind her head.

She sat up, rubbing her eyes as she remembered where she was. After several hours of posing, she had bedded down on Rufus's couch with a blanket while he continued working from photographs. He had offered his bed, but she had refused, partly because the sheets hadn't been changed in months, and partly because she didn't want him to get the wrong idea.

She yawned again, and ran fingers through her hair, untangling the worst of it.

"Hey, sleepy! How do you like your steak and eggs?"

Looking over the back of the couch, she saw Rufus grinning at her from the kitchen, spatula in hand. He still wore the clothes he had worn last night. She wondered if he had even gotten any sleep. Her stomach grumbled at the wonderful smell. "Rare."

"Rare it is!" He turned back to the stove. "Scrambled?"

"Whatever's easy." Whiskey shrugged. "Mind if I shower?"

Rufus waved at her. "Go ahead. I'll hold your steak until you're done."

She headed for the bathroom under the stairs. Curious, she examined the painting she had posed for as she passed. It looked like her in a rudimentary sort of way, but the dragon twining about her arm was real, separating from her skin to roar at the viewer from above her shoulder. She absently rubbed the tattoo as she continued on her way.

The bathroom echoed the loft in that it was long and narrow. She locked the door, stripped, and started the water. Once it was a tolerable temperature, she climbed in and let it wash over her.

She had used Rufus's cell phone to call Castillo the night before. Contingencies had been put in place as soon as they had moved into the house in Felony Flats so she doubted anyone would be there. No one knew whether Valmont would be able to follow anyone back; everyone had been directed to abandon it for safer ground.

Margaurethe was probably worried sick. Whiskey picked up a bar of soap, and lathered her skin. Maybe she could have Castillo or Reynhard call and let her know all was well.

A sick feeling rolled around her gut as she washed, a familiar sensation she had grown used to over the years. For most of her time on the streets, she had thought it was caused by being orphaned, poor and homeless; somebody decent people scraped off the bottom of their shoe. Lately she'd had reason to question that assumption. Since she had finished the *Ñíri Kurám*, she had begun analyzing so much in her life, comparing it to the imported memories she now held.

Elisibet had felt much the same. The only way she had made the feeling go away was by taking action. In her case it meant extreme violence, but take action she had. Whiskey wondered if that was the issue here. Running away, living on the streets, the easiest way to survive was avoidance—turn a blind eye to people getting robbed or beaten, ignore the right thing in favor of the easy way.

Living with her pack the past few months, Whiskey had been forced into a leadership role. She couldn't sit back, let others act for her, or let her pack run roughshod over the Humans to which they felt superior. After so many months being in charge, running away from Margaurethe had put Whiskey back into the position of avoidance. She hated the feeling. There was only one thing she could do to get rid of it, and that was to call Margaurethe herself.

Whiskey snorted, and rinsed off. While the idea soothed the ugly sensation in her gut, her heart sped up with trepidation. *There's just no winning.* She located the shampoo, and washed her hair. For good measure, she gave both her hair and body a second wash before shutting off the water. She dressed in yesterday's clothes, tidied up after herself, and left the bathroom.

"I was beginning to wonder if you'd gotten lost." Rufus grinned at her.

Whiskey shrugged. She sat at the dining table.

Unperturbed by her lack of response, he piled eggs onto a plate, handing it to her. "Eat up."

"Thanks." Whiskey cut into the steak, mouth watering at the sight of pink blood pooling beneath her knife.

He sat across from her. "You earned it. I know it's not easy sitting still for that long."

"Earned it, huh? You did all the work."

Rufus chuckled. "For the record, it's fun. No work involved."

She smiled, and applied herself to her food.

Once breakfast was finished, she watched him collect their plates. "Mind if I use your cell? I want to call the padre."

He hesitated a moment. "Uh, no." Placing the plates in the

sink, he turned the water on. "But I'm having trouble with the cell phone."

Whiskey frowned. That was the first she had heard of it. "Okay. Is there a pay phone somewhere around here?"

Rufus glanced over his shoulder at her, squirting too much dish soap into the filling sink. "You can use the apartment phone. It's over under that stack of newspapers by the TV."

She thanked him, and went to locate the landline, his strangeness already forgotten. Rufus was an odd bird sometimes.

CHAPTER SIXTEEN

Unable to sit and worry at the house, Margaurethe visited the construction zone of her new headquarters. A former hotel, the building that now housed The Davis Group had the luxury of a glass and marble lobby, an entire city block of meeting space, two levels of garage, and a dozen floors of guest rooms. Multiple kitchens on two floors sweetened the deal, allowing Margaurethe to host lavish state dinners while simultaneously maintaining a cafeteria for future employees and an executive dining room. A hand holding her bright orange construction helmet for fear of it tipping to her nose, she leaned over the latest diagrams with the floor foreman as he pointed out specific details.

"You wanted to expand the health club facilities, but there

ain't a lot else we can do. We can't get the pool any deeper without taking out part of the second floor beneath it." He stabbed a gnarly finger at one area, and then thumbed up the next page to reveal the floor below. "That would mean moving the waterworks down another level, which would put it there." He turned, gesturing toward what had been meeting rooms in one corner of the lobby. "You'll lose the locker rooms and that conference space."

Margaurethe pursed her lips. She had wanted to keep the meeting area here for impromptu gatherings, a place where her people could come to meet with the unanointed at a moment's notice. And the locker rooms were a vital employee perk. The majority of her workforce would be Human, and much inclined toward loyalty for a company that gave them such benefits as secure storage for their personal belongings and free meals. "I can deal with a four-foot pool if I have to." She thought a moment, taking the pages from him, and once more exposed the third floor. "Perhaps if we lengthened it? If we moved the spa here," she poked the paper, "and turned the pool this way," she twirled her finger in a circle to indicate a one-hundred-eighty-degree turn, "we could afford to have a longer pool with a higher lap distance."

The foreman thought a moment. "Actually, I remember seeing something in a magazine once. A pool that had its own current to swim against." He traced the current pool location. "I'd have to look into it, but this area would be big enough for two or three, side by side."

"Really?" Margaurethe pulled out her phone, and entered a note to check on the idea.

"Yeah. You'll be able to use the existing plumbing. Wouldn't have to worry about length for laps since you swim in place." He glanced at her with a grin. "I'd need updated blueprints to work from if you go that route."

"I'll take care of it."

He nodded. "In that case, we'll stay focused on the residences and offices upstairs, and keep the crew renovating the lower levels. Until we have something solid, we'll avoid the second and third floors."

"Thank you. You're continuing to work twenty-four hours a day?"

"Yep." He rubbed the back of his neck. "Just like you wanted. We'll have this place done in record time."

"Excellent. Are the elevators working? I've a mind to check out the penthouse."

"Not these." He waved at the bank of four elevators in what would remain the public area. "The elevator company finished their renovations last week, and I had 'em locked off. Didn't want anybody messing up the work." He escorted her away from the worktable, around the corner, and through the framework of a future wall. "Use these in the service area. And watch your step up there!"

Margaurethe smiled. "Thank you, I will." Her smile faded as the elevator doors closed. She fished out her cell phone to see that no one had called. The adage "No news is good news" ran through her mind, though it didn't decrease her worry.

The elevator opened to a barrage of hammering and sawing. She exited into a small service area on the sixteenth floor. Two doors had been propped open, one to the corridor, and one into what had been the hotel's Presidential Suite. Considering some of the quality hotels Margaurethe had enjoyed in the past, she had found the title somewhat misleading. This one had not even had a proper bed in it, relying on a pullout couch for sleeping, or the rental of connecting suites.

She stepped into the suite, aiming for its claim to fame— a magnificent view of the Willamette River. This was the only balcony on this floor, and ran the length of the room. The doors had been opened to combat the smell of sawdust and wallpaper glue. She went outside. A chill breeze swept over her, and she leaned into the freshness. It had not rained since the night before, but the air still smelled so clean. She marveled at the scent.

Margaurethe went to the banister, checking it for stability before leaning upon it. Far below, traffic on Naito Parkway was brisk. The corner pedestrian crossing light chirped for the vision impaired, audible at this distance even without her sharp hearing. Across the street sat Tom McCall Waterfront Park, a concave expanse of green grass marred only by a dirt walkway along the river's edge leading from the running path on the left to the marina on the right. Though the air was still cold, the park held a number of people seeking to reacquaint themselves with sunlight.

This would be Whiskey's view every day, the foyer to her residence would take up the room behind Margaurethe. Her dwelling itself would utilize half the floor. In the corner across from the main elevators would be a security station monitoring access, and the remaining space would be Margaurethe's residence. *Elisibet would have loved the view.*

Her cell phone rang, and she hastily answered it.

"Margaurethe?"

Glad of the banister, Margaurethe sagged against it at the sound of the familiar voice she had not heard in over three weeks. A thousand questions flooded her thoughts, clogging her throat with their sheer number. "Whiskey."

"Yeah, it's me." Pause. "Is everything okay? What's all that noise?"

Margaurethe hurried to close the sliding glass doors, muffling the majority of the construction noise. "I'm at the new building. They're doing some work."

"Oh."

Margaurethe could almost see the blond head dip in acceptance, her expression uncertain. She smiled at the vision. "Are you well?"

"Oh! Yeah, I'm fine. That's why I called, to let you know I'm okay."

Her heart thumped, and she felt a lump forming in her throat. "Thank you for the consideration. I was quite worried when I heard the news."

"You heard? About Valmont?"

Margaurethe smiled, walking back to the banister to stare out over the water. "Yes. Father Castillo called, all atwitter. He thought I should know what happened." She did not bother to mention her altercation with him, not wanting to break this tenuous connection between her and Whiskey.

"Ah, the padre. Right."

She heard the disgruntlement in Whiskey's tone. Apparently

Margaurethe wasn't the only one who'd had her fill of the priest these days. "He assured me your pack is safe. Have you had time to contact him?"

After a few moments pause, Whiskey said, "Not yet. I wanted to call you first."

Tears sprang into Margaurethe's eyes, and she brought one hand up to her mouth. *At least I haven't completely alienated her.* "Then thank you again. I know how important your friends are to you. I'm honored that you would notify me before finding them."

Noises on the other end almost made Margaurethe smile. Again she saw Whiskey in her memory, bashful and blushing at the praise. She opened her mouth, wanting to ask when Whiskey would come home, but pressed her fingers to her lips to prevent the words. Despite the incredible danger Whiskey was in because of Valmont, this was a conclusion she needed to arrive at on her own. Castillo had been right; Margaurethe would throttle the very spirit out of Whiskey by holding on as tightly as she had. Though it hurt to her soul, she had to relax her grip.

"I should call the padre."

As hard as it was, Margaurethe denied the urge to beg otherwise. "Yes, you probably should. He's quite concerned for you, too. I assume the younglings will also need reassurance."

"Yeah, probably."

She stood, listening to Whiskey's gentle breathing. Margaurethe wasn't the only one loathe to disconnect. "Do you need anything?" she finally asked. "Money? Transportation?"

"No, I'm good. Rufus has a car. Once I find out where the others are, I'll have him drive me there." After another long interval of silence, she said, "I'll…I'll see you later then?"

"Of course, Whiskey. My door is always open to you. Never forget."

"I won't." There was a suspicious sniffle. "Bye."

"Goodbye, *lúkal*," Margaurethe murmured, ending the conversation before she started crying.

She turned toward the river, both elbows on the balcony as she filled her lungs with the crisp, clean air. It bolstered her, forestalled the desire to weep with relief—not just the easing of her immediate concerns, but also the bone-deep alleviation of worry that she had irreparably damaged her budding relationship with Whiskey. The phone call told Margaurethe that the obstacles were not insurmountable, that she still had a chance to sway Whiskey, to work with her and keep her protected from all those that would have her dead.

All was not lost.

Margaurethe stared across the water, not truly seeing the highway traffic on the bridges, the green hump of Mt. Tabor, the white peak of Mt. Hood in the distance beyond.

Dorst had yet to call. She assumed it was because Whiskey remained on the loose from even his hunting talents. He was probably frantic in his search—or at least as frantic as an assassin could get. Margaurethe chastised herself for the light chuckle escaping her lips. Dorst, the dangerous broken man, followed Whiskey around like a puppy. He had followed Elisibet around in the same manner until Margaurethe had told her lover how uncomfortable she felt in his presence. After that, Margaurethe rarely saw him.

She had sometimes wondered what would have happened if she had not driven him away from his precious mistress's side. Would he have been in the palace when Valmont came to destroy Elisibet? Would he have saved her from certain death, defended her against the traitorous man whom she had called friend? Unlike Margaurethe, would he have been there on time?

Did he feel shame, like she did, for not being there to save Elisibet?

Margaurethe swallowed against the bile in her throat. This sudden emotional connection between her and Dorst tasted much too bitter. She had always wondered why he had come to save her before the Purge swept through the capitol city and palace, though she had never given it deep thought over the years. Far easier to assume he had done so out of loyalty to Elisibet than that they shared a common life-changing mistake. Besides, that time and those feelings would engulf her as they had done then if she examined them too closely.

She heard the banging and power tools once more as she forced herself to the present. Turning away from the spectacular view, she made her way back inside, the sound magnifying as she opened the sliding doors. There was nothing she could do here, and a number of things she could work on elsewhere.

Making a to-do list in her head, she picked her way through Whiskey's entry foyer, and headed for the elevator.

CHAPTER SEVENTEEN

"How long have they been here?" The question was asked with some urgency. Margaurethe attempted to hustle up the front walk without appearing to be rushed. She didn't want to give the impression of not being prepared for her unexpected guests, nor did she want them peeking out the windows to see her flapping about in hysteria. She had assumed the American Indian contingent would send an emissary, not travel here en masse.

"Half an hour, give or take." The captain of her guard strode beside her. "As soon as they announced themselves, I had them brought into the living room. Alicia has served them coffee and cookies."

Margaurethe wrinkled her nose. "Americans and their coffee. I certainly hope she had the sense to heat water for tea."

He gave her a slight grin. "She did, *Ki'an Gasan.*"

"Good. Call Reynhard and ask him to come. I don't want him to reveal himself, but I want him here for backup in case it gets nasty." Despite the crucial nature of this meeting, she paused at the door. She took a deep breath, smoothed her clothing, and adopted an air of calm. At her nod, the guard stationed there opened it for her.

A multitude of strange jackets hung from the normally empty coatrack in the corner of the otherwise barren foyer. Margaurethe glanced behind her as her captain closed the door, and took up a position there. Giving him an encouraging nod, she squared her shoulders, and flowed into the living room.

A half-dozen people waited for her, one being Alicia who was leaning over a frail-looking man in one of the armchairs. Another woman squatted beside them, her long hair flowing free about her shoulders, helping Alicia serve the elder. A man and woman sat on the couch, balancing coffee cups on their knees, and a third man stood by the large window. He had seen her walk by, and Margaurethe felt a measure of smugness for having not revealed her true nervousness while outside.

Alicia looked up, eyes widening with relief. She straightened and approached Margaurethe. "*Ki'an Gasan* Margaurethe O'Toole, I'd like you to meet the *We Wacipi Wakan.*" The security detail *cum* herald began the introductions. "This is Mr. Saghani of the Inuit and Ms. Alopay, of the Apache—" she indicated the two on the couch, "Mr. Chano is from the Chinook, and Ms. Lega represents the Lakota," gesturing to the elder man and woman at the armchair, "and Mr. Deganawidah is from the Iroquois."

"Just call me Degan, everyone else does."

Margaurethe dipped her head in understanding, and turned back to the security guard. "Thank you, Alicia. That will be all."

Not needing a second command, Alicia fled the room.

Margaurethe smiled. "It's a pleasure to meet you all. I must say I'm rather surprised that you deigned to come here."

"As was I." Alopay gestured from the couch at the others, indicating she'd had not much to do with this state of affairs.

Saghani sitting beside her did not grace the sarcastic words with much of a response. He merely grunted in disagreement. His input caused Alopay to flush, her broad face twisting into a grimace.

Degan stepped forward, offering his hand. "It seemed the thing to do once we knew who had made the request." He was the best dressed of the group, wearing dress clothes and polished shoes. He had foregone a jacket for a traditional robe of colors; it hung on him like a medieval cape, though not as long, tied at one shoulder.

Margaurethe shook his hand. "My apologies. I hardly wanted to uproot you from your...territories during winter. Were your travels difficult?" She went to the tray set on the coffee table, pleased to find a pot of hot water, and her favorite herbal tea awaiting her.

"Not for most of us, no." Degan gestured to the elder. "Fortunately, Chano actually resides in this area, so he hadn't far to travel."

Finished preparing her tea, Margaurethe took the remaining armchair. "I'm glad of that."

Chano looked ancient. His iron-gray hair was mid-length, but wispy in the way that suggested the onset of baldness. A carved walking stick rested beside his chair. Margaurethe visually scanned the others, noting that only the Lakota woman looked younger than her. Saghani was well on his way to becoming an elder, and Degan and Alopay were at least a couple of centuries senior.

Margaurethe gently reached out and touched the minds of her people. Her visitors could easily join together and overpower her. She was glad she had had someone call Dorst. At least with the help of her guard she would be able to avoid being compelled by this collection of powerful Sanguire.

The eldest, Chano, coughed and cleared his throat. When he spoke, his voice was rough with the echo of age. "Why did you ask for us?"

"A number of reasons." She wondered how to bring about the topic of Whiskey's future. "Publicly, I'm here to set up a corporation called The Davis Group. We'll be exploiting a number of technological and software communication patents I own."

"Interesting choice of words—exploiting."

Margaurethe cocked her head at Alopay. "I realize that Human whites have done horrible things in the past. I was not involved. Please don't insult me in my own home."

Alopay's jaw jutted outward. She made a move to stand, no doubt a prelude to a bitter tirade followed by the requisite dramatic departure, but Saghani grunted again. Alopay snorted. She set her cup down, crossed her arms over her chest, and sat back.

Pleased to see directness had not destroyed this tenuous beginning, Margaurethe gave a regal nod of thanks to Saghani.

"And privately?"

The Lakota's voice was so soft that Margaurethe almost didn't catch it. She looked at Lega who still knelt beside Chano, holding his plate of cookies. "What do you know of Mahar's prophecy?" At Lega's blank stare, Margaurethe continued, "It's European."

Saghani spoke for the first time. "Your worst tyrant is supposed to come back from the dead to unite all the Sanguire as one."

"White Crow Woman?" Degan looked startled.

Margaurethe looked around the room. Her guests all appeared faintly awed. "Who is White Crow Woman?"

"Her story is somewhat similar." Lega stared off in thought. "She's in many of our different myths and legends. A woman who tried to bring all the tribes together peacefully, but died in the attempt. It's said she'll return someday when we've matured enough to accept her."

Dare I use this as a way to gain their acceptance of Whiskey? Margaurethe set the idea aside. Considering Alopay's obvious animosity, she decided not to attempt to sway the council without doing serious research first. "Elisibet Vasilla ruled the European Sanguire centuries ago. After she died, Oracle Mahar prophesied her return. It's said she will unite all the Sanguire as one."

Degan had yet to overcome his astonishment. "And you think you've found her?"

Margaurethe inhaled deeply. "I have."

Several of them exclaimed in surprise. Alopay's response was more of an earthy denial. "Bullshit."

"Whiskey?"

Margaurethe stared at Chano, fear and animosity overriding her common sense. "Who told you that name?"

The elder smiled, revealing one missing tooth. "My great-grandson knows her."

"Nupa."

He nodded.

She cursed inwardly, her suspicions regarding the young American Indian verified. "That's why you came here, isn't it? To confirm what he's been telling you?"

Chano gave her a look of commiseration. "She's a child, so very young, and so very powerful."

"Wait? You knew about this?" Degan demanded. He took a step closer to the gathering. "You knew that this…Whiskey was White Crow Woman?"

"I had my hopes, the hopes of an old man, nothing more."

Alopay shook her head, her braids waggling back and forth. "She can't be. She's not Indian."

"Nothing in the story says she has to be," Lega supplied.

Saghani stood. "It does in our myths."

"And ours," Degan added.

Margaurethe stood as well, raising both hands to placate them. "And she is."

"What?" Alopay's head spun around as she stared at Margaurethe.

Movement at the doorway caught Margaurethe's awareness, and she saw her captain scanning the room for danger in the midst of the tumult. She waved him away. The sensation of amber and steel caressed her mind, indicating Dorst had arrived. She hoped he would stay out of the way unless she called for him—these people might not appreciate his humor nor his appearance.

"Whiskey's mother's name was Nahimana. We don't know much beyond the fact that she married Gareth Davis, and bore Whiskey in North Carolina. She died in an auto accident about fourteen years ago."

"Nahimana." Lega tasted the name. She glanced around at the others. "North Carolina. A branch of ours?"

"It's possible," Degan answered. "You keep pretty extensive records. Should be easy to check the rolls."

Saghani regarded Margaurethe. "Back to the conversation—publicly you're starting a company. What's the other part of the story?"

She studied them. Chano looked amused, Alopay disgruntled. The others watched with attentive inscrutability. "I intend to put Whiskey in power, and support her in a bid to take over the Euro Sanguire."

Several minutes passed as another round of exclamation and dissidence ensued. No one directed their diatribes at Margaurethe so she remained silent as they hashed things out amongst themselves. The majority of the discussion took place in a language she didn't know anyway, which made it easier to simply observe. It was an interesting experience. American Indians were always aloof and stern in public; this rabble-rousing and whooping and yelling among them now seemed a rather untidy way to gain consensus. Even old Chano was bellowing his point of view, his lungs nowhere near as infirm as his appearance suggested.

After twenty minutes, the room calmed. But Alopay still fumed, having stood and marched over to the window to glare outside.

Chano brushed his fingers across his brow before peering at Margaurethe. "We will see if we can find this Nahimana among us. If she lived, she had family who would know if she had married and carried a child."

"And if she did?"

"Then this Whiskey is ours. You cannot take her away to rule your people. She must stay here to follow her path."

Margaurethe frowned, mind racing. "But…I *know* who she is, know who she was. She remembers Elisibet. This is her destiny."

"Her destiny is hers to follow, not yours to direct. If she wishes to travel to Europe, and rule your people then that is her wish." Lega tilted her head. "You cannot take her. She must decide."

Slightly relieved at the concession, Margaurethe nodded.

"And we must meet her." Saghani glared at the others. "We

can't confirm she's White Crow Woman until we do. If she is, we'll need to make the proper gifts."

"That is going to prove problematic." Margaurethe searched for the words to explain the current situation.

Chano took care of the issue. "But not today, not yet. First we must discover if she's truly one of our people. Then we will know whether we must move forward or not."

The others agreed with his announcement.

Degan stepped forward. "In the meantime, you have our permission to base your corporation in our country. We'll have a treaty drawn up for your approval and signature within the week." He smiled. "Be warned. We'll demand a percentage of your new hires be Indian."

"I have no problem with that. The corporation will be more than able to supply your people with jobs."

Chano nodded approval. He handed his empty cup to Lega who set it and the plate of uneaten cookies aside. Struggling to his feet, he leaned heavily on the walking stick, Lega at his elbow. "And if we want one of our own on the board of directors?"

Margaurethe smiled. "Then it shall be done."

Her quick response left a favorable impression on Saghani whose face became a little less sour. He declared, "I have a flight to catch."

"Of course." Margaurethe played the hostess, assisting her guests out into the foyer. Alopay refused to be placated, snatching her buckskin jacket from the coatrack before Margaurethe could retrieve it for her. She stepped outside with them, scanning for Dorst and not finding his strange persona anywhere in view. All but Alopay shook her hand before climbing into the beat-up, old van in which they had arrived.

Chano was last, the paper-thin skin of his hand dry against hers. "Don't become blinded by your goal, young woman. Take a closer look at your prophecy; perhaps it's not as clear-cut as you believe." He climbed laboriously into the passenger seat of the van.

Margaurethe didn't know how to respond. She closed the door behind him, and remained outside in the cold breeze until the van coughed to a start and rattled down the drive.

"My! That was most intriguing."

She turned. Behind her, Dorst watched the vehicle disappear. She said, "Thank you for coming on such short notice. I wasn't certain how they'd react."

Dorst bowed. "It was my absolute pleasure, *Ki'an Gasan*."

His excessive nature made her glad she had asked that he remained unseen. If he had insulted these people so early in the game, she would have been forced to scrap her plans, and scramble for some other way to attain her goal. Still, she wondered about Chano's last statement.

"Shall we go inside?" Dorst gestured for her to precede him. "I could do with a spot of tea."

"Of course." Margaurethe returned to the warm house, finding she had more questions than she had started with before the meeting.

CHAPTER EIGHTEEN

Four days passed before Margaurethe had a calm moment to think about what Chano had said at their parting, four days spent nailing down the financial accounts for The Davis Group, and transferring patents to its control. The Portland *Saggina* would have reported her presence to the *Agrun Nam* by now. There was no more need for discretion. She had reassigned the majority of her stocks and investments to the new corporation, planning to continue her growing communications empire to the benefit of Whiskey.

When she finally had time to look over Mahar's prophecy, she saw what she had always seen—her lover would return and reunite her people, saving them even as she destroyed them.

How she would destroy them was unknown, and had been much speculated upon over the centuries. Mahar had been whisked into seclusion, and never seen again. Questions put to the *ensi'ummai* went unanswered. It soon became common assumption that Mahar had passed the veil, though her fellow oracles insisted she lived.

Some people felt the foretold destruction meant another Purge, one aimed at those who had been responsible for the Sweet Butcher's death, for had not she been merciless and brutal in her regime? Surely she would retaliate against her enemies. Even Margaurethe had found that the most likely possibility, thinking that the new monarchy would rise out of the blood and ashes of the old.

That argument was no longer valid. Whiskey didn't have a high opinion of Elisibet, despite possessing her memories and power. The idea of Whiskey at the head of a military force, intent on destroying everything the Euro Sanguire had built in the intervening years since her absence, was unfathomable. If she was a vengeful returning monarch, it would make sense to take such action, but she was not. Besides which, she was far too compassionate to tear down centuries of growth over such pettiness.

The myth of White Crow Woman opened a completely different line of reasoning. How could Whiskey be both the second coming of the European Sanguire and the American Indian peoples? If she went to Europe to rule, she could hardly bring the tribes together under one leader. They were already united under the *We Wacipi Wakan*. For that matter, the Euro Sanguire already had the *Agrun Nam*. Which people was Whiskey destined to unite according to prophecy?

A light tap at the door interrupted her circular thoughts.

"*Ki'an Gasan*? The *We Wacipi Wakan* sent a courier." Her captain stood at the door. "He won't speak to any of us, but I'm certain he's not a threat."

How appropriate. Think of them, and they arrive. Standing, Margaurethe gestured. "Send him in."

He stepped aside, waving someone forward.

He wore what appeared to be the full traditional garb of a

Plains Indian, complete with a headdress of eagle feathers that would have looked at home in a museum. Sun-browned skin could be seen between the breechclout and leggings, and he wore a buckskin vest with colorful bead and quill decorations. Crooked in one arm was a lance, and a sheathed knife hung on a tether around his neck. He approached her desk, holding something toward her.

Margaurethe took the bundle of leather, soft rabbit fur tickling her fingers. She jerked her head at her captain who remained hovering in the doorway. He looked disapproving, but closed the door, leaving her alone with the newcomer.

Setting the bundle on the desktop, she opened it to find a pipe, a carved and decorated stick about thirty centimeters long, and a roll of parchment. Not wanting to give insult, she nevertheless had no clue how to respond. She looked at the Indian. "I do not wish to offend, but I have no idea what these things represent."

A faint smile caressed his lips. "The stick is the *We Wacipi Wakan's* offer of a treaty between our people. The pipe will be the one you smoke when you negotiate and finalize that treaty with them. The treaty itself is enclosed."

She nodded, spreading out the rabbit fur. "Is there something I should do in return?"

"Keep the pipe and the treaty, return the stick to show acceptance of the initial offer, and send a gesture of good faith in return to be held until the pipe is smoked."

Margaurethe wondered what to send back. "This 'gesture.' Will it be returned when we finalize the treaty?"

He smirked. "Yes. 'Indian giver' was a term used for the whites who gave us gifts and then took them away. We have honor."

His light acid tone informed her that she had offended anyway. Reaching behind her neck, she undid the clasp on the golden locket she always wore. She placed it on the fur, removing the pipe and parchment. Closing it, she handed the bundle back to him. "I've worn that locket every day for the last three hundred seventy-five years. It belonged to Elisibet, and is very precious to me. I entrust you and your people with its care."

Her words surprised the sarcasm from his face. "I'll keep it safe," he promised somberly.

"Thank you."

"The council will contact you next month to arrange a negotiation."

Before she could respond, he turned and strode out of the room. Her captain peeked in to check on her, and then closed the door.

Disconcerted by the abruptness of the courier's departure, Margaurethe picked up the parchment to see what they considered good treaty terms. They had already discussed employment of a percentage of natives, and made mention of a member on the board of directors. Those points were firmly outlined in the document, as well as the stipulation that Whiskey not be coerced to leave the country. Margaurethe raised an eyebrow.

Next was a request for a portion of native contractors to be hired. That might take some doing, at least at first. Headquarters had been all but completed, so she had no need to hire more construction companies. She would have to do some digging to see what contractors the Indians had available. Once the dust settled, she could begin transferring whole divisions into the area— construction, warehousing, shipping. This clause of the treaty would be dependent on what skills the *We Wacipi Wakan* had to offer.

The final request was a tithe of ten percent of profits split evenly between the council's coffers and local charity. "Ten percent?" Margaurethe sat down, staring at the paper. "Do they realize how much money they're asking for? We have billions of dollars in assets." While Margaurethe had no issues with donating to charitable organizations or assisting the Indians in their progress, it was obvious the *We Wacipi Wakan* had no monetary understanding of an international corporation. Perhaps they only saw The Davis Group as a start-up, and thought there would be much more to spare.

"Five percent." She drew a line through the number ten, and put a five above it. "Half for the council, and half for their charities. Whiskey will make the final determination of which charities receive funds." Scribbling the change under that, she ran the back of the pen down the page as she looked it over. Satisfied, she set it aside, and emailed her lawyer to have him draw up an initial contract.

With that business concluded, Margaurethe fielded a few emails from the new human resources director. The poor Human was having fits about some of Margaurethe's demands. A number of her people had no formal work history, having been with her for decades. On paper it looked like the majority of her security staff had never previously worked a day in their lives.

The foreman's report made her smile. All was completed except the health club itself. The installation of the side-by-side current pools was going well, but their last-minute inclusion had put construction behind schedule and above budget. She returned his email, assuring him that so long as his people were not purposely lagging, she had no issue with the incurred cost. The construction crew had worked long and hard, completing the massive undertaking in record time. She made note to add a bonus to the final payment to the company. With the headquarters completed, another project had already begun on another bulding a block away that would contain a small warehouse and shipping outlet, and she was looking to break ground in Hillsboro for a large research and development lab come spring. Soon, she'd be moving everyone downtown, and selling this house.

Margaurethe sighed, and leaned back in her chair. Since that single phone call, she had not heard from Whiskey. It had been two weeks. Castillo had stopped giving her reports, forcing her to rely on Dorst for information. She couldn't blame the priest; she had been quite confrontational at their last meeting. His resultant outburst had shocked her so much, she hadn't had the heart to contact him herself.

Perhaps she had read too much into the call. She felt her brow furrow, and her lips pursed into a frown at the thought. *Perhaps it's time for you to get off your delicate duff, and call her yourself. It could be she's waiting for you to take the next step.*

She stared at the mocking phone on her desk in silent debate. Several minutes passed before she finally muttered, "Well, it's not going to dial itself." She snatched it up, quickly dialing the number from memory before she could stop herself.

The phone rang once. Again. A third time. Margaurethe thought Whiskey had seen the caller ID, and purposely ignored the incoming call. *Did the priest tell her of our argument?* Before she could get a good head of steam up at the thought, someone answered.

"Margaurethe?"

Her heart thundered in her chest so loudly she wagered Whiskey could hear it on the other end despite the loud clamor of music in the background. "Yes." After a long moment of silence, she asked, "Did I call at a bad time?"

"What? No! No. I just didn't expect—" She covered the mouthpiece and shouted. The music quieted, either from someone turning it down or her leaving the area. "It's good to hear your voice."

"It's good to hear yours." Margaurethe didn't know what else to say, bereft of words.

"Is everything okay?"

"Yes. Yes, everything is fine. I simply found myself thinking of you, and wanted to call." *Goodness, I sound like a* ñalga súp.

"Ah, okay." Hesitant silence. "I'm glad you did."

Margaurethe wondered what to say. Hearing Whiskey's voice was fine, but it was not enough. Enough for what, she didn't pursue. "I was—I—" She rolled her eyes, sighing as she slumped back into her chair. "I'd like to see you, if it's possible. Perhaps have coffee somewhere?"

Whiskey faltered for so long, Margaurethe thought they had been disconnected. "I'd like that."

Heart soaring with joy, Margaurethe sat up. "Really?" she blurted. With an inward groan, she closed her eyes, and pinched the bridge of her nose. Dorst paraded through her memory. *"How juvenile."*

"Yeah."

Whiskey's chuckle charmed her. "You know the city much better than I. Do you have any suggestions?"

"There's a coffee shop in southeast, on Hawthorne. It should be safe there."

Meaning Valmont had not been spotted in the area. Margaurethe brought up her calendar, scowling at the stack of meetings she had lined up. "I'm busy for the next two days. How about Thursday afternoon?"

"Okay. Thursday's good." Whiskey paused. "Ten a.m.?"

"I'll be there."

"Sweet."

The ever-present awkwardness once more claimed conversation. After a full minute, Margaurethe reluctantly said, "I suppose I'll let you go then."

"Okay. I'll see you Thursday."

"I look forward to it."

They said their goodbyes, and Margaurethe set the phone down. She automatically blocked the time on her calendar, knowing the date and time would be etched upon her heart. She stared blankly at the computer screen.

Some time later, she shook herself, seeing several incoming emails from HR and one from the foreman. "Honestly! I believe it's time to hire a personal assistant." Forcing herself back to work, she set her hopes and memories to the back of her mind.

CHAPTER NINETEEN

Whiskey remained inside the coffee shop, not wanting to brave the drizzling rain despite an overhead patio covering the outdoor seating area. She had insisted on coming alone. To keep her pack safe, this shop was nowhere near the vicinity that Valmont had been searching. Besides, with Margaurethe at her side, they would be able to take down anyone that threatened them. She cast out with her mind, looking for Sanguire that were not visible, finding no indication that Margaurethe was near.

She stared out the rain-streaked window at passing cars. The last thing she had expected was a call from Margaurethe. Since the first days after Whiskey had left the house—*you mean ran away*, her mind supplied—Margaurethe had not attempted contact, preferring to speak with Castillo and Dorst about Whiskey's health and safety. Whiskey had thought Margaurethe saw too much of Elisibet within her, that she would much rather take care of problems at a distance instead of having Whiskey underfoot. Living with the constant reminder of your ultimate loss had to be difficult. It had been easier for Whiskey to not call or speak to her, procrastination a well-worn habit.

Since being away, Whiskey had come to realize she had acted like a snotty twelve-year-old rather than the adult she proclaimed to be. She had begun to challenge her observations about Margaurethe's feelings and motivations. After speaking with Margaurethe on the phone the other day, all sorts of emotions had come to the fore—concern, caring, empathy. Whiskey had run the poor woman through the wringer, yet no recriminations had been shouted at her for her childish behavior. When Whiskey had closed the connection, she had felt a little of the ugly feeling in her gut fade away. If that wasn't an indication of what her next actions should be, what was? When Margaurethe called to ask her out for coffee, how could she say no?

"Is anyone sitting here?"

Whiskey glanced up sharply, surprised anyone could sneak up on her. Her automatic frown faded in recognition, and she felt a dozen butterflies conducting a skateboard exhibition in her stomach, flipping and sliding and rolling through the nervous turmoil. "Uh, no. Go ahead."

"Thank you." Margaurethe smiled, and sat across from her. "You look well."

God, she's beautiful. The years have been good to her. Whiskey shook her head to clear it. "I'm...fine, thanks." Forcing herself to look away, she recalled thinking the same thing when she had first seen Margaurethe, both as herself and as Elisibet.

"Where is everyone?"

Whiskey tensed, preparing for conflict about her safety. "The padre dropped me off. I told the others to stay away, to keep them safe."

Margaurethe's eyes hardened, but she said nothing, taking a sip from her coffee.

Whiskey let out a subtle breath.

"I was thinking," Margaurethe said, her voice rich with the Irish. "We were never introduced properly to one another." She politely reached across the table. "Hello. I'm Margaurethe O'Toole."

Startled into nonaction, Whiskey stared a moment before tentatively accepting the contact. "Whiskey." Smooth skin met her palm, warmed from the coffee cup. A smile broke out upon her face at the absurdity, and she fought an urge to giggle.

"It's a pleasure to meet you, Whiskey." Margaurethe raised an eyebrow, returning her smile. "The name suits you."

The compliment unsettled her. She heard Cora's voice on a cold Seattle street talking about her name—*I like it. Are you well-aged, slow and smooth? Or are you young and rough, burning your way down?*" Banishing the thought, Whiskey shrugged one shoulder, and leaned back in her chair, stretching her legs out before her. "Thanks. I think your name is beautiful." Comfortable behind her bland mask, her heart fluttered in her chest at the sweet smile on Margaurethe's face.

"Thank you." Margaurethe's voice had taken on a husky timbre. "I'm pleased you noticed."

Whiskey almost smelled the change in the air, a seductive odor underlying Margaurethe's delicate perfume. Her body responded of its own accord, a gentle pulse of arousal flickering in her belly, quelling the skateboarding butterflies. "How could I not notice?" she murmured.

Margaurethe sipped her coffee, an air of amusement about her. "And how is Cora these days?"

The change of topic shattered Whiskey's burgeoning desire. She had a moment of muddled confusion before her mental cogs slipped back into gear. Despite very clear and intimate memories, she had never actually touched Margaurethe other than handshakes. Clearing her throat, wondering if she had even received the signals she thought she had, Whiskey stuttered. "Um... she's all right. The others are too."

Nodding, Margaurethe looked away. "That's good. She seems rather taken with you."

Whiskey's mood soured. "Yeah, I guess so." She let her eyes trail over the pedestrians outside the window. They drank their coffee in silence.

"By the way, I wanted you to know we've moved out of the house in northwest."

"Really? That building is ready?"

Margaurethe waved a hand, indicating the ambiguousness of her announcement. "For the most part. Residences are complete, as are a majority of the offices. We're finalizing details for R&D, and the recreation center is still under construction."

Whiskey smiled. "Recreation center?"

"Oh, yes." Margaurethe nodded, returning the smile. "An entire floor devoted to it, as a matter of fact. I'd say two-thirds of the floor is dedicated to the exercise area. Then we have a small patio, child care and a handful of rooms available for gaming."

"Gaming? What kind of games? A pool table? Arcade?" Whiskey felt a *frisson* of excitement at the prospect, though she had not decided whether or not to return. *Duh! Of course, you will. Don't be stupid.*

"Certainly, if that's what you wish. The specifics haven't been finalized yet."

Whiskey chewed her lower lip as Margaurethe continued speaking.

"We've begun hiring locally. A number of my people have started the process of transferring here so that they may continue their research. I expect we'll be fully staffed and running in two months."

"Wow." Whiskey gave a low whistle. Her memories of Margaurethe held nothing to indicate such efficiency. Granted, Margaurethe had run the immediate household, and had done it well, but *she* had never given Margaurethe much in the way of power, not willing to release even a crumb of her might to the woman she treasured above all others. "That's pretty impressive."

Accepting the compliment with a slight preen, Margaurethe thanked her and sipped from her cup. "As soon as you decide to return, we can also utilize the lower ballroom levels for movie nights and parties." She frowned, raising an eyebrow. "What do you call them here? Raves?"

"A rave?" Whiskey stared, mouth open. "You'd host a rave?"

"No, you'd host the rave, *lúkal*. The building belongs to you." Margaurethe continued speaking, ignoring Whiskey's dumbfounded reaction. "A budget is already in place for your entertainment. Keep in mind, however, that the same budget is needed for proper dinner functions and speaking, so you can't spend the year's amount for one party."

Not knowing what to say, Whiskey said nothing as she tried to wrap her mind around the fact that she owned a building with a health club and a place to have a rave.

"Do you miss it?"

She released her preoccupation at Margaurethe's faint question. "Miss what?"

Margaurethe nodded her head toward the window. "Out there. Do you miss it?"

Whiskey watched cars pass by on SE Hawthorne Avenue. This was an eclectic section of town with large old houses just past a district of quirky, ratty businesses. Tie-dye and batik, wool and cotton were the costume of the day, and any number of former hippies wandered by in their sandals and dreadlocks, kerchiefs and ponytails. "I do sometimes. I didn't spend much time out here, though." She looked at Margaurethe, wanting to make her understand, not knowing if she was capable of it. "I stayed downtown when I was here; only for about a year before going up to Seattle."

Margaurethe looked away, a little crease manifested between her brows.

She was thinking so hard, Whiskey almost heard the mechanisms in her brain. Grinning fondly, she followed Margaurethe's gaze out the window at a trio of teenagers bearing backpacks. They looked like they hadn't eaten in days. "Most of us weren't in such a bad way."

"Really?" Margaurethe asked. "No home, no food, no money. That can't be pleasant."

Whiskey snorted. "Out there I relied on me. I stood or fell on my own."

"It sounds lonely."

The words opened a chasm in Whiskey's heart as she realized for perhaps the first time that it had been lonely. "No." She forced herself not to squirm with the lie. "It's freedom."

Margaurethe didn't argue. Instead she asked, "So how long did you spend on the streets?"

"Six years, give or take." She surprised herself with the automatic response. She had never been so loose-lipped about her past before—not on the streets, nor in the foster homes she had frequented as a child. *Damn. Am I losing my edge?*

"Six years." Margaurethe clicked her tongue, her tone concerned. "Where did you sleep in winter? I know the climate hereabouts is rather mild, but certainly it became cold enough to need a warm place to stay."

Whiskey shrugged. "I don't know. Here and there. Abandoned houses and stuff. There was an all-night club I went to most of the time." She grinned. "Sometimes I'd get picked up by people. I spent two weeks with a nun last February. Sister Rosa. The padre set it up. She did her damnedest to convert me, but I couldn't handle the ridiculous rules."

Margaurethe propped her chin in her hand, elbow on the table, and studied her. "That couldn't have been safe."

Whiskey set her cup down, and drew in her legs. Leaning both forearms on the table, she peered at Margaurethe. "Life's not safe. Anyone who says so is deluded." She waited, almost afraid to breathe, expecting an argument. Her reward was a bright smile, and her heart leaped in her chest.

"Very true. If it was, it would be—" She paused to think. "Boring."

"Mundane."

"Mediocre."

Whiskey nodded in grudging respect. "Yeah."

They examined one another for several minutes, the silence at their table absorbing all other noises and distractions. Whiskey inhaled deeply at the almost alien sense of safety and trust she felt, the part of her that was always on edge relaxing as it hadn't since she had left the house weeks ago. Time stood on edge, not quite toppling over into the next second. She wanted to reach out with her mind, to connect with the sensation of heated woodsmoke and mulled wine, but held back. Castillo had drilled into her fairly early that forcing a connection was considered rude, and she didn't think she could stop at a polite brush of request. She would want to delve deep into Margaurethe's soul.

Another sensation eased into her consciousness. A pressure

from outside them, behind her. Margaurethe's absorption wavered, noting the intrusion, easing herself away from their tableau of two. As their connection abated, noises and odors rushed forward to fill the vacancy, causing Whiskey's head to reel.

Margaurethe straightened in her chair. "I have to go." Her smile became flirtatious, and she slightly cocked her head, her dark bangs brushing across her forehead. "Call me if you need anything?"

Whiskey's eyes narrowed at the questioning tone. *Does she think I won't?* Given her tendency to distance herself from Margaurethe, however, it was no wonder she was uncertain whether or not Whiskey would actually contact her. "Can—" She paused, and cleared her throat, feeling like an idiot. "Can I call you just to talk?" Heat suffused her face.

"That would be wonderful." Margaurethe stood. "I'll see you later."

Whiskey watched her leave, winding through the tables and outside into the light rain shower. Margaurethe turned once to wave before disappearing around a corner and out of sight, leaving Whiskey with a strong desire to follow.

Shaking herself at the abrupt departure, Whiskey remained seated. Her view fell upon Margaurethe's discarded cup. Entranced, she pulled it toward her, noting a faint smear of lipstick on the lip. She did not have to bring it to her nose to catch the faint aroma of makeup and perfume and a spiciness that made up Margaurethe's scent.

She wanted to go home, but *home* was a word that had not held any real meaning for her since she was a child. Home was comfort and stability and love. Whiskey stared out the window. Home now was Margaurethe.

CHAPTER TWENTY

As soon as she was out of Whiskey's sight, Margaurethe's smile melted into a snarl. She had no need to search for him; he stood boldly on the corner by a small theater.

"Ah, Margaurethe! Another pleasant surprise!"

She marched up to Valmont, and slapped him hard across the face. A Hispanic woman gasped, and pulled her small daughter quickly past. Margaurethe ignored the bystanders. "I told you to stay away."

Valmont rubbed his cheek, an impudent grin on his face. "I must say you've got good follow-through. Have you taken boxing lessons recently?"

Margaurethe growled, putting every ounce of will into the

effort to sheathe her teeth. Around them, Humans sauntered from shop to shop, oblivious to the simmering violence in their presence. "How did you find her?"

His grin widened into a full smile. "Funny you should ask. I got to thinking the other night—you remember—when we ran into one another at Tribulations." At her faint grumble, his devilish smile grew. "Anyway, I figured that if anyone would eventually meet with her, it would be you."

"You followed me."

"Oh, no, no, no." Valmont chuckled. "I had you followed...by a private detective I hired when I arrived in town."

Margaurethe cursed. No doubt his lackey was Human, as well, making it all but impossible for her to find.

"I know you miss her."

A statement more than a question, it shocked her from her self-castigation. "Very much." Her lips pressed together at the admission, her wrath with Valmont sinking beneath the sea of annoyance for letting him get past her guard with such ease.

Ignoring her stiffness, he glanced back to the coffee shop where Whiskey had remained. "I miss her too."

She scoffed, a gentle sound that nevertheless reached his ears despite heavy vehicle and foot traffic. "I doubt she'd say the same of you if the situation were reversed."

"True." He nodded, a rueful grin stretching his lips. "She was a wonderful opponent."

She watched as he peered down the street, inadvertently baring his neck. The sudden desire to attack, to rend the tender flesh there almost overwhelmed her. She shook from its intensity. Looking away from the temptation, she reeled from her weakness, her temptation. No matter how much she wanted his destruction, doing so on a public street in an American city would have vast repercussions. "Why are you here?"

He turned back to her, a smile in his voice. "Perhaps the *Agrun Nam* wanted an unbiased approach."

Margaurethe shook her head. "If they did, they would have done better than to call for you."

"Why? You know what she was like. You, of all people, can't deny what you witnessed firsthand."

She swallowed against her fury. "I don't deny her actions. She knew no other way."

It was Valmont's turn to scoff. "And any other ways presented to her were summarily ignored. I know. I was her chief advisor." He waved a hand to forestall her response. "She may have been a powerful leader to our people in the beginning, but she became obsessed with her power. Toward the end, she listened to no one, making rash decisions that were such a detriment to our people that it has taken us centuries to rebuild."

She crossed her arms over her chest, holding herself. "And you *killed* her!"

A rotund man blinked at them, scuttling out into the street to avoid passing too close on the narrow sidewalk. Margaurethe turned and walked away, rounding a corner.

"Aye, I did," Valmont said to her back, following her off the busy street. "And I'd do it again if faced with the same choices!"

She stopped when she deemed them safe from eavesdroppers, but did not respond.

Valmont sighed. "I'm sorry. My purpose isn't to fight with you. It's just…it's been so long since I've seen you. I've missed you too, Margaurethe."

The words unexpectedly eased her animosity, reminding her of a time of friendship before the breaking, before the death that had divided them forever. Her chin settled on her chest, a slight frown pursing her lips. "I've missed you, as well."

The rain dribbled down upon them, drops coming faster and with more substance. Margaurethe had forgotten her umbrella, but did not want to give Phineas a coronary by bringing Valmont into his presence. "Shall we find someplace a little less exposed?"

"Certainly." He thumbed over his shoulder. "How about that coffee shop?"

Scowling at his cheek, Margaurethe led him down the residential side street in silence. They walked at a leisurely pace. "I hear you've spent quite a bit of time in South America recently?"

"That I have." He settled into the small talk with ease. "I've had an estate down there for a number of years. And you?"

Margaurethe shrugged, pulling up the collar of her jacket. "Here and there. No one place stands out above the others."

"Itinerant lifestyle then, eh?"

"Yes. It's easier." She smoothed a nonexistent wrinkle from her sleeve, not wanting to fall for his tricks. Valmont had a handsome and open face, one he used to his advantage. Many people found it easy to believe his lies, ignore his treasons, and follow his practical and knowledgeable lead. She had vowed to never be subject to his spell again after he had murdered Elisibet.

Minutes and city blocks ticked past before he spoke again. "Why do you think the *Agrun Nam* called me?"

She did not answer, noting the increase of traffic at a crossroads ahead.

"Come now, Margaurethe. There can be only one reason." He touched her elbow, pausing them in place. "They believe the prophecy is true, and she has returned to lead again."

She pinned him with a sharp look. "And what are your intentions?"

"I intend to ensure history does not repeat itself."

Cursing, she spun around. The nameless horror that had filled her soul all those years ago threatened to consume her in fire and hatred and a joyous thirst for revenge. "I will defend her to my death, Valmont."

"You misunderstand me." He held out his hands in supplication, palms toward her. "I will do everything in my power to sway her from repeating past mistakes. I was young—we all were. If it is true, if this girl is Elisibet, I'll not hesitate to put her over my knee should she need a reminder of her place."

The incongruous vision filled her mind, easing the black cloud of death away. Despite the righteous malevolence she felt toward him, she snorted a laugh. "That scenario would be worth paying to see."

"Wouldn't it?" Valmont smiled, even teeth white against the darkness of his skin. "I know you don't believe me. There's no reason you should, given the circumstances. I just want you to keep an open mind."

"So that you understand fully, if you try to cause her any hurt, I will kill you as I should have before."

They stared at each other, eyes locked, challenge given, received and accepted.

He nodded. "I would expect nothing less."

CHAPTER TWENTY-ONE

"*Sañar.*"

Looking up from her late brunch, Bertrada Nijmege glanced at the interruption. One of the servants stood at her elbow, a tray in one hand. The item on it seemed incongruous with the surroundings of her dining room, which duplicated Victorian splendor to the finest detail.

Her scowl served to enhance her bird of prey features as she set her knife and fork aside to take the cellular phone. Needing no order to leave, the servant whisked away, closing the door quietly behind him.

"Hello?"

"It's her."

Bertrada sat forward in her chair, eyes sharpening. "You're certain?"

"Yes. There's no doubt."

She slumped against the back of her chair, closing her eyes for a moment. *The bitch is back.* A distant part of her chortled at hearing the old pop song, doubting it had been written for such an occasion.

"*Sañar?*"

Bertrada's eyes opened, not seeing the room before her. Instead, the old *Agrun Nam* hall hovered in her vision, the one that none of them had set foot in since Elisibet's death. Faintly, she heard the echoes of her beloved's screams as the flesh was stripped from his body before them, heard the questions put to him in that detestable honeyed voice.

"*Sañar*, are you still there?"

"Does she remember?"

There was a pause. "I'm not certain."

"Do you think she'll develop any memory?"

"Again, it's uncertain. That she's even returning is unheard of. We're not aware of anyone who has." The caller stopped talking for another few moments. "It could be that she won't become the Sweet Butcher again."

Bertrada's eyes hardened. "Regardless, she'll pay for her crimes if I have to kill her every time she bloody well shows up."

"Yes, *Sañar.*"

She sighed, rubbing the bridge of her beaky nose. "How long before you'll know for certain?"

"Unknown. *Ki'an Gasan* Margaurethe has made things... difficult."

"Margaurethe." Bertrada cursed. "She'll be trouble."

"I know, *Sañar.* I've a few ideas on how to keep her occupied."

"Good. Implement them. As soon as you can, bring this... *person* before the *Agrun Nam.* We'll take it from there."

"We, *Sañar?*"

"Who my allies are does not concern you." Bertrada's voice sounded furry with rage. "Don't overstep yourself."

"Yes, *Sañar.*"

She suppressed her fury, knuckles white on the phone. "Call

me when you have further information." Hitting the disconnect button, she forced herself to set the phone gently on the table rather than throw it across the room. Her teeth had extended during the conversation, and she wished she could see the Sweet Butcher now, taste her flesh and blood as she tore Elisibet's throat out.

Time ticked past as Bertrada regained control of her emotions, her breathing coming easier. Inhaling deeply, she let the last vestiges of her wrath fade away. Soon. Thwarted by the *Agrun Nam*, her personal revenge had been put aside for the expediency of Valmont's solution. It would not happen again.

"I will have you, Elisibet."

CHAPTER TWENTY-TWO

Margaurethe stood in the center of her new office, hands on her hips. What had once been conference space on the second floor had been renovated into a reception area and two massive offices for the president and CEO of The Davis Group. The room smelled of fresh paint, plaster and new carpet. Behind her was a tree-strewn view of the river, winter-bared branches reaching to the terminally gray skies. The upper third of Mt. Hood peeked over the top of the raised highway on the east side.

Her desk phone rang, and she silently congratulated the workmen on getting the communications up and running. Muffled construction noises in the distance indicated that industry still continued on the third floor. She sat down in the plush leather desk chair, and picked up the phone. "Yes?" She responded after listening, "That's fine. Have all deliveries go to the loading dock. Security will meet them there."

The sounds increased in volume as the door opened, and she looked up to see Dorst sweeping into the room.

"Of course. Thank you." Margaurethe set the phone on its cradle. "How did you get past my receptionist?"

Dorst craned his head to look over behind him, frank surprise on his face. "Oh! Was there supposed to be someone at that large desk out there?" When he turned back to her, his gaunt face was split into a grin. "Silly me."

Margaurethe grimaced, not bothering to become annoyed with her new receptionist's inability to catch him. The man was an enigma, and had probably given Harry Houdini lessons on escape and disappearance.

He bowed, and looked about the room. "My, you certainly have done well for yourself, haven't you, *Ki'an Gasan*."

"How is she?"

"Who?" Dorst pinned her with an inscrutable look.

Not wanting to play his little games, Margaurethe raised an eyebrow and lowered her chin to glare at him.

He laughed, wagging a finger at her. "Ah, there's no frolicking with you, is there?" He plopped himself in an inglorious heap on the couch under the window. "Has anyone told you that you should 'lighten up'?"

She remained silent, waiting.

"Oh, all right!" Shifting his weight, he stretched his arms over the back of the couch. "She's fine. Safe. Well. Better?"

"Much." She made a show of going over files in her briefcase.

"That Human artist has been painting her, it seems. She's over at his apartment every two or three days to sit for him."

Margaurethe looked up, cocking her head. "Is he that good?"

Dorst gave her an expression of grudging respect. "To be sure, he's not up to the standards of some of the great masters of the past, but he has an interesting style."

"Perhaps we should commission an official portrait from him."

He sniggered. "Only if someone rides roughshod upon the

young man. He has this unfortunate tendency to add some rather fantastical elements to his work."

Margaurethe made note of the information. "He has a portfolio online, according to the background search we did on him. I'll look into it, and see if he's acceptable enough for a state portrait."

Dorst raised his chin slightly. "Of course."

"Have you had a chance to look around here? Check out the security?"

"I have!" Dorst brought his long, thin hands down from the couch, and rubbed them together. "I particularly enjoy the multi-level security offices and armories. Are you expecting a war?"

"Shouldn't we?" Margaurethe asked, looking up from her desk. "Considering who will be in residence, I think it behooves us to have every method in place to protect her and ourselves."

"No Purge this time, eh?"

She felt her stomach drop at his words. "No. No Purge this time. We're no longer in a Sanguire homeland. If a mob mentality forms, they'll have to deal not only with our security staff, but the Human riot and S.W.A.T. teams."

"Who knew Humans could be so handy to have around?"

Margaurethe ignored his flippancy. "Do you have any suggestions?"

Dorst propped his feet up on the conveniently placed coffee table, arms once more spread wide across the back of the couch as he stared at the ceiling. "As far as security is concerned, no. Providing the majority of them are Sanguire, it shouldn't be an issue." He peered at her, the movement bird-like in its execution. "Do you plan on reprising her personal guard?"

"I do. She'll have two guards with her at minimum, over and above the staff assigned to various posts and patrols." She paused to check a drawer, pulling out a single sheet of paper. "In fact, this is your security clearance and computer access codes. I'd like you to go over the personnel files of those I've flagged for the job, let me know if you have any reservations."

"Certainly!" He jumped to his feet, and came to take the paper from her. Scanning it, he nodded and handed it back, passwords apparently memorized.

Margaurethe returned it to her drawer. "I've drawn up a rudimentary budget, and have allocated funds to a number of departments, including intelligence. That department will be a branch of security, but autonomous from it, and will answer only to the president and the CEO."

Dorst's smile was sly as he bowed to her. "And where will this department be based?"

"You tell me."

He paused, his grin fading for a brief moment before widening even larger. "I've noticed a pair of rooms down in the bowels of this building. They don't appear to be earmarked for anything."

Margaurethe smirked. "Do tell."

"Basement levels two and three, over in the northwest corner."

She booted up the building floor plans on her computer, quickly locating the two areas in question. "You're right. One was used as accounting storage, and the other the shipping office before we took over the building. Do you want them both?"

Dorst fairly buzzed with excitement at the prospect. "Oh, *may* I?" he asked in a breathless voice.

Margaurethe chuckled. "They're yours. Do you want any work done on them?"

"Oh, no! I'll make the necessary adjustments myself." He thought a moment, tapping a long finger against his lower lip. "Perhaps I'll enlist those colorful younglings residing with my *Gasan*."

"Just remember, this is a corporation, not a monarchy." *Yet.* "You have a budget, and will need to account for every penny of it in your quarterly reports."

He scoffed, giving her a disgusted look. "I know how to make the numbers add up, and the books look proper. Never you mind."

With an odd sense of fondness, Margaurethe watched him return to his scheming. She wondered what it was about him that had scared her so when she was young. Putting aside the thought, she asked, "Do you want to reside here? As you know, the top floors are available for a select few to remain on the premises."

Dorst raised an eyebrow, speculative. After a slight hesitation, he said, "No, I don't believe I'll need to. But thank you so much for the offer, dear *Ki'an Gasan*. And now, I really must go. Things to see! People to do!"

She gave his proper bow a graceful nod, and then he was gone.

With the thought still fresh in her mind, Margaurethe accessed her web browser and did a search for Rufus Barrett. He was fairly popular if his placement on the search engine list was any indication. Clicking the link brought her to a dark and dreary web page. He had multiple galleries to view, each named after one of the seven deadly sins.

"How trite." She accessed the gallery entitled Wrath, finding a series of photorealistic paintings of very angry-looking people. The predominant colors were blacks and crimsons, the subjects tattooed and pierced beyond what was considered the norm even in this day and age. She saw why Dorst suggested Barrett needed a firm hand. Dark leathery wings sprouted from the shoulders of a shaggy man in one photo. In another a morose woman held a demon child that looked at the viewer with yellow cat eyes.

Despite the absurd nature of his subjects his portrayals were impeccable. The soul-deep weariness in the woman's eyes made the ridiculous child seem believable. If Barrett could paint a portrait of Whiskey with such distinction, Margaurethe would gladly display it in the lobby. She would have to restrain the artist's more fantastical nature, but the right amount of cash might be enough of a bribe to assure success.

Margaurethe clicked the "Contact Me" link. Perhaps it was time she had an interview with young Mr. Barrett.

CHAPTER TWENTY-THREE

Castillo stared with dismay at the disaster in the kitchen. Someone had wanted cookies in the middle of the night, and had proceeded to use every pot and pan in the house to make them. He picked up a frying pan thick with burnt cookie dough, and stared. "All right, that's it." Dropping the pan back onto the stove with a *clank*, he strode into the common room of their latest safe house.

A former warehouse in Gresham, two of the four floors had been taken over by the pack. Though less luxurious than a traditional house, it at least had running water and working bathrooms. The change in lifestyle had not impressed Daniel or Cora, both of whom had lived in the bosom of their families until striking out with Fiona Bodwrda. Fiona's house in Seattle had been the height of affluent luxury into which Daniel and Cora had fallen with ease. The others were used to sleeping urban rough, however, and Valmont had not been seen beyond Portland in his search for them. It was hoped that the change of both venue and city would confuse his attempts further, so the hardship was accepted without complaint.

Music blared from a set of Bose speakers in one corner of the common room, and one of Rufus's friends played along with an electric guitar. The large flat-screen television added to the cacophony, displaying a disaster movie of Biblical proportions. Alphonse and Whiskey circled the pool table, attempting to trounce one another. Cora sat on the couch, not watching the television, intent on Whiskey's every move.

"Whiskey."

She looked up from the green felt. "What's up, Padre?"

He crossed his arms over his chest. "The kitchen's a disaster area."

Whiskey cocked her head, looking at her gaming companion.

Alphonse shrugged, chalking the end of his cue. "Kit and Frank wanted cookies, and nothing nearby was open," he said, speaking of two of Rufus's Human friends who had taken to hanging out at all hours of the day and night.

She looked around the room, noting Kit on the guitar. "Hey, Kit!"

The Human either ignored her, or could not hear her shout over the level of noise.

"I'll take care of it, Padre." Whiskey leaned her stick against the nearest wall, patting his shoulder as she went by. "Kit!" When he did not respond, Whiskey turned off the music. "Dude, I'm talking to you."

Kit remained focused on the guitar, continuing to play.

Castillo saw Alphonse and Cora both scowl at the Human's disrespect. Neither interfered, however, knowing Whiskey to be their leader. If she wanted their help, she would give the order. Castillo abruptly realized that he had fallen into the same habit as the others. Two months ago, he would have found out who was involved with the mess, and demanded they clean it up himself, not go to Whiskey to take care of things. *When did this happen?*

Whiskey, annoyed at Kit's refusal to answer, unplugged the guitar from the amp. "I said I'm talking to you."

"Hey! Who died and made you God?" Kit stood, radiating annoyance. He reeled in his cable.

A scoff escaped Whiskey as she stared at him. "Dude, you have no idea."

"Yeah, whatever. Rufus might fall for all that vampire princess bullshit, but I don't." Holding the end of the cable, he moved to plug it into the amp again.

Whiskey blocked him. "You and Frank made a mess in the kitchen. Go clean it up."

"No. Frank did it. Tell him to clean it."

Castillo inwardly winced. Whiskey had been taking a crash course in leadership since inheriting the pack. That and her memories of the Sweet Butcher made her brutal when faced with such obstinacy. A hardcore background on the streets had not helped soften her tactics.

Her eyes narrowed, and she pushed Kit back from the amp. The force was strong enough to make him take three steps. "I'm telling you."

Kit was a large man. He registered a split second of surprise that she had the strength to move him at all, before his face turned ugly. "Fuck you."

"You can't get that lucky."

In a move reminiscent of a number of television cop shows, Kit reached for her. Whiskey grabbed his questing hand, spun him around, and twisted his arm to the breaking point behind his back. Hampered by the guitar, unable to combat her Sanguire speed, Kit yelped and dropped to one knee. Whiskey used the opportunity to wrap her other arm around his throat, leaning over his back.

Nupa sauntered into the room from parts unknown, a beer in one hand, and raised an eyebrow. "That's got to hurt." He smirked at Alphonse, who returned the smile.

"You're going to pack your guitar, and you're leaving. Don't come back. Ever." Whiskey spoke softly into his ear, letting him save a little face since he had no idea the gathered Sanguire could hear every word. "Understood?"

"Fuck you," he grunted as Whiskey applied pressure to his arm.

"You want to keep playing guitar? Or do you want me to do permanent damage?"

He growled. "All right! Let me go!"

Castillo didn't trust him, and Whiskey paused to assess Kit's truthfulness. A flicker of resignation crossed her face, and she did as he asked, though it was apparent she thought he would put up a fight. Castillo saw a flash of glee in the Human's eyes as he was released.

Kit stood, whirled, and attempted to deliver a roundhouse punch. It didn't connect. He stared in shock at her hands wrapped around his fist, stopping his attack a foot away from her face. Whiskey twisted his arm, and a sickening *crack* echoed over the sounds of the television. Kit crashed to the ground with a wail, guitar clanging against the cement floor as he grabbed his upper arm.

Taking a shaky breath, Whiskey stepped back. "Alphonse, take out the trash."

Eager, Alphonse dropped his cue onto the pool table, and approached.

"Don't hurt him," Whiskey admonished.

Castillo smiled. Leave it to Whiskey to show such viciousness, yet be concerned for the Human's welfare. Alphonse's enthusiasm dampened, and he waved for Nupa to give him a hand. They carted the wounded man out of the room.

"Sorry, Padre." Whiskey ran a hand through her hair. "We'll clean up the kitchen."

"You don't have to do that."

"Yes, I do." She shrugged, looking around the large room. "You're not a nursemaid or a butler here. There's no reason you should have to play housewife to a bunch of brats."

He felt pleasure that she understood his growing frustration with the current state of affairs. Paying homage, he bared the side of his throat to her. "Thank you."

Nupa and Alphonse returned from their task. Thwarted in his wish to add more injury to the insult, Alphonse instead collected Kit's amplifier, and tossed it out the nearest window.

A satisfied smile crossed his face at the resultant crash from the street three floors below.

"C'mon." Whiskey gestured everyone toward the kitchen. "Let's clean up that mess for the padre."

Castillo watched them file into the other room, Cora drifting quietly along behind. Taking full advantage of the situation, he sprawled across the couch, picking up the remote control to turn down the television volume.

He considered Cora's recent demeanor. There had been a lot of strain between the two women, strengthening as the weeks had passed. He had been surprised that the two had carried on for as long as they had. Occasionally, he had caught the glances Whiskey shot Cora when she thought no one was looking. They had been an odd combination of speculation, distaste and fondness. She had never spoken of her feelings, but he could tell the relationship had been more physical than emotional, at least on Whiskey's part. Margaurethe O'Toole's arrival had been a death knell, and Cora had known it. Her jealousy had grown exponentially until Whiskey had been forced to take the matter in hand. Since then, they had slept in separate beds. Cora's daydreams of being Whiskey's queen were unrealistic from the beginning, but her youth had not allowed her to see the reality of the situation.

Castillo heard noise downstairs, and got up from the couch. It sounded like someone knocking. He glanced at the kitchen door, and decided to deal with Kit on his own. Whiskey had not enjoyed the need to trounce him; no reason to make her do it twice. He trotted down the stairs. Not bothering to look through the peephole, he threw open the door.

Zebediah stood there, face pale. A dark-skinned hand held him by the collar. Castillo visually followed the brown hand, down a brown clothed arm, to the charming face of a brown man whose hair was scattered about his scalp in short dreadlocks.

"Hello. I found this at the supermarket down the street." Valmont smiled. "I was wondering if Jenna Davis could come out to play?"

CHAPTER TWENTY-FOUR

Deep bitter chocolate stabbed at Whiskey, sharp against her mind. She dropped the pan she had been transferring to the sink. It clattered in slow motion, banging along the floor as the others turned toward her. Then the sensation was gone. Reaching out, she attempted to make contact with Castillo, and found herself blocked by a faintly familiar feeling. She knew if she pressed harder, she would smell the slightest hint of steel along with the touch of silk in her mind.

Valmont.

"Shit!" Grabbing Cora, Whiskey pushed her toward the door. "Get out! Run! Valmont is here!"

Alphonse bolted from the room, leaving the water running in the sink.

Nupa, having not lived with the constant threat as long as the others had, did not move as quickly. Whiskey grabbed him. "Get upstairs, wake Daniel. He's napping in the back. Both of you get out any way you can."

Nodding, he hastened to comply.

Whiskey hustled down a back set of stairs, bursting out into the alley behind the warehouse. Cora was already there, and Alphonse was at the corner, peering around the building. Whiskey danced from one foot to the next in urgent anticipation, preparing to attack when she heard footsteps running for the door. Relieved to see Daniel and Nupa, she gestured for them to run ahead of her.

The pack reached the corner and paused.

"Zeb went to the store. Do you think—?"

Whiskey laid a hand on Alphonse's shoulder. "If he was followed, it's too late. The padre will try to keep him safe. We have to go."

He looked mutinous, but nodded.

Whiskey did not like the idea of leaving Zebediah or Castillo behind, but it was that or get caught. It felt cowardly. She could not be taken by Valmont. She had no choice. "Let's go. We'll call the padre when we're away from here."

Following her orders, the pack disappeared into the night.

***

Margaurethe looked up at the knock on the door. She had turned out the overhead lights in her office, relying on the desk lamp and the soft glow of the streetlights to illuminate the room as she worked. Wondering who would be here at this hour, she called, "Come in."

A security guard poked his head into the room. "My apologies for the interruption, *Ki'an Gasan*, but there's a Catholic priest and a young man here to see you. One says his name is Father James Castillo?"

She stood bolt upright, blood pumping fiercely through her veins. The priest would not come here without good cause. "Thank you. Send them in."

The guard nodded, and pulled back, opening the door wider.

Castillo's complexion more resembled curdled milk than his Mediterranean heritage. Behind him came one of the young brothers belonging to Whiskey's pack, appearing ill-at-ease and shaky.

As soon as the door closed, Margaurethe came around the desk. "What happened?"

"Valmont found us." Castillo glanced at the youngling. "He found Zebediah at a store, and followed him back to the warehouse."

Margaurethe reached out, using the edge of the desk to stabilize herself. "Whiskey?"

"She got away with the others." Castillo wiped his face with a trembling hand. "I was able to hold him off long enough to warn her."

"Thank goodness." Margaurethe tottered back to her chair, and collapsed into it with a sick feeling. "Would he have been able to track her from there?"

"I don't know. If they found a car, perhaps not." Castillo looked at the youngling beside him. "Can we sit down, *Ki'an Gasan?*"

Startled at her lack of manners, Margaurethe exclaimed. "Oh! Of course! Sit." She picked up the phone, ordering sandwiches and soft drinks brought to her office.

"Thank you, Ki'an Gasan." Castillo waved Zebediah to the couch. As the youngling dropped onto it, he sat at one of the chairs in front of the desk.

"You're sure she wasn't seen?" Rising, she walked to the chair beside Castillo, and sat beside him.

Castillo tugged at his beard with a shaky hand. "I can't be certain; I have no idea how long he was in the area. We were in Gresham, and all of *Sañur Gasum* Dorst's reports indicated he remained in Portland." He glanced over at Zebediah, whose head sagged in his hands. "He wasn't pleased that she evaded him. I think we can safely say she got away."

"Have you been in contact with Reynhard?"

"No. *Sublugal Sañur* Valmont took both our cell phones. Besides, even if I'd called, it could have been him compelling me."

Margaurethe cursed. Standing, she returned to her phone to call Dorst.

"Oh, I must say I'm so pleased to see you, Father!"

Growling, Margaurethe set the phone down. She turned to see Dorst closing her office door.

He smirked at her, and paid his respects. "My apologies, *Ki'an Gasan*, but I'd heard from security that you had some unexpected guests. I thought I'd come up to have a look."

"How did Valmont slip your surveillance? He made it to Whiskey's front door."

"Did he?" Dorst looked impressed. "I really must interview that private detective he's hired. For a Human, he certainly knows his job." He bustled forward, taking a seat on the couch uninvited. Reaching out, he tipped Zebediah's chin up, and gave him a long look. "You'll do."

Exasperated, Margaurethe threw her hands into the air. "Shall we focus on the here and now, Reynhard? Whiskey is on the run, and without protection. We need to find her!"

He released Zebediah, and looked at her, surprise on his face. "Have you attempted to phone her?"

Margaurethe sputtered a moment before forcing herself to silence. Of course not. She had spent so many weeks trying not to force Whiskey into a corner that it hadn't occurred to her to simply make the call.

"In any case, if she doesn't answer, I can track her via her cell phone." Dorst glanced over at his young companion on the couch. "I learned that brilliant little trick from you."

Zebediah didn't have the energy to react, simply giving Dorst a nod.

With belated grace, Margaurethe returned to her desk chair and dialed Whiskey's number.

"Hello?"

Relief ran through her at the sound of the tentative voice. "Are you all right?"

"I'm fine. We're fine! We're in the car. How did you know?"

"Father Castillo and your young friend, Zebediah, are here. They're safe." Her last words were for both Whiskey and the people in her office.

"Oh, thank God! We were so worried—" Whiskey covered the mouthpiece to relay the information to the others.

Dorst rose and strolled to the door to answer a soft knock. A security officer wheeled in a table piled with sandwiches, soft drinks and a pot of water for tea.

"What should we do now? Can we meet them somewhere?"

As the others availed themselves of the repast, Margaurethe sighed. "Will you come to me? At least stay the night, get some decent sleep and food."

The silence of suspicion met her request.

"I've never lied to you, Whiskey. I promise I won't try to make you stay here. Come, stay the night, you can leave in the morning." When there was no response, Margaurethe added, "It's not like you have anywhere else to go, and it's late. Let your people rest. They'll be out of danger here."

Appealing to her sense of responsibility did the trick. "Okay. What's the address there?"

Margaurethe had no idea how she held it together long enough to convey the information without breaking into a celebratory cheer.

"We'll be there in about twenty minutes."

"I look forward to seeing you again, *lukal*." Margaurethe released a pent-up breath. "When you pull into the drive, give your keys to the security officer. They'll park your car in the underground lot. Valmont can't get to it then."

"Okay. See you soon."

Margaurethe notified security of Whiskey's time of arrival, and the need for additional measures to be taken until she was safely inside. More phone calls ensued as she had the kitchen make more food, and housekeeping prepare rooms for the others.

"You'll be staying, Father?"

Castillo blinked in surprise. "If it won't be a bother, *Ki'an Gasan*."

She smiled, too happy to be insulted by his confusion. "No bother. We've plenty of rooms to fill."

Dorst had no compunction against needling her. "Don't forget Ms. Kalnenieks. She'll need a room, as well."

Margaurethe's smile faltered. "I thought that—" She looked at Castillo for confirmation.

The priest flushed, and pulled at his beard. "Um, no. Whiskey and Cora are no longer…" He hesitated, trying to think of a polite way to relate his news.

Zebediah saved the day. "They ain't cut buddies anymore. Whiskey dropped her."

Margaurethe didn't know what to say. Her adolescent desire to fall in love with a queen once again warred with the adult reality that Whiskey was a teenager and needed so much more than that from her. It also occurred to her that up until now, she had never heard Zebediah speak; that his first words to her would be ones that had the potential to unlock her heart was uncanny.

She set aside the weird sensation for the businesslike approach she had adopted over the decades. Standing, she brushed her clothing into place. "I'll go see to the room assignments. You three stay here. Reynhard, now's the time to interview the father and the youngling. We don't know if Whiskey will stay much longer than tonight."

"Understood."

Margaurethe left her office, unable to keep the smile from her face as she made her way to the elevators.

CHAPTER TWENTY-FIVE

Despite the chill weather, Margaurethe waited patiently outside the front entrance of The Davis Group. The drive was a covered half-circle, partially protected from the eternal fall of rain. In deference to the new arrival, security had been ramped up. All other entrances to the building were locked down, and a half-dozen officers waited outside with her. She knew that four armed Sanguire stood on the roof, vigilant against anyone following Whiskey's car onto the front apron.

A decrepit sedan slowly turned into the drive, reflecting more damp dust than blue paint in the overhead lights. It rolled to a stop in front of the security escort. Whiskey's wan face stared at Margaurethe from the passenger side. She held out both hands, beckoning for Whiskey to come. After a scurry of conversation within the vehicle, the doors opened and the younglings spilled out onto the pavement.

"Let's get you inside. Quickly!"

Whiskey hustled with the others through the main revolving doors. Once inside, she and the others gaped at the modern marble lobby, making entry somewhat difficult for those behind.

Margaurethe smiled. This was the first time Whiskey had actually seen the building she owned. As much as she wanted to take the time and tour her around, Margaurethe knew they made quite handsome targets with the lit windows against the blackness of night. "Come along. We'll get you some food, and then to your rooms."

She and four of the guards herded their charges toward the bank of elevators. One stood open, held there by another security officer. Margaurethe pushed the button for the fifteenth floor. With so many occupying the wood and brass car, she did not bother to speak.

The pack stepped out onto the fifteenth floor foyer, staring around at the residential lounge while Margaurethe dismissed the guards. As one, the younglings gravitated toward a well-stocked buffet counter giving off wonderful aromas. Margaurethe stayed back with a smile as they marveled at the selection. Despite protestations of starvation, none of them attempted to eat. Margaurethe found their willpower interesting. Their unruly habits indicated a lack of self-control, yet here was discipline.

Whiskey looked back at her. "Is it okay?"

"Of course." Margaurethe held both hands out, urging them forward. "It's for you."

A strange look crossed Whiskey's face. She turned and nodded at the others, who promptly snatched up plates and dished up a late dinner.

Margaurethe drifted toward the beverage section, taking a bottle of water from the cooler. Whiskey's control over her people interested her. Not unexpected, considering Whiskey's level of power, but intriguing. She didn't let them run rampant despite their appearance of irascibility. Elisibet had also been quite adamant about control.

Sitting at a table, Margaurethe listened to the younglings chatter as they commented on their dining options. Elisibet wouldn't have allowed such gregarious twaddle. She would have been ever on the lookout for insult. Whiskey joined in with her pack, laughing at a comment from Nupa, and tossing a bread roll at Alphonse's head. Even the ever-subdued Cora laughed at someone's comment as she helped herself to the salad. After everyone plated up, they found the soft drinks and ice cream machine. More prattle followed, until they finally had all they wanted.

Whiskey waved to a large table where the four of them could comfortably sit. While they settled down to the business of eating, she came to Margaurethe's table. "Thank you. We hadn't gotten around to having dinner yet."

"You're welcome. Father Castillo and Zebediah have already eaten. They should be here shortly." Margaurethe nodded toward Whiskey's plate, indicating she should eat.

For several minutes, Whiskey appeased her hunger rather than attempted to speak. After she had made a sizable dent in her meal, she wiped her mouth on a napkin, and looked at Margaurethe. "So, what is this place?"

"The building, or the room?"

Whiskey waved around them. "This. This floor."

Margaurethe scanned the area. "This is the residential lounge. It serves three meals a day, and has snacks available throughout the day and night."

"Residential." Whiskey paused to drink from a soda bottle. "I remember you saying people lived here. Who?"

"Mostly Sanguire at this point. We have some primary research specialists who prefer to live near their work." Margaurethe nodded toward a man exiting the elevator and walking down the hall. "Some of the security officers, Phineas, any number of people."

"And you?"

She nodded at Whiskey. "Yes, I as well. I have an apartment on the sixteenth floor."

Whiskey nodded in thought, stirring a puddle of ketchup with a steak fry.

Margaurethe smiled, watching her profile, happy beyond all reasoning that she was there. "You have one upstairs too."

"Yeah?" Whiskey grinned. "Cool."

Pleased at the positive reception, Margaurethe returned the grin. "We have one- and two-bedroom units available, as well as studio apartments on the eleventh floor. I've taken the liberty of preparing two of the doubles for the young men in your group, and single dwellings for Father Castillo and Cora. Is that acceptable?" She held her breath, hoping that Zebediah's news was correct.

Whiskey's good humor flagged, as she glanced at the table her pack occupied. "Yeah. That'll be fine."

Margaurethe released a silent sigh.

An elevator opened again, and Dorst, Castillo and Zebediah exited. A shout from the younglings made all conversation impossible as they jumped up to welcome their comrades.

It gave Margaurethe pause to witness the priest receiving hugs and jostling from the gathered children. She had expected it from Whiskey, but not the younglings. It seemed their time away had solidified their coterie. She sighed again, realizing that the time to separate Castillo from Whiskey had long passed. He may not have given her his oath of fealty, but it was all but done. To pursue a way of removing him from influence would widen the rift between her and Whiskey, a rift that may now actually be closing.

The next twenty minutes consisted of everyone explaining what had happened to them. Their excited air wearied Margaurethe even as it amused her. She truly enjoyed seeing the energized Whiskey reenacting the moment when she realized what had happened, though the thought of Valmont getting so close made Margaurethe shiver. Eventually, they ran down, stomachs sated and adrenaline fading.

"I think it's time for everyone to consider going to bed."

Whiskey looked at Margaurethe, smothering a yawn. "Yeah, you're probably right. Where's everybody going to stay?"

Margaurethe, with Dorst's help, escorted the pack to their various destinations. She had made certain to put them all on the same floor, so they did not have far to go. Alphonse and

Zebediah were across the hall from Castillo on one wing, with Nupa and Daniel across from Cora on the other. Whiskey made arrangements for them all to meet back at the residential lounge at a certain time the next day.

Back at the elevators, Dorst took Whiskey's hand in his. "It is a delight to see you safe and sound, *Ninsumgal*."

"Thanks, Reynhard." Whiskey tightened her grip. "We'll talk tomorrow, okay?"

"Of course." His elevator arrived, and he bowed deeply before disappearing within.

Truly alone for the first time since Whiskey's departure from the house weeks ago, the two women stared at each other.

"Up."

Whiskey blinked. "What?"

Margaurethe smiled. "We're going up."

"Oh!" Whiskey turned and pushed the call button.

A few moments later, an elevator opened for them. Margaurethe gestured Whiskey in first. She pulled an electronic key card from her jacket pocket, and inserted it into the slot on the panel before pushing the top floor button. Once it lit up, she removed the card. "If you should decide to stay, you'll get one of these, as well. It's the only way to access the sixteenth floor from any elevator."

Whiskey nodded.

The elevator opened onto a short corridor. In the left corner stood a sleek wooden security counter. A guard behind it came to his feet as they exited. "Good evening, *Ki'an Gasan*."

"Good evening, Francis." Margaurethe turned to her companion. "You remember Whiskey. She'll be staying in the *Ninsumgal*'s suite tonight."

Francis nodded at Whiskey. "Yes, ma'am. It's a pleasure to see you again, *Ninsumgal*."

Flustered, Whiskey stood speechless. Rather than keep her in the spotlight, Margaurethe thanked Francis. Using her key, she unlocked a large set of double doors, gesturing for Whiskey to precede her inside.

The tiny antechamber held two doors, and Margaurethe opened the right one. "This is your suite whenever you're here.

No one else will be residing here, so if you wish to leave personal belongings behind, feel free." Margaurethe stood back to watch her reaction.

Whiskey stepped hesitantly into the long room, mouth opening in surprise. The entry room had casual seating placed throughout its expanse, and a small bar and bathroom to one side. Its function was to hold those visitors deemed safe, while also keeping them out of Whiskey's private quarters. If necessary, small receptions could be held here for her and her closest friends.

Margaurethe followed her inside.

Reaching the center of the room, Whiskey turned slowly around. "This is really big."

"This is just the entrance and sitting room." Margaurethe chuckled at Whiskey's incredulous look. Waving to a door at the far end, she said, "Through there you'll find the rest of your apartment. The largest bedroom has a master bath and sunken tub. You'll find the belongings you left behind at the house there along with some additional items."

Whiskey gaped. "And this is all mine?"

"Yes, it is."

Nibbling her lip, Whiskey turned to take it all in once more. When she came back around, she cocked her head at Margaurethe. "Where are you sleeping?"

"My quarters are next door." Margaurethe smiled. "The captain of the guard has a smaller apartment across the hall from us, where the security station is. You should only see security or myself up here."

Whiskey nodded absently, scanning the room.

Moving closer, Margaurethe reached out to take Whiskey's hands, snagging her undivided attention. "I won't demand, or make assumptions regarding your actions and decisions. But I do need to ask you to stay." She squeezed Whiskey's hands at the expected roll of her eyes. "I must at least make the attempt, *m'cara*. You know this." She smiled. "Please. For your safety, and the safety of your friends. For my state of mind, please seriously consider staying here."

Whiskey blinked at her, and swallowed. "I'll—" She cleared her throat. "I'll think about it. Really think about it."

Margaurethe stepped toward the door. "Thank you. I'll leave you then. Good night and sweet dreams, Whiskey."

"Good night." Whiskey took a step toward her, and stopped, uncertainty crossing her face. "And thank you."

"Of course." Margaurethe curtsied. "It is my absolute pleasure." She left Whiskey standing in the elegant sitting room, positive she wouldn't get a bit of sleep the entire night.

CHAPTER TWENTY-SIX

"And this is the recreation floor."

Whiskey exited the elevator with the others, seeing exercise machines through the glass wall before her. Margaurethe had insisted they have a look at the building right after breakfast, and so they had been given a whirlwind tour of business offices, parking structures, ballrooms and R&D laboratories. This had been the first floor that looked remotely interesting, though the employee cafeteria had been noteworthy.

With a good night's rest, Zebediah had gotten over his scare and was back to his rascal self. "Oh, sweet! Swimming pools!" He opened the door to one side of a security desk, and dashed inside, followed closely by Cora and Alphonse.

"Just finished!" Margaurethe called after them. She mirrored Whiskey's grin, and held the door open for the rest. "They look small, but you can set a current to swim against. This is the cardiovascular room."

Whiskey entered the room with the equipment, seeing what Zebediah had spotted from the hall—another set of windows that revealed a sunken room beyond with multiple pools. The door to it had just snicked closed, though it didn't muffle the *whoop* of excitement from the brothers as they promptly stripped to their underwear and cannonballed into the water.

"And the pools." Margaurethe opened that door, revealing a set of steps down into the tiled area. Waving to the left, she indicated another set of steps up to a second tiled level. "We moved the original Jacuzzi to make room for more swimming areas. Since we had the room, we added another."

Castillo carefully averted his eyes as Cora, wearing nothing but her panties, carefully stepped into one of the hot tubs. "Have you included weight equipment?"

"Oh, yes." Margaurethe led them through the room, up a set of three steps, and through a door. "The weight room is here, with state of the art equipment and free weights. There's a small room farther on for massage appointments." Turning, she pointed out the floor-to-ceiling windows. "And a couple of smaller gymnasiums to use for yoga, general exercise. Those rooms take up two floors, so one can play racquetball or basketball, though the courts aren't regulation."

"Wow." *And this is all mine?* She'd spent so much time trying to keep her people entertained without putting them in danger, she had never considered the implications. Taking a leadership role with the European Sanguire would be brutally difficult, yes, but there were perks. Here her pack would be safe from harm. She would still have to keep close tabs on them, but they would have the opportunity to eat well, sleep without worry, and perhaps do something with their lives should they decide.

Margaurethe's arm looped through hers, interrupting her thoughts. Grinning at the smile she saw on Margaurethe's face, she considered another bonus. *Not to mention a chance to get to know her better.*

"Let me show you the rest of the floor."

Accompanied by Castillo, Whiskey allowed herself to be led out into the hall, past the bank of elevators. The security desk was occupied, of course, and it looked like the officers had a room in the corner. Double glass doors led outside.

"A patio and garden," Margaurethe murmured, continuing around the corner.

Daniel drifted toward the inviting sunlight, stepping outside.

"Down this hall we have eight rooms for gaming, half of them open to the corridor. At the end is the child-care facility."

Whiskey gave her guide a sharp look. "Child care?"

Margaurethe nodded. "Oh, yes. I've learned through the years that the better you treat your employees, the more loyal they'll be. I include child care in every facility. Women tend to shorten their maternity leave, and work longer hours knowing their children are safely cared for on the premises."

Whiskey's first thought was for her best friend in Seattle. Pregnant and homeless, she'd probably already had the child. Whiskey missed Gin fiercely, but knew that their time was past. The chaos of learning she was Sanguire and going through the *Ñíri Kurám* had put a wall between them. Whiskey's involvement in the accidental death of Dominick, a teenager attached to Gin's street family, had forever closed the door on their friendship.

"Are you all right?"

She shook herself, realizing she had stopped walking. "Sorry. Thinking about something else."

Margaurethe did not pry. She nodded, patted Whiskey's forearm and continued down the hall. They passed an open area with two pool tables, another with arcade games, and a third with comfortable seating and a large flat-screen television. "Shall we sit down a moment?"

Castillo backed up a step, preparing to return to the others. "I'll go check on Daniel."

"No." Margaurethe held out her hand to him. "I'd like you to stay, as well, James. You're one of Whiskey's advisors, and should be privy to this conversation."

The use of Castillo's given name surprised Whiskey. It surprised him, too, as he stood a moment with mouth agape.

Over and above the concern that she needed an advisor in this discussion, Whiskey found his demeanor funny enough to grin. "C'mon, Padre. Sit down." She followed her own advice, and dropped onto a couch.

He raised his chin, and joined Whiskey. Margaurethe sat in an armchair facing them. "Now that you've seen the property, do you have any questions of me?"

Whiskey wondered which of her thousands of questions should be spoken first. "Where does the money come from?"

"The majority of the capital comes from my own companies and accounts." Margaurethe stared off into the distance, deep in thought and memory. "I've spent decades focusing on communication technology and software. Over the years, I've held contracts with a number of governments, and my equipment can be found as close as the nearest cell phone, and as far away as the Hubble telescope."

Whiskey felt her jaw drop open. "The Hubble? Really?"

Margaurethe smiled. "Yes. My past research and development teams have been brilliant. When the first advances in computers came out, I made certain to buy into them." She laughed, a musical sound that brightened the room. "To be sure, we're not talking major portions of any space-faring satellite or Earth-bound computer. A simple line of command code, or a particular transistor or chip on a motherboard is all there is."

"Your work is impressive, *Ki'an Gasan*." Castillo looked at Whiskey. "It's rumored that she's the richest European Sanguire in the world."

Whiskey could find no words. From a modern perspective, it made sense that the Sanguire would expand and grow with the industrial advantages. With the same person making the investment decisions for hundreds of years, it seemed a sure thing even considering stock fluctuation. "Do you have any business competition from other Euros?"

"No." Margaurethe shook her head.

She sat back. "No? I'd think that half the conglomerations in the world are headed by our people."

Castillo shook his head. "You'd think wrong. To my knowledge, *Ki'an Gasan* Margaurethe is the only private individual to have done so."

"But—" Whiskey looked from one to the other, sitting up from her slump. "But why? Look at all the money to be had, all the power!"

Margaurethe smiled. "Money and power amongst Humans isn't that important."

Castillo's somber look validated Margaurethe's words.

Racism. Unable to sit still, Whiskey jumped to her feet and paced the room. "How do they survive then? How do they get money for food? For personal goods?"

"Many do dabble in the stocks," Margaurethe said, standing as well. "Most have ancestral lands. Our families do not grow as quickly as Human ones, so we've not had much reason to 'make money' for the sake of shelter or food. Most properties are working farmlands paying Humans wages to do the work. Those that have been overrun by urban growth have sunk their inheritance into real estate. There are many ways to get by without having to…" She trailed off.

"Without having to sully their hands by working with Humans instead of having Humans slave for them," Whiskey finished. She saw the feudal form of governance surviving through the Middle Ages with a population of people who had been born and raised within its framework.

Margaurethe's answer was simple. "Yes."

Whiskey stopped at the window. It overlooked the patio and garden. A few trees and hedges ran along the far wall, presumably the end of the building. Despite the late winter cold, there were a number of green plants soaking up sunlight. Daniel sat on a wooden bench under the shade of a hedge, reading a book.

Superimposing itself over the view was an image of Elisibet's gardens somewhere in Eastern Europe, the place where Margaurethe had first been drawn to the Sweet Butcher. All that was needed to complete the scene was a fountain in which the young handmaidens could play. She closed her eyes, remembering the sight of the youthful Margaurethe, dripping with water after being splashed by a playmate, and a grin touched her lips.

A few seconds later, she opened her eyes to see Daniel instead of Margaurethe. Sighing, she turned back. "Why didn't you do the same?"

Margaurethe cocked her head in thought. "Because I needed to prepare for you."

"Prepare?" Whiskey walked back to the couch, but didn't sit.

"Yes. I knew you would return. And I knew you'd need a stable treasury, and a way to communicate with your people. What better way than to become the world's largest telecommunications technology corporation?"

There was something else, something she avoided saying. Whiskey studied Margaurethe a moment, searching for a lie and not finding one. "So. What happens now?"

Margaurethe glanced at Castillo on the couch. "That depends entirely upon you, Whiskey." She returned her stare. "If you stay, you'll become the president of a corporation. As you learn how to do the job, you'll be given more control. As you gain more control in business, you'll do so in politics. I've already been contacted by the *We Wacipi Wakan*, and they wish to make a treaty with you. Soon the other governments will do so, as well."

None of which has anything to do with the European Sanguire. Whiskey frowned, scrubbing the back of her neck with one hand. "But what about the *Agrun Nam*? What about the prophecy?"

Taking a moment to consider her words, Margaurethe finally said, "They'll come into line or they won't. I think that your destiny is much bigger than retaking control of the *Agrun Nam*."

"Bigger?"

Castillo cleared his throat. "Rather than setting her at the head of a single government, you mean to have her lead all of them?"

Margaurethe's smile was wondrous as she quoted Mahar's prophecy. "She'll save the Sanguire, even as she destroys them."

Rather than fall down, Whiskey flopped back onto the couch.

"That would definitely destroy things." Castillo stroked his beard in thought. "Sanguire culture has changed dramatically over the last hundred or so years. What you suggest will hasten the demise of the multigenerational feudal compound."

Margaurethe made a noise of agreement. "We must have something come out of it. As it is now, our younglings are running like wild wolves among sheep. Our natural tendency to treat Humans as prey has forced our people to remain within their antiquated lifestyles." She threw her hands up in exasperation. "Humans breed like rabbits compared to us! If we don't find a way to gain control of modern society, our people will never survive."

"So, you interpret the foretold destruction as Whiskey bringing the Sanguire out of the Dark Ages?"

"I do." In an easy gesture, Margaurethe took Whiskey's hand in her own. "I've discovered that every Sanguire nation has a similar myth or prophecy. We know that you're Elisibet reborn; of that there is no doubt. But what if you're also destined to unite all Sanguire, not just the Europeans?"

Only Margaurethe's hand on hers kept Whiskey from jumping up to run away. She'd had enough trouble coming to terms with being the Euro *Ninsumgal*, now she was supposed to rule the world? Too many thoughts and emotions ran through her. She found it difficult to follow a single train of thought. "Can I have a moment with the padre?"

Margaurethe studied her a moment, worry upon her face. She raised her chin in capitulation. "Of course. I'll check in on the children in the pool."

Whiskey squeezed Margaurethe's hand before releasing her. She smiled. "Thanks."

Mollified, Margaurethe returned the smile before leaving them.

As soon as she was out of earshot, Whiskey turned to Castillo. "What do you think?"

"I think she may have something, at least as far as the method of destruction Elisibet's return could cause. It's been debated for centuries, and this makes sense."

"But what about the rest?"

He shrugged. "That I can't tell you. I haven't had the opportunity to do the research. I'd have to look into it myself to give you a comprehensive answer."

Whiskey looked away, leaning forward to put her elbows on her knees. She stared at the floor between her feet. "What the hell do I do, Padre?"

"Knowledge is power. Stay. Learn." He shifted beside her and when he spoke again, his voice was closer, quieter. "In the short term, you'll be safe from Valmont's clutches. Your people can live and play without care. Eventually, you'll take control. If you don't like the path set before you, you'll have the strength and knowledge to step aside when you decide to."

She chewed her lower lip, mulling over his words. Last night she had slept the sleep of the dead, fully relaxed for the first time in weeks. One thing she had not told Margaurethe about her time on the streets was always having to be alert, the many sleepless nights. Having to worry about the next meal, the next crisis, the next attack, always took its toll. It would be nice to lay that particular burden down, even for a short time.

But how many others will take its place? Whiskey had no idea what sorts of decisions she would have to make as head of a corporation. Thanks to *her* memories, she knew the problems with which a despot had to deal. But a business? *Do I really have a choice?*

A door opened, and a dozen Human children ranging between two and six years of age walked by the open room, chattering excitedly. Each was clothespinned to a bright colored rope as two young women escorted them down the hall. They all carried some manner of towel or plastic toy. Trailing behind them, a third woman toted an inflatable pool.

Castillo watched them pass. "I certainly hope Cora has dressed herself."

Whiskey chuckled. *Maybe I don't have a choice just yet, but I can at least change things here and now for the Humans I can reach.* "Let's go find Margaurethe, and tell her we'll be staying."

CHAPTER TWENTY-SEVEN

Margaurethe sipped her tea as she stood at her office window, staring out over the park in front of the river. It had become one of her most enjoyable views. Sunlight remained strong, though lack of cloud cover had made temperatures drop. From what she'd been told, the worst days of winter were in February, and she could see why.

Today was a day to celebrate. Whiskey had decided to stay. Margaurethe felt a grin widen on her face. Right now Whiskey was upstairs in her apartment, probably playing some horribly violent video game with her pack, or raiding the residential lounge for food and drinks. It was a momentous day.

Her phone buzzed, indicating an incoming message from her receptionist. She returned to her desk, and answered it. "Yes?"

"Mr. Rufus Barrett to see you, ma'am. He has an appointment."

"Please send him in." She looked up from her desk as the door opened. Her receptionist ushered in an unruly looking blond Human. Walking around the desk, she held out her hand. "Rufus Barrett, it's good to see you again. How have you been?"

If he was surprised by her sudden familiarity, he didn't show it. "I'm good, *Ki'an Gasan*. I'm glad to hear that Whiskey's decided to settle down for a bit."

"As am I." She gestured for him to be seated on the couch. A tray sat on the table, and she proceeded to pour coffee for him. "I was quite worried while she was away."

"Yeah, she had a few scary moments out there." He looked around the office. "This is really a nice place. She said there were apartments upstairs?"

"Oh, yes. I have a few researchers and specialists that prefer to live near their work. This seemed the best choice." She offered him a cup and a plate of cookies. "You'll love these. I brought my chef over from Europe last week, and he's been baking up a storm."

"Thanks." Rufus made a show of tasting one, and rolling his eyes in enjoyment.

Tedious. If he wasn't a friend of Whiskey's and an excellent artist, she would send him on his way. "I've asked you here to discuss an official portrait."

"Portrait?"

"Yes, of Whiskey." She sipped at her tea. "I've a mind to put a life-sized painting in the lobby. It will be the first thing anyone sees as they come in via the main entry."

He stared blankly at her for a moment, his mind obviously running through the potential income and publicity. Setting the plate of cookies down, he cleared his throat. "I'm not sure my art would be...um...appropriate for a business building."

Margaurethe nodded. "I do understand. I've seen your portfolio online, and have heard about the pieces displayed in your windows." She hid her smile at his startled look. "While I certainly don't want to suppress your creativity, I think we can come to an equitable compromise that won't cause you to...how do Americans say it? 'Sell out'?"

Rufus snorted in laughter. "I'd appreciate that, though the idea of having my work displayed so prominently is an excellent motivator."

"No doubt. Of course, it will be labeled with your name and contact information." She smiled behind her teacup at the greedy flash on his face. "I'd have a few stipulations, however."

His avarice crashed, and he warily studied her. "What would they be?"

She set her cup down, and reached for a crisp. "For one, I'd require you to work here. We can supply all your needs for the piece; you won't be out of pocket for the expenditures."

"That's not a problem."

"And you'd have to...shall we say, 'tone down' the fantastical rhetoric of your style."

Rufus nodded, frowning. "Which part of my style are you referring to? I refuse to work with bright yellows and greens. If you're looking for something upbeat and cheery, you should probably speak to someone else."

Margaurethe lightly patted his hand. "Oh, no, no. As I said, I like your style now. I'm referring to wings, fangs, iridescent cat's eyes, that sort of thing. The photorealism is wonderful, as is the dark atmosphere you convey. I don't want to lose those aspects in the artwork."

He looked relieved, the lines about his mouth no longer as deep. "And you'll have final say throughout?"

"Of course." She let him consider before sweetening the pot. "I'm thinking to pay something in the range of ten thousand dollars."

He choked a moment at her offer, coughed, and cleared his throat. "That—That sounds...fair."

Margaurethe smiled, knowing he generally received four or five hundred for everything he had created to date. "Then I'll have my lawyer draw up a contract, yes?"

Rufus paused, frowning as he went over the conversation, obviously searching for something that would indicate he was being taken. He nodded. "Of course."

"Excellent! It should be ready by tomorrow afternoon. May I call you when I have it?" Margaurethe stood.

He hastily set his coffee cup down, and rose. "Yeah, that would be great."

She reached forward and shook his hand. "Thank you." Directing him toward the door, she continued, "I believe Whiskey is upstairs in her apartment. Shall I have security show you the way there?"

"Oh, yeah. Thanks."

Considering he would never get up to the floor without a security escort, she found his agreeable nature humorous. She opened the door, and waved him out. "Helen, can you please have security escort Mr. Barrett to Whiskey's apartment on the sixteenth floor?"

"Yes, ma'am." The receptionist picked up her phone.

"It's been a pleasure speaking with you, Mr. Barrett. I'll call you soon."

Rufus, still looking a little awestruck, smiled. "Um…yeah. Thanks."

Margaurethe left him in the foyer, closing the door. She leaned against it, and closed her eyes. *This has been a wonderful day.*

***

Whiskey's first day in residence was similar to living at the old house with all the security staff Margaurethe had brought along. Instead of sitting in the small living room playing video games, however, the pack now congregated in the sitting room of her apartment. The only apparent difference was the upscale atmosphere. Whiskey had requested a couple of gaming consoles and a large television screen, which now hung from the wall by the door. Couches and chairs had been rearranged to center on the entertainment, and the wet bar had been stocked with snacks and drinks purloined from the residential lounge. Alphonse had been banned from playing mumblety-peg indoors, and the balcony saw heavy usage as the smokers in the crowd stepped outside to partake of their habit.

Sitting on a bar stool, Whiskey received a bottle of soda from Zebediah, then spun around to watch Nupa and Daniel play another round of a street fighter game. Zebediah returned to an armchair to watch them duke it out. Cora had elected to remain in her new apartment for the afternoon, but had promised to meet them for dinner. With the new quarters, she had increased the physical distance between Whiskey and herself. Whiskey could hardly blame her, and felt slightly guilty for enjoying Cora's absence.

"Hey, is this party for everyone?"

Whiskey saw Rufus enter the room through the open door. "Hey! What's up?" She went to meet him, pulling him farther into the room. "You want something to eat or drink?"

"Love a drink." Rufus ogled the fine furnishings as she led him toward the bar. He gave a low whistle, barely heard over the roar of the digital crowd as Nupa thrashed Daniel's avatar. "Not a bad crib. Things are looking up, huh?"

She chuckled, and rummaged inside the small refrigeration unit under the counter. "A bit. You want a beer?"

"Yeah." He sat on the stool she had vacated, still focused on the interior decorations. "Penthouse, huh?"

"Yep." She pulled out a bottle of Mexican beer, opened it, and set it down before him. "I've got half the floor. Margaurethe has most the other half, and security is across the way."

Rufus took a drink. "Yeah, they escorted me up here. No access without a key." He turned to wiggle his eyebrows at her. "What are my chances of getting one?"

Whiskey laughed. "Slim to none. I can't even get keys made for these guys." She waved at her pack. "Don't worry. You're on the permanent guest list. Just ask any of the security officers; they'll bring you up if I'm here."

"That's good to know. I'd hate to think you'd shun me because I'm better looking than you." He winked.

She shook her head at his joke. Coming back around, she sat on the stool beside him. "So, how'd you know to come here? Did the padre call you?"

"No, actually your *Ki'an Gasan* did. I've just come from an interview."

Whiskey raised her eyebrow. "You looking for a job?"

"Nope. But she's offering me quite a lot of money to do a life-sized portrait of you to hang in the lobby."

She felt a flush rise across her face. "You're kidding."

"Nope. No joke." Rufus laughed at her expression. "This is what happens to royalty, you know. Just remember us little people when you're running the world, okay?"

Whiskey grimaced, rolling her eyes. "I'm not royalty."

He tipped his bottle at her. "Whatever you say, *Ninsumgal*." He took a swallow.

Considering Margaurethe's plans for world domination—Whiskey suddenly heard in her mind an overused cartoon quote regarding that very same topic—she had no quarrel with his remark.

"Oh, that reminds me." He dug into one of the many pockets of his paint-spattered cargo pants. "I finished your painting this afternoon."

"Really. That's cool." Whiskey watched him rummage through his pants. "It looked pretty hella last time I saw it."

"Yeah, it turned out really good." He pulled a crumpled envelope from his pocket, delight on his face. "Just in time for a gallery showing I have lined up in a few days. I liked it so much, I talked the owner into letting me add it to the others I'd selected for the showing."

Whiskey set her soda down, and took the envelope with a frown. Inside was a card with a photo of one of his pieces. "An invitation? For me?"

Rufus nodded. "Yeah. You know. I figured since you're gonna be there in portrait, you should be there in person too."

A mix of pleasure and sorrow washed over her as she attempted to hand the invitation back. "I can't go, Rufus. You know I've barely been able to keep one step ahead of Valmont. You don't want a team of three dozen security officers there."

He pushed her hand away, his smile fading to seriousness. "I don't care about the security, Whiskey. You deserve to be there as much as I do. It's one of my better pieces." He grinned. "Besides, considering who's running the show here, why would you need anybody? Just have Margaurethe come with you; she's badass enough to kick Valmont to the curb if he should show."

Whiskey studied the invitation.

Seeing her begin to waver, Rufus leaned closer. "C'mon. It'll be great! Free food!"

She snorted, a wry smile curving her lips. "Appealing to the pragmatic?"

"If it'll get me what I want."

Her eyes automatically unfocused, seeing him differently. What he wanted seemed harmless enough. Not giving herself the chance to back out, she said, "Okay. I'll be there."

"Great!" Unable to help himself, he slapped her on the arm, surprising both of them. "I've got a few more invitations to get out."

"Okay." Whiskey set the invitation on the counter. "I'll see you at the opening if not before."

"Sweet!" Rufus drained his beer, and stood. "Do I have to use a key to get back downstairs?"

Whiskey smiled. "No, just call the elevator up. It'll take you to the lobby."

"Thanks. See you in a few days."

She waved him off, her brow furrowed in thought. He had a good point about Margaurethe being plenty strong enough to take on Valmont. Between Whiskey and Margaurethe, Valmont wouldn't stand a chance if he tried something. That would, of course, mean that the two of them would have to join together to fight him.

At the idea of feeling the warm woodsmoke and mulled wine again, Whiskey licked her lips. Since that initial meeting months ago, both she and Margaurethe had been careful not to attempt a connection. She wondered if Margaurethe craved it as much as she.

"Yeah!" Whiskey started as Nupa sprang to his feet. His feet shuffled as he mimed punching someone out. "Whitey takes a dive! Skins rule the day!"

Daniel gave him a disgusted look, and tossed the game control down.

While Zebediah chimed into the celebration, demanding a chance to take on the winner, Whiskey nodded. *I'll ask her to go to the opening at the meeting we have lined up tonight.* She hopped off her stool, and approached her squabbling pack members, ignoring the faint hope that Valmont would track her to the art gallery.

CHAPTER TWENTY-EIGHT

Hesitant, Whiskey stood in the foyer of the executive offices. A window to her left overlooked the front entrance. She drifted closer, realizing that she stood directly above the arc of the drive. From here she saw the street corner and rush-hour traffic on the Morrison Bridge, as well as the lobby and main reception desk inside. A pedestrian stood at the corner, waiting for the light to change. He turned, glancing back at the building, appearing to look right at her.

Whiskey stepped back, suddenly feeling naked. Anyone walking by would see her silhouetted against the light. Swallowing, she felt her demeanor sour with her stomach. She had thought that agreeing to stay would ease some of her fears, but new ones had popped up in their places. At least running away had afforded her a little anonymity. She no longer had that luxury as anyone seeing her here would know who she was.

Catching movement from the corner of her eye, Whiskey turned to see Dorst's arrival through the double doors of frosted glass. Smiling, she went to him, interrupting his flourishing bow with a hug. "Reynhard!" Without thought she reached forward with her mind to brush against his, her trepidation fading with the caress of amber and steel. "It's been a while. How are you?"

"My goodness, it has been some time, hasn't it?" Dorst returned her embrace. "I'm quite well, my *Gasan*, and enjoying this magnificent new location. Are you?"

"Yeah." Whiskey smiled, releasing him. "It's pretty cool."

"Very good. That is the most important thing."

Despite his sarcastic tone, Whiskey knew he truly meant what he said, and that she was well and happy was of utmost importance to him. Someday she vowed to discuss *her* with him, to see if what he had felt for the Sweet Butcher was anything like what he felt for Whiskey. Most of the time she felt confident of his response, but not today.

"Shall we go in?" he asked, waving an arm at the door. "I believe the others are already there."

Whiskey nodded, forcing her insecurities aside. He led her toward one of two doors, opening it for her. She paused on the threshold, fingers tracing the name plaque on the wall.

Jenna Davis, President

Shivering, she walked into her office for the first time.

Dorst was correct, both Castillo and Margaurethe were already present. The padre sat on a brown leather couch beneath a window the length of the room, and she in the chair before the desk. Both stood and turned toward the door as she entered. Castillo's bow barely registered to Whiskey. All she could see was Margaurethe's bright smile.

Margaurethe came forward, looping her arm through Whiskey's. "Welcome! I hope you like the decor."

Whiskey forced herself to look around the room. One wall was floor-to-ceiling bookcases already full of leather-bound tomes. A section even held aged yellowed scrolls. All the sitting arrangements were dark brown leather with mahogany incidental tables beside them. The massive wooden desk was polished to a rich sheen, and engraved with designs. It looked antique. Against the wall behind it stood another set of full bookcases, and a smaller desk of a lighter colored wood, stained and pitted with age. It looked familiar. She pulled away from Margaurethe, frowning as she went to it. Her hands stroked the ancient surface, lightly rubbing a scorched spot. She remembered almost lighting it on fire in a flash of pique centuries ago.

"This is *hers*." Whiskey turned toward Margaurethe, searching for confirmation. "It was in our—*her* sitting room."

"Yes. It was one of the few things in the palace that survived the Purge." Margaurethe had clasped her hands before her, eyes shining with unshed tears. "It belonged to her father. I could never get her to part with it though it clashed with everything else in the room."

A multitude of emotion ran hot and cold through Whiskey. The tenderness and joy at Margaurethe's careful preservation warred with the intense hatred she felt toward anything to do with *her*. The Sweet Butcher had been a callous monster, but even *she* had been loved. Whiskey felt Elisibet rising up within, pleased that Margaurethe had been able to salvage something of her father. The dichotomy threatened to overtake and drown her.

"Shall we get on with it then?"

Whiskey's head shot up, and she stared at Dorst. He looked blandly back. Swallowing the lump in her throat, she nodded thanks for the timely interruption. A smirk curled the corner of his lips.

Similarly affected, Margaurethe took a moment to gather her wits. "Yes, of course." She shot Dorst a glare that bounced off him. Bustling around the desk, she opened a file folder, revealing the ever-present paperwork. "Whiskey, if you'll sit down?"

Obeying the request, Whiskey settled into the comfortable desk chair.

Hovering over her, Margaurethe spread the documents out before them. "These contracts basically state that you're accepting the position of President of The Davis Group. They outline your duties to the corporation, as well as the corporation's duty toward you. You'll be given access to the accounts, but I ask that you at least take an online finance course before using your card."

It took a moment for Whiskey to realize Margaurethe awaited a response. "Oh. Um…okay."

Margaurethe smiled. "Father Castillo, you'll be our notary. Reynhard and I will be witnesses." She looked at Whiskey. "Do you wish to read them prior to signing?"

Whiskey frowned as she stared down at the papers. "I don't think I'd even understand them." She glanced back at Margaurethe. "Is there anything I should be worried about in there?"

The smile became impish. "No, nothing untoward, I promise."

She nibbled her lower lip. "Okay then." Picking up a handy pen, she stopped to gawk at it a moment. It was black and gold, and heavy enough to make her think it was made of the real thing rather than some cheap yellow metal. "Let's do it."

Several minutes later, after everyone had had a chance to sign and dot their i's, and Castillo had stamped it all and entered the information into his Notary Public book, Margaurethe collected the paperwork. "Let me be the first to congratulate you."

Whiskey shook her and Castillo's hands. Dorst simply rolled his eyes at them, making her laugh.

"Next on the agenda…" Margaurethe gestured for Whiskey to stand and come around the desk.

Curious, Whiskey did so and was startled when Margaurethe dropped to her knees at Whiskey's feet.

"I, Margaurethe O'Toole, *Ki'an Gasan* of the European Sanguire, recognize *Ninsumgal* Jenna Davis as my liege and ruler. My dagger, my blood, my heart is yours, my *Gasan*, to do with as you will."

Whiskey looked wildly about the room, finding a very satisfied look on Dorst's face. *Fealty! She's swearing fealty to me, just like he did.*

Remembering that she was supposed to respond in some manner, she cleared her throat. Her mind blanked a moment before she recalled what she had said to Dorst last fall. "Your dagger, your blood, your heart are mine to do with as I will. In return, I swear to treat you as you treat me, respect with respect, trust with trust, loyalty with loyalty." The look on Margaurethe's face indicated she had said the right thing. When she remained on her knees, Whiskey recalled something else from her first round with Dorst. "Rise," she hastily added.

"Thank you, my *Gasan*."

Castillo replaced Margaurethe at Whiskey's feet. Once more she went through the process, this time ordering the padre to stand promptly. "I think I need to sit down."

Margaurethe smiled. "It is a bit much, isn't it?" She escorted Whiskey to the couch. A tray sat on the coffee table, and she poured coffee, tea and a hot chocolate for Whiskey. "Now that the niceties have been concluded, we must discuss our next steps."

Castillo accepted a coffee. "The *Baruñal* Ceremony?"

"Among other things." Margaurethe handed tea to Dorst. "First we must have the local *Saggina* come in for a proper introduction."

Whiskey paused, chocolate halfway to her mouth. The *Saggina* was the local ambassador for the European consulate. "Won't that let the *Agrun Nam* know where I am?"

"Indeed." Dorst sipped his tea, little finger delicately poised to one side. "And no doubt confirm that you are the prophesied return of our *Ninsumgal*."

Shooting a glance at Margaurethe, Whiskey said, "I thought we were trying to avoid that."

"In the beginning, we were. But it's time to cease hiding." Margaurethe offered cookies to everyone. "Now that you're in residence, you can be well-protected. It's time to admit you're here in Portland, that you exist. Our next political steps will involve you making treaties with other Sanguire nations, and we cannot allow any hint of impropriety to be bandied about."

Castillo nodded. "Following Euro law, we should report our presence to the *Saggina*. That will put you into a position of power rather than have anyone arguing you snuck around like a thief in the night."

"Exactly." Margaurethe nodded.

Whiskey scowled. "But I thought we decided I probably wasn't European. Do I still have to follow your law?"

Margaurethe smiled. "Ah, but you won't be reporting your presence here. *He* will, as will young Daniel." She pointed at Castillo.

"Oh, well played, Margaurethe." Dorst lightly patted his free hand against his thigh in applause.

Castillo looked back and forth between them a moment, before giving them a slow nod of comprehension.

"What am I missing?"

Dorst leaned forward, setting his teacup down. "The father is your advisor, and in danger of attack from *Sublugal Sañar* Valmont. For his safety, the *Saggina* is to be brought here. The official introduction will take place in your presence, though you will not be included in that respect." He smiled. "You're American! The *Agrun Nam* have no claim on you, nor can they attempt to make one."

"But they'll know who you are." Castillo grinned. "I knew who you were when I first saw you. Every Euro Sanguire has seen official portraits of the Sweet Butcher, even those born after the Purge. The *Saggina* will have no doubt."

These finer points of politicking made no sense to Whiskey. She gave them a perplexed look, and shook her head. "If you say so." She took a bite of cookie. "But why is Daniel involved in this? Why not any of the others? Is it because he's older?"

"No, he's European." Dorst poured himself another cup of tea. "As you know, all European Sanguire must report in to the local authorities. Daniel has been here with you for six months. It's high time he attended to the political and legal niceties."

Margaurethe patted Whiskey on the knee. "I've made an appointment for tomorrow afternoon at two. Be sure to have Daniel ready."

"Okay."

"Our next concern is the *Wi Wacipi Wakan*. I met with them two weeks ago, and they sent a courier with their treaty requests." Margaurethe pulled a piece of parchment from a briefcase on the floor beside her. She handed it first to Whiskey who read the list before passing it to Castillo. "For the most part their demands are well within reason. I think their only true concern is that we coerce Whiskey into leaving the country."

"Why?"

Margaurethe smiled at her. "Because even if we don't know for certain that you're European, we do know you're American Indian. To that end, you fall within their jurisdiction." She looked at the others. "They are aware of our prophecy, and have a myth of their own."

Whiskey thought a moment, hardly listening. "Did any of them know my mother?"

"I don't believe so. They had planned on doing some research to locate your family."

Family. Whiskey had a vague memory of walking through the house as a child during a garden party. Many people were present, talking to her, caressing her hair, helping her locate her parents where they danced in the living room. Had they all been Sanguire? Would any remember a little blond girl with a floppy teddy bear clutched in her arms?

Castillo handed on the list of demands to Dorst. "I don't know enough about business to offer much in the way of suggestions here."

"That's quite all right. I do." Margaurethe watched Dorst peer down his nose at the parchment. "The majority of them are well within our capacity to offer. It's the profit percentage that's at issue."

Whiskey had hardly glanced at that point, but knew enough about American history from television and movies to know that natives had been sorely misused over the centuries. "Why is it a problem? They've never had much in the way of money. And I'd gladly offer a percentage to local charities."

"Yes, but you're not seeing the larger picture. Ten percent of our profit is worth millions. I'm fairly certain they don't understand the amount of money we're talking about here. They don't strike me as greedy guts."

Millions? Whiskey felt those skateboarding butterflies return, and she set down the half-eaten cookie. The whole idea of being responsible for the amount of money Margaurethe played with on a day-to-day basis terrified her, yet here she was—president of the corporation, and owner of a shiny new credit card with no limit.

"What are you suggesting instead?" Castillo leaned forward, staring intently at Margaurethe. "We're in their territory, and Whiskey is a member of their people. What compensation do we offer for permission to conduct business here and keep Whiskey safe?"

"Five percent." Margaurethe held up her hand, though no one was inclined to interrupt. "That would put a million plus into their coffers annually. And half of that five percent goes to charities of Whiskey's choice."

Whiskey veered away from her nervousness, latching onto the idea. There were a number of youth and adult homeless resources in Portland that could benefit from an influx of cash— Green House, Outside In, Blanche House, Sisters of the Road Cafe. She might even be able to funnel some of it as far away as Seattle and the Youth Consortium that had helped her over the years. "Okay. We go with five percent and half of it for charity."

Margaurethe appeared pleased. She took the treaty parchment from Dorst, and filed it back into her briefcase. "Excellent. I'll arrange a time for them to visit. I'll suggest a few days; they can stay upstairs. Mr. Saghani has to come from northern Canada, so it may take him some time to arrive."

Whiskey felt out of her element. She had a sudden urge to flee for the familiarity of her pack. "Is there anything else?" She flushed under the intent observation from Margaurethe.

Apparently understanding Whiskey's need to get away, Margaurethe spoke quietly. "No. I think that's all for right now."

"Okay." Whiskey shot to her feet.

The others stood, as well. "Can you come down tomorrow morning? We need to discuss furthering your education." Margaurethe paused, slightly flushing. "We could have lunch together before meeting the *Saggina*."

Whiskey swallowed, feeling her apprehension fade at Margaurethe's obvious nervousness. *Glad it's not just me.* "Yeah, okay. I'd like that."

Margaurethe smiled. "Thank you. Around ten?"

"Uh-huh." The fleeting shyness disappeared as all three of them bowed or curtsied to her as she stepped away from the table. "Oh, God, can you guys not do that?"

Dorst gave her a smug grin. "It's proper etiquette, *Ninsumgal*. Surely you don't wish us to treat you with disrespect."

Whiskey faked a scowl. "Then don't do it when we're alone!"

Castillo chuckled. "Point taken."

"Yes, my *Gasan*." Contrary to his words, Dorst bowed again.

Grumbling, Whiskey made it to the door before looking over her shoulder. The men fussed over the tray, collecting used cups and brushing crumbs from the furniture. Only Margaurethe watched her, a look of pride and contentment on her beautiful features. Their eyes met. Unable to help herself, Whiskey caressed Margaurethe's essence with her own.

The sensation of heat suffused her, the homey smell of wood-smoke and mulled wine made her inhale deeply. She smiled, no longer a bundle of nerves and confusion, the sensation filling her with confidence. She pulled her mind away from Margaurethe's and left the room.

CHAPTER TWENTY-NINE

Margaurethe paused at Whiskey's office door, tugging at her jacket and brushing nonexistent lint from her shoulder. Helen, the receptionist, pretended to not see her, for which Margaurethe was exceedingly grateful. Deciding that she was presentable, she knocked lightly and let herself in.

Whiskey stood at the bookshelves, craning her neck to see who had entered. She wore black leather pants and boots, and a skin-tight emerald-green camisole that revealed the dragon tattoo crawling up one arm. A tattered denim jacket lay draped across the back of one of the chairs. Margaurethe smiled, wondering how difficult it would be to get her young charge into at least a business casual wardrobe.

Whiskey held up a thick leather-bound book. "Looks like I've got a lot of catching up to do."

"And you'll have plenty of time in which to do it." Margaurethe closed the door behind her. "Did you sleep well last night?"

Her question was met with a sardonic grin. "Eventually." Whiskey carefully put the book back in place, and turned to fully face Margaurethe. She looked down then, and studied her Doc Martens, giving a light shrug. "Last night was kind of…I don't know. Terrifying? Humbling?"

Margaurethe watched as Whiskey sighed and turned away to stare out the windows onto Naito Parkway. She enjoyed the dichotomy of rich carpet and mahogany settings surrounding Whiskey's dark wildness. She stood so regally, head held high despite the leathers, subconsciously daring anyone to say something against her presence here. Though she looked a pauper everything about her screamed nobility. Feigning casual disinterest, Margaurethe noted the stiff neck and clenched jaw, the discomfort in her surroundings. Whiskey fought so hard against showing weakness. In many ways she was so much like Elisibet.

"I imagine it can be." Margaurethe moved closer, standing beside her. "You now have it within your power to do some real good in the world, and I think your experiences to date may dictate exactly how much good you'll do. Don't let this mantle of power overwhelm you. That's why you have advisors; we're here for you." She paused. "*I'm* here for you."

Whiskey's eyes caught Margaurethe's. They stared at each other for long moments, and Margaurethe was reminded that this was not her Elisibet. This was someone else, someone with different life experiences and viewpoints. Despite the wrenching pain she felt at the loss of her lover, Margaurethe also felt a trembling within, a shivering stillness of expectation.

"Thanks." Whiskey smiled. "I'm going to need all the help I can get."

The tableau broken, Margaurethe realized she had stopped breathing, and inhaled. "Then I suppose we should get started. Shall we?" She gestured toward the large desk with a smile.

Whiskey nodded, and sat down while Margaurethe collected one of the other chairs to sit beside her.

"First you need a username and password to log into our network. You noticed the office in your apartment?" Margaurethe opened a desk drawer, and pulled out a folder.

"Yeah." Whiskey looked at the paper Margaurethe produced. "I sign this?"

"Yes. We have a company policy regarding network and Internet usage." She went down the document, point by point, and had Whiskey sign it.

Several more papers were produced, numerous policies on safety and security that had to be signed. Informational details regarding the company, a slew of personnel reports on the more crucial employees in the building, and a dossier of Whiskey's personal guard. By the end of an hour, Whiskey was awestruck. "God, is every day going to be like this?"

Collecting the latest round of documents, Margaurethe smiled. "Not every day. Once we get you up and running, you'll spend more of your time in meetings rather than paperwork."

"That's not much better!"

Laughing, Margaurethe lightly rubbed Whiskey's shoulder. "You'll get used to it." She chuckled again at the grumble she felt beneath her hand, and patted Whiskey once before moving on to the next topic. "Now for your education. I've set up a few tests so we can ascertain where you are academically."

"Not far. I hit the streets by the time I was twelve." Whiskey shrugged. "I loved reading in the library in Seattle, but I haven't had a lot of formal classes since fifth or sixth grade."

Margaurethe nodded. "As I assumed. Let's get you logged into the system, shall we?"

Whiskey obediently signed onto the computer.

"This computer is a mirror of the one in your home office, so anything you see or create here will be there." She pointed out the icons on the desktop window, explaining the program uses and documentation available. "And this one is the educational testing program. When you click on it, you'll be taken to a page that allows you to choose between a number of subjects— mathematics, science, arts, literature, philosophy and culture. I'd like you to take at least one of these tonight after we meet the *Saggina*, and two or three each day until you've completed them all."

Clicking on the icon, the program started, and Whiskey peered at the subjects. "Sanguire politics and culture, too?"

Margaurethe studied her profile, feeling a slight smile curve her lips at the familiar vexation on Whiskey's face. *Yes. So like Elisibet.* "Those as well. Keep in mind, we're not testing to current American educational standards. These tests are to European Sanguire standards, which are much more extensive."

Whiskey groaned. "I'll never pass this stuff."

"You don't have to 'pass,' Whiskey. There's no failure here. This is just a measurement tool, like a ruler."

Scratching the back of her neck, Whiskey slumped back in her chair and looked at Margaurethe. "Followed by schooling, of course."

"We have to get you up to snuff, or you'll not do anyone good." Margaurethe could not help it; she reached out to touch Whiskey's mind, the deep smell of roses filling her. "Cheer up, *m'cara*. It won't last forever."

"That's the second time you've said that."

Margaurethe cocked her head. "Said what?"

Whiskey leaned forward, one elbow on the arm of her desk chair. "That's the second time you've called me *m'cara*."

Flustered, Margaurethe pulled back. Her heart sped up as she realized Whiskey was correct. She had used her pet name for Elisibet without thought. "I'm—I'm sorry." A flush heated her throat and cheeks, and she stood so quickly she wavered. A hand grabbed hers, stabilizing her, and she saw that Whiskey had risen, as well.

"It's okay. I don't mind. I'm not offended." Whiskey stopped her rapid speech, took a deep breath, and squeezed Margaurethe's hand. "It's kind of nice, actually."

Margaurethe could not decide whether to be pleased or saddened. Did Whiskey enjoy the feelings, the memories that pet phrase evoked? Her adamant denial of all things Elisibet contradicted that possibility. *Am I opening the door for more heartache?*

Carefully, Margaurethe closed down the mental connection between them, light as it was. She smiled at Whiskey, holding tight to the hand in hers before releasing it, ignoring the faltering look on Whiskey's face. "Thank you. I'm glad you think so."

Whiskey studied her, pursing her lips.

Margaurethe stepped around the desk, putting distance between them. "Shall we get lunch? I believe your chef has come up with something spectacular for this afternoon's entree."

After a pause, Whiskey nodded. "Sure. Okay." She scrubbed the back of her neck again. "Let me log off the computer."

As she did so, Margaurethe collected her tattered emotions. *Whatever am I thinking?*

CHAPTER THIRTY

Whiskey sat at the head of a conference table in one of the lobby meeting rooms, tapping her fingers against the wood. Beside her, Daniel wore casual slacks, looking out of place with his dark blond mohawk and visible piercings, tugging at the unfamiliar polo shirt he had been forced to wear for his meeting with the *saggina*.

Not nearly as out of place as Whiskey felt. This morning she realized that she had nothing in her wardrobe resembling business attire. The thought of putting on a slip and skirt made her skin crawl, and she had never owned such clothes. After completing one of Margaurethe's aptitude tests, she had perused the Internet in search of stylish attire. Most of it would make her look or feel like an idiot. Now she prepared to meet the Euro Sanguire ambassador to Portland, Oregon, wearing black leather from head to toe. It would make for a hell of a first impression.

"*Ninsumgal.*"

Whiskey looked up at one of her personal guards standing inside the door.

"*Ki'an Gasan* Margaurethe and *Saggina* Alfred Bescoe are on their way. His car just pulled up onto the front apron. He has two bodyguards with him."

Her stomach fluttered, and she nodded thanks. *Maybe having a personal guard is worth the trouble if I can get advance warnings like this.*

Daniel took a bracing breath. "Wonder where the padre is."

"He said he'd be here." Whiskey scanned the lower levels, finding a multitude of unfamiliar Sanguire in her search. Dark, bitter chocolate, and amber and steel grew stronger. "He's on his way. Reynhard's coming, too." She relaxed. No matter the danger, with Dorst and Margaurethe at her side Whiskey felt nearly invincible. She looked curiously at Daniel. "Didn't you do this before when you were with Fiona?"

"Once or twice. Most the time it's an opportunity to hear long lectures on the youth of today, and what the *saggina* won't stand for on his watch."

Whiskey nodded, considering the differing circumstances. They were not here as a group of young toughs this time.

The guard responded to something on his radio, and directed the other to open the double doors. Voices from the lobby grew in volume as the group neared the meeting room.

"...highly irregular," a man said.

Margaurethe answered. "I can certainly appreciate the inconvenience, Alfred. But, as you know, I have no desire to put my people in peril, and *Sublugal Sañar* Valmont has already attacked my man."

"I don't doubt your veracity, my dear, but can this fellow be trusted? I can't imagine *Sublugal Sañar* Valmont attacking anyone unless that person stood between him and his search."

Whiskey frowned, annoyed with his familiarity. "*My dear?*" *Has he forgotten who he's speaking to? And why's she calling him by his first name?* She got to her feet, as did Daniel, waiting for the group to make their way inside.

"Ah, here he is now. Father Castillo, *Sañur Gasum* Dorst, may I introduce you to *Saggina* Alfred Bescoe?"

They all came to a stop in front of the open doors of the meeting room, perfectly timed for Whiskey to see the government official grow pale as he stared at Dorst.

"Dorst?" A squeaky rasp came from his throat, and he cleared it. "*Reynhard* Dorst?"

"One and the same!" Dorst rushed forward, putting Bescoe and his guards on high alert as he grabbed Bescoe's hand. Gripping it tight, he shook it for all he was worth. "So sorry for not having informed you of my presence here. I've been a bit busy."

Rattled in both mind and body, Bescoe noticed his bristling guards, and held up a hand to stop them from doing something stupid. "It's...it's a pleasure to meet you."

Whiskey smiled, glancing over to see amusement on Daniel's face. *Leave it to Reynhard to make it a circus.*

Too bemused by his proximity to the most dangerous known European Sanguire, Bescoe hardly looked at Castillo as the priest stepped forward to meet him.

"Shall we sit?" Margaurethe nodded toward the conference room. "I have coffee and tea prepared."

Bescoe consented faintly.

"Excellent." Dorst hooked his arm through the *saggina*'s, and ushered him inside. "I do so enjoy those gingersnaps that come from the kitchens. You really must try them."

Swallowing, Bescoe muttered something in agreement, his wan countenance beginning to flush. Dorst monopolized the man for the next ten minutes, insisting on seating and serving him. In an attempt to get away, Bescoe resorted to the only thing possible given the circumstances—looking around the room. He eyed Daniel, blinking at the contrast between business casual and punk piercings, before glancing at Whiskey.

His mouth dropped open. She didn't realize his skin could get any whiter.

Dorst returned from the buffet table of drinks, and fussed

over Bescoe for another moment before noticing his abrupt lack of concentration. He looked at Whiskey, a radiant smile crossing his face. "Oh! How impolite of us, Margaurethe! We've yet to introduce everyone else."

Margaurethe smiled. She set her cup of tea down at the chair beside Whiskey. Passing behind her, she placed a hand on Daniel's shoulder. "I apologize, Alfred. This is Daniel Gleirscher. He arrived in town at the same time as Father Castillo. He's the other Euro I mentioned."

Bescoe's mouth worked, his attention never leaving Whiskey.

"And this is Jenna Davis. She's American, so she's not part of the proceedings here. However she is the president of The Davis Group, and should be present."

"Hi." Taking Dorst's lead, she smiled easily at the terrified official, and came around the table. It was difficult not to laugh as he leaped to his feet, almost spilling his coffee down his expensive suit. "It's a pleasure to meet you."

He stared at her outstretched hand as if it were a viper.

"Oh, really, Alfred. Is that any way to treat a stranger you've just met?"

Dorst's voice so close to his ear made Bescoe jump. After an audible gulp, he shook Whiskey's hand with trembling fingers.

"Much better." Dorst patted him gently on the shoulder. "You look a little ill. Perhaps you should sit down?"

Bescoe dropped into his chair.

Margaurethe smiled, patting Whiskey's chair. Whiskey returned to it, and sat down. She spared a look at Bescoe's guards who also seemed distressed as they stared at her.

"Now, Alfred, Father Castillo and Daniel were in Seattle several months ago. I'm certain you've heard some odd rumors from there."

"Rumors?" Bescoe tore his gaze away from Whiskey. "Yes. Yes! Rumors from Seattle."

Whiskey felt amazement as she saw the already terrified man become even more so. She hadn't thought it possible. Knowing it was because he thought her to be Elisibet, she felt slightly sick, no longer finding humor in the farce.

"Suffice it to say that both of them ran into Ms. Davis there.

They arrived here six months ago." Margaurethe gestured toward Whiskey. "As you can imagine, they chose not to inform you of their presence for rather obvious reasons."

"Yes." Bescoe swallowed, flinching away from looking directly at Whiskey. "Yes, of course. I can understand that now. I don't believe any penalty shall be laid upon either of them for not reporting their presence immediately."

Dorst clapped, and Bescoe shrank away from him. "That is a relief, isn't it, Padre?"

"Thank you, *Saggina*." Castillo leaned his elbows on the table. "We do appreciate your leniency in this matter."

"As do I," Whiskey added. She frowned as Bescoe slumped into a cower. Unable to think of something to do to ease the man's fear, she turned to Margaurethe.

"And I believe you've now ascertained why Valmont is in Portland, and what he's searching for?" Margaurethe patted Whiskey's upper arm as she spoke.

Bescoe refused to look up from his lap. "I do."

"If it's any consolation, Alfred, I don't expect you to keep this quiet. Valmont knows I'm here for the same reason, and has no doubt already reported his findings to the *Agrun Nam*. There's no need for secrecy any longer."

The relief in Bescoe's features was plain.

Margaurethe continued. "Should he approach you for information, please give it freely, and—"

Whiskey interrupted her with a wave, and leaned forward. "*Saginna* Bescoe, please look at me."

The man struggled with himself, but finally pulled his eyes up to hers.

Speaking softly so as not to terrify him further, Whiskey said, "I don't want to see you or your people hurt over this. Tell Valmont whatever he wants to know, okay?"

Bescoe blinked at her, confusion twisting his features. When his face cleared, he frowned at her in thought.

Probably looking for the lie that would put him in danger. Being the spitting image of the Sweet Butcher had its bad points, foremost among them gaining trust from potential allies. She reached out with both hand and mind, though she sat several chairs away. Her fingers brushed the wooden surface, her mind gently caressing his tightly closed mind. "I understand that you'll have to report this to the *Agrun Nam*, and they may give you orders to do something we'll all regret. But I am serious—I don't want you hurt over this."

He stared a moment longer, and cleared his throat. "Thank you."

She nodded, pulling back from his essence. Given the need, she knew she could take him in a one-to-one duel. She wondered if her confidence was hubris, or reality.

"Do you have any questions for Daniel or Father Castillo?"

Bescoe glanced at the men in question. "No, I don't believe I do."

Whiskey touched Daniel's mind, and nodded toward the door. Glad of the respite, he took no time in leaving, not even bothering to say goodbye to the *Saggina*.

"May I warm up your coffee?" Dorst peered at Bescoe's cup. "Oh, dear! You haven't even started, yet."

"Reynhard." Dropping her chin, Whiskey shook her head.

Dorst ceased his servile posturing, grinning. Her warning plain, he nodded, and sat down.

Bescoe's earlier fear eased back into his countenance. He glanced sidelong at Dorst beside him, then back to the head of the table. Whiskey could almost read his mind—*She controls the Sweet Butcher's chief assassin?*

"Allow me to summarize the situation as it stands, Alfred." Margaurethe clasped her hands upon the table. "You've already given me permission to open a branch of business here in Portland, which I've done. A number of European Sanguire have already made themselves known, as well as the *kizarusi* that arrived with them to sustain our increased population. Legally speaking, this company is international, not European, and is run by an American." She waved gracefully in Whiskey's direction. "As long as the Euros in house do not break our law in the city and surrounding areas, we're fine. This building and Ms. Davis are not your jurisdiction. Is that understood?"

He pursed his lips, a calculating look on his face. "It is."

"Then I believe we have nothing further to discuss."

"I agree." Bescoe pushed back his chair, discreetly moving it away from Dorst. "Thank you for insisting I come, my dear. It's been most illuminating."

Whiskey grimaced at Bescoe's familiar tone again. *Maybe I should scare the crap out of him.* As the others around the table rose, she stood as well.

"Allow me to escort you out." Castillo came around the room, becoming a buffer between Bescoe and Dorst.

That alleviated the man's anxiety, and he flushed with relief as he made his farewells, careful to not approach either Dorst or Whiskey for a handshake.

Once he and his guards had left, and the doors closed behind the entourage, Margaurethe sank into her chair. "I think that went off quite well."

"Indeed." Dorst drifted toward the buffet table and the cookies.

Whiskey, tired of acting the benevolent ruler, hopped onto the conference table, swinging her booted feet. "How do you figure? He's scared to death."

"Whatever's wrong with that?"

She grimaced at Dorst. He chuckled, and bit into a gingersnap.

"His fear will keep him from plotting against you too soon. Right now, he's concerned we'll destroy him. Even though he'll tell the *Agrun Nam* and Valmont everything, we don't have to worry about him taking an active hand in any attempt to assassinate you. A few months down the road, we'll have cause to worry, but by then you'll be well protected." Margaurethe leaned back in her chair, hands in her lap and head tilted as she regarded Whiskey. "You really shouldn't have been nice to him. He'll view it as weakness."

Whiskey scoffed. "I don't want people to be afraid of me."

"Sometimes fear is necessary to keep people in line."

Frowning, Whiskey stared at Margaurethe. "Did you learn that from *her*?"

Margaurethe blinked, searching her distant memories. "Aye, I did."

"Look where it got her." Not liking the turn of conversation or the stricken expression flashing across Margaurethe's face,

Whiskey hopped off the table. "I'm going to head upstairs, maybe take another test."

"And I shall return to my own work." Dorst clutched a napkin full of cookies in one hand. "Good afternoon, my *Gasan*."

Too disgruntled by her thoughts and feelings about the Sweet Butcher, Whiskey didn't take him to task for his formality. "See you later, Reynhard." She chose not to collect a few snacks for herself.

"May I join you?" Margaurethe had risen, and now stood beside her, bearing a contrite look.

Feeling like an ass, Whiskey turned toward her. "I'm sorry. I didn't mean to hurt you."

Margaurethe smiled. "I know." She placed her hand on Whiskey's upper arm. "I understand. Shall we go upstairs? I need to introduce you to your chambermaid."

Whiskey's mind flashed to the pretty little things in linsey woolsey that had kept the palace clean during the Sweet Butcher's heyday. "You're kidding."

"No, you need someone to keep your quarters clean, and it can't just be whomever walks in off the streets." Chuckling, Margaurethe wrapped her arm around Whiskey's. "Come on. It'll be fine."

Knowing she would not like it, Whiskey nevertheless allowed Margaurethe to pull her along. *What are my chances of running away again?*

CHAPTER THIRTY-ONE

Whiskey spent the majority of the uneventful elevator ride wondering how she had become so exhausted after a mere half-hour meeting. She vowed to become a hermit, refuse to leave her apartment, and conduct all business through video channels. *It sure beats being on display.*

As they stepped onto the sixteenth floor, one of Whiskey's guards stood.

"Has she arrived?"

The woman at the security desk nodded. "Yes, *Ki'an Gasan*. She's inside."

Margaurethe moved toward the apartments, but Whiskey pulled away. She went to the security station. "Sasha, right?"

Pleased to be remembered, the guard raised her chin. "Yes, *Ninsumgal*. Sasha Kopecki."

Whiskey committed the name to memory. "Thank you for being here."

Sasha smiled. "I'm honored, *Ninsumgal*."

"No. That would be me." Feeling somewhat easier with herself after the fiasco downstairs, Whiskey turned back to Margaurethe, and followed her inside.

Margaurethe picked up the phone behind the bar, using the building intercom system. Then she pulled down a set of glasses, and opened the refrigerator.

Whiskey stripped off her jacket, tossing it across a chair as she made her way across the room. Opening the patio door, she stepped onto the terrace. The cool, bracing caress of wind felt good against her heated forehead. Overhead, she saw the morning clouds had dissipated, leaving behind blue sky. The park below held angular shadows, stretching across the grass as they sought the water's edge.

"Here you go."

"Thanks." Whiskey accepted a tall glass of orange juice from Margaurethe. She drank deep, the citrus quenching her thirst. "So, what exactly does a chambermaid do? Just clean up the place, like a maid?"

"For the most part. She'll also be responsible for keeping your clothing laundered and in good repair, fix meals and run errands."

Whiskey stared into her half-full glass, not liking the idea of a stranger being in her private space. "I don't know…"

Margaurethe laid a hand on her wrist. "She's gone through an extensive background check, I assure you. I've personally interviewed her. She comes with wonderful credentials."

A strange voice caught Whiskey's ear, and she turned to see an older woman standing just inside the door.

"Whiskey, may I introduce Sithathor."

The woman knelt, iron gray head bent. "*Ninsumgal*."

Her voice held a pleasing mellow tenor. The accent sounded familiar, and Whiskey's initial embarrassment at the deference warred with an attempt to place the sounds. An elegantly raised eyebrow on Margaurethe's face brought her back to the present.

"Oh, um, it's a pleasure to meet you, Sithathor. Please rise."

Sithathor regarded her, the corners of her mouth crinkled in amusement as she smoothly regained her feet. She clasped her hands before her, deep golden brown skin contrasting against the pale blue sari she wore. Whiskey studied her, noting gentle lines etched in the weathered face.

Sithathor was the oldest-appearing Sanguire she had ever met. Try as she might, though she recognized the accent, she could not find a corresponding memory of the woman in *her* memories. "Have we met before?"

Margaurethe bristled as she awaited an answer.

"No, *Ninsumgal*, we have not. I am honored to be considered for such a high position. Please accept my thanks." She bobbed in a curtsy, amusement never leaving her eyes.

The way she pronounced her words, the oddness of her name, it all came together where Whiskey had heard it before. Of course the memory belonged to the Sweet Butcher. "You're Egyptian, aren't you?"

"Yes, *Ninsumgal*, I am."

"Did you know *Nam Lugal* Nahib?"

Sithathor's visage reflected gentle sadness. "I did not have that particular honor, *Ninsumgal*. I left Egypt for the east long before your dynasty originated."

Margaurethe shifted, no doubt alarmed. Apparently, she hadn't realized the potential threat of a woman who shared the same homeland as the man the Sweet Butcher had publicly executed for treason. She stepped forward to a more advantageous defensive position beside Whiskey.

Whiskey shook her head. "That wasn't my dynasty."

Sithathor cocked her head to one side. "You are not Elisibet Vasilla reborn?"

The aftertaste of tart orange juice in her mouth turned sour. "Unfortunately, I am."

"Then for will or ill, it was your dynasty, though the person you are now had no control over the person you were."

Whiskey was unable to find an argument. Succinct, the statement absolved Whiskey of all *her* wrongdoings, yet made her ultimately responsible for her future decisions.

Sithathor's words did not ease Margaurethe's defensive stance. If anything, it made her more suspicious.

Touching Margaurethe's mind, Whiskey soothed the ruffled feathers, still keeping most of her diligence focused on the elder woman. She then touched Sithathor's mental defenses. "Would you mind if…?"

"Of course not, *Ninsumgal*. My life is yours."

Startled at her overt acceptance, Whiskey hesitated. She had only seen such unconditional approval from Dorst. *Is he somehow involved with this woman?* She skimmed the surface of Sithathor's mind, finding the same level of devotion as that of her chief assassin. *How weird.* At least with Dorst, there was a history involved; she found nothing recognizable in Sithathor's essence. She had never met Elisibet before.

Whiskey pulled away, allowing Sithathor her privacy. "Have a seat." She stepped inside and gestured toward the sitting area.

Sithathor moved forward, and sat with an elegant economy of movement, politely holding her hands in her lap. She gave Whiskey her full concentration, hardly noting Margaurethe's presence.

Joining her, Whiskey fought a bout of self-consciousness at the frank appraisal. Margaurethe perched on the arm of the sofa beside her, and laid a welcome hand on her shoulder. Having never conducted an interview before, she searched frantically for something to say. "So, Margaurethe said you've been through a pretty deep background check. Can you tell me about yourself?"

"Yes, *Ninsumgal*. I've been most fortunate in my life. I was born into the kingdom of Pahlavi Shapur, the King of Persia, though my family originated in what is now called Egypt. I toiled for His Highness as a serving woman until his death."

Whiskey struggled with the name, trying to connect it to her admittedly spotty education. "Persia?"

Sithathor smiled. "Yes, *Ninsumgal*. It was a very long time ago. Shapur I, as he became known, died in 272 A.D."

"Wow, that was a long time ago." A blush followed close on the heels of Whiskey's words. She kicked herself for being crass to a woman who had seen the turn of two millenia.

Margaurethe chose this moment to speak. "Certainly you're not saying you're over two thousand years old, Sithathor."

The Egyptian's grin widened, and she gave a slight nod in agreement. "I am indeed, *Ki'an Gasan.*"

Whiskey frowned at Margaurethe's light scoff. She thought back over her lessons with Castillo.

"You don't look a day over twelve hundred."

Sithathor raised a chin. "Thank you, *Ki'an Gasan.* I can well understand your disbelief, but I've yet to reach the *Ñri Izisíg*, the Path of Fire."

"Path of Fire?" Whiskey looked from one to the other, searching her mind for a reference.

Margaurethe answered first. "We age slowly over the centuries, but when we reach the end of our life cycle, we follow the Path of Fire."

"We burn out," Sithathor supplied.

Whiskey found the easy way she spoke of aging to her death in a matter of months disconcerting. "No one's made it to two thousand?"

"Very few, *Ninsumgal.*"

They sat in silence as Whiskey digested the information. Eighteen was about a fifth of a natural Human life cycle. Next to Sithathor, Whiskey wasn't even out of swaddling clothes.

"Shall I continue, *Ninsumgal?*"

"Yes, of course." Whiskey attempted to focus on the interview.

Sithathor wove a tale of travel that rivaled Marco Polo's. She had spent decades in India with her brother, working with Susruta, one of the first Human surgeons, and had researched Buddhism with a Chinese pilgrim named Huan-Tsang. Eventually she made her way to the Asian Sanguire empire where she served Empress Tairo-no-Mitsuko.

A flash of memory from *her* broadsided Whiskey. An Asian woman knelt before her in full Japanese regalia; her slender form hid an immense level of power, a siren's call to the Sweet Butcher. Distracted by the recollection, it took a moment for her to realize that Sithathor had stopped speaking. She cleared her throat, forcing her attention back to the present. "You said you served her for several decades. When did you leave the, ah, empress?"

"In the fourteenth century."

Knowing enough of Sanguire history from her extended historical sessions with Castillo, Whiskey found another possible connection.

"Didn't the empress sign a treaty with the European Sanguire in the fourteenth century? Did you travel with her entourage?"

Sithathor's mouth drooped in regret. "No, *Ninsumgal*. I had already left the employ of Her Most Exalted Empress by that time. I've spent the intervening years as a pilgrim of sorts, in the manner of Huan-Tsang."

Whiskey's natural paranoia reared its head, honed from years of living on the street and enhanced by memories of a different time. Odd that Sithathor would come so close to meeting *her*, yet miss the encounter by a hair. Had she heard of the Sweet Butcher's excessive violence, and left the Asian realm before Mitsuko made her pilgrimage? Or had Sithathor's absence held a more sinister meaning?

Her unfortunate ability to see webs of deception, plot entwined within plot made distinguishing reality much more difficult. Half the time, Whiskey had no idea what was true, and what was imagination as far as court intrigue was involved. She refrained from rubbing the bridge of her nose.

Sithathor had extensive experience serving Sanguire royalty. She came across as loyal, though loyalty without cause seemed odd. Having had no extended contact with the European Sanguire, why would she be so dedicated to a woman she had never met? Margaurethe had grilled her at least once, and Sithathor had made it through a thorough scrutiny from security. Her presence here indicated that her credentials had been thoroughly verified.

Whiskey straightened. One more question to ask. She unfocused her vision to catch any nuance of Sithathor's response. "Do you mean me or my friends, family and allies any harm?"

Surprise radiated from Margaurethe beside her, but Whiskey remained focused. She needed to ascertain whether or not this woman was a danger. She had always been able to tell if someone was lying, and her experience with Fiona had taught her well. To get the necessary responses, she had to ask the proper questions.

Sithathor's expression was solemn. "No, *Ninsumgal*. I would never do anything to hurt you or your realm. I wish only to serve you in whatever capacity I may."

Nodding slowly, Whiskey recognized the truth in the statement. She looked at Margaurethe. "So, what will her duties be?"

CHAPTER THIRTY-TWO

Margaurethe stared out over the city as she cradled her teacup. It was a weekend, so traffic was sparse on the street below. Her sensitive hearing picked up the sounds of a multitude a few blocks away. One thing Portland boasted was a quantity of marathons, and they all started from the World Trade Center.

Phineas had called ten minutes earlier to tell her that Ms. Lega's plane had arrived on time, and they would be on their way from the airport soon. The rest of the *We Wacipi Wakan* had arrived over the prior week, and were assigned apartments on the fifteenth floor for their stay. At this point, none had run into Whiskey because she remained in seclusion. Sithathor had taken over all the duties necessary for pleasing a high-ranking

Sanguire, including keeping the apartment kitchen and sitting room stocked with everything her *ninsumgal* should require. There was no need for Whiskey to venture into the residential lounge for food or drink, and Whiskey was more than happy to idle in her quarters rather than roam the building.

It had been a week since Sithathor's first day, and Margaurethe still marveled at the way Whiskey had taken over the initial meeting. It had galled Margaurethe that she hadn't made the nationality connection between Sithathor and Nahib, one that Whiskey had picked up almost immediately. She wondered whether it had been Whiskey's street smarts or Elisibet's political acumen shining through. Elisibet had lasted as long as she had because of her ability to see people; her downfall had been trusting a friend who had turned traitor. There had been speculation that Elisibet would have survived well into the eighteenth century had Valmont not assassinated her.

Some while later there came a light tap at the door.

Margaurethe set her cup down, glancing at the time on her computer. *Goodness, where'd the time go?* "Enter."

Her chambermaid opened the door. "Ms. Lega has arrived."

"Thank you, Maya. I'm on my way downstairs." She returned the young *kizarus's* smile, and left her office. "I won't be back until later this evening. Don't bother with supper, I believe we'll be eating in the executive dining room."

"Yes, *Ki'an Gasan.*"

Her receptionist met her in the sitting room, a leather-bound notepad and multiple file folders clutched to her chest. "Good morning, ma'am." She handed over the folders. "Here is your copy of the contract, and the large lobby conference room is prepared. I've rearranged all of today's appointments, and have left messages with the *We Wacipi Wakan* to join you there."

"Thank you, Helen. I couldn't do this without you." Margaurethe led the way out of her quarters, and knocked on Whiskey's door.

Sithathor opened it, curtsying to Margaurethe. "I'll tell her you're here, *Ki'an Gasan.*"

Musing about a woman who claimed to be over two thousand years old, Margaurethe watched her glide across the sitting room and into the apartment beyond. She couldn't find anything positive at the moment. After Sithathor's introduction, Margaurethe had asked if she should be replaced, but Whiskey had been adamant against the idea.

Her concerns vanished, overcome by a leap of adrenaline as Whiskey entered. The longer they worked together, the more the sight of Whiskey affected her. She had begun having rather erotic dreams of late, always starting with Elisibet and fading into Whiskey at the end. The dreams left her aching, and her first sight of Whiskey every day resulted in heart-pumping embarrassment. Today was no different. Flushed, she looked away to regain some equilibrium.

"Morning."

Margaurethe clutched the folders to her chest, much in the manner of Helen beside her. "Good morning. I've heard that our last guest has arrived. Are you ready?" She forced herself to look at Whiskey, appraising her clothing, easily seeing Sithathor's influence.

Whiskey shifted uncomfortably on her feet. She wore jeans instead of baggy cargo pants or leathers, and a cream dress shirt. Her chambermaid had not been able to part her from her boots, though to do Sithathor credit the burgundy leather had been polished to a high sheen.

"You look wonderful."

Blushing, Whiskey tugged at the cuff of her shirt. "Thanks. Sithathor insisted."

Margaurethe smiled, setting aside her displeasure at the newcomer's ability to shape the future of the Sanguire race. "It's probably for the best. While we're not officially discussing the treaty, we should make the attempt at making a good first impression."

Whiskey grunted, running her hands down the unfamiliar denim on her thighs. "Let's get on with it then."

Chuckling at her discomfort, Margaurethe noted Sithathor in the doorway behind Whiskey. "We shan't be back for dinner, so there's no need to prepare anything."

Sithathor curtsied. "Of course, *Ki'an Gasan.*"

Whiskey reached the coatrack by the front door, and scooped

up her leather jacket. She glanced over her shoulder at her chambermaid, giving her a look of challenge, and receiving only a smile in return. "You'll still make baklava, right?"

"As promised, *Ninsumgal.*"

Margaurethe watched Whiskey grin, giving her chambermaid a wave as she led them out of her apartment. She spared a single glance for Sithathor, and followed, closing the door behind her.

In the elevator, Helen gave Whiskey the leather binder she carried, explaining it was their treaty offer, as well as a notepad and pen for her to take notes. Whiskey's personal guard met them in the lobby. Helen remained in the elevator, and security escorted Whiskey and Margaurethe to the meeting room.

***

Whiskey's nerves were shot. She had spent most the night worrying about this meeting, and had barely gotten to sleep before Sithathor had awakened her. *Probably just as well. I'm not sure I should have been having that dream.* She did not remember much of it, but her level of arousal had been off the charts when she had opened her eyes. Seeing Margaurethe in the sitting room had reminded her of the prurient nighttime vision, increasing her jitters.

She tugged at the collar of the unfamiliar shirt, damning Sithathor for making her wear it. The jeans felt uncomfortably tight compared to the loose-fitting pants she wore as a matter of course. Grabbing her leather jacket had been more an act of security than anything, its well-known heaviness shielding her from the unknown. Those skateboarding butterflies had come back. As they neared the meeting room door, the bugs increased their antics. Whiskey almost wished she hadn't eaten the piece of toast Sithathor had forced on her for breakfast.

Taking a deep breath, she nodded to the guards flanking the doorway. One opened the door, and stood aside to allow her and Margaurethe inside.

Several people milled about the room. Only one had chosen to sit down, and he looked very old, older than Sithathor. A carved walking stick leaned against the conference table beside him. Nupa had just served him a cup of coffee and a croissant. Whiskey raised an eyebrow at seeing a member of her pack here. It took a moment for her to recall that Nupa was actually Chano's great-grandson. *Of course, he'd be here.* He had been spending quite a bit of time with his grandfather rather than hanging out with her and the others in her apartment.

She visually scanned the rest of the crowd, easily putting names to faces. Margaurethe had done an excellent job of describing them. Alopay scowled in a corner, speaking to the dapper Degan as she glared at Lega across the room. Saghani approached them in sock feet, his sealskin mukluks parked at the door. Nupa's was not the only familiar face. Castillo chatted up a trio of women nearby. The number of bags, and recently discarded jackets indicated that they were the new arrivals. Whiskey frowned. All the other members of the *We Wacipi Wakan* had been here for days. Only Ms. Lega had been absent. *Who did she bring with her?*

Conversation died down as the occupants noticed them. All faces turned toward Whiskey and Margaurethe, and Whiskey swallowed against the abrupt desire to lose her toast. The gentle *snick* of the door closing behind her was overloud to her senses, cutting off her avenue of escape. Most of the Indians studied her with impassive faces, even Nupa, but two of the three women with Castillo held different bearings. A slow smile grew on one, and the other gave an audible gasp.

"Jenna?"

Whiskey stared at the second woman who stepped closer. She threw Margaurethe a panicked glance, automatically taking a step back.

"My God, Jenna, is it you?" The woman stopped, one hand held out in supplication. She looked to be in her thirties, not much older than Margaurethe.

It took a moment for Whiskey to find her voice. She croaked, then cleared her throat. "Yeah, I'm Jenna." Margaurethe's hand on her lower back bolstered her confidence, and she straightened. "But people call me Whiskey."

The woman smiled, taking another slow step closer. "You look just like your mother." She turned her head to look at the others. "Doesn't she?"

The smiling woman nodded. "Not 'just like,' *ina*. I see some of her father in her." She, too, moved closer, impish glee sparkling in her dark eyes.

The first one scoffed, though with humor as if they argued many times without allowing their disagreements to affect their relationship. "You need glasses, *cunski*. She's the spitting image of Nahimana or I'm a goose."

"So we'll be serving goose for dinner?" She laughed at the exasperated look she received. "My apologies, Jenna. It's been so long since we've seen you. We thought you dead with your parents a dozen or more years ago." She glided forward, taking Whiskey's hand. "I am your aunt, Zica. Your mother was my sister." Wrapping her arm around the older woman beside her, she continued, "And this is your grandmother, Wahca."

Whiskey felt faint. The room spun a moment, and she was certain she swayed and stumbled. Her heart pounded in her ears, drowning out exclamations of surprise. When she focused once more on her surroundings, she was seated, a sea of brown faces around her. Alopay's and Degan's expressions were calculating in an acerbic way. The two old men watched impassively, and Nupa remained by Chano's side, appearing concerned. Lega stood close. The other two knelt before Whiskey as Castillo arrived with a glass of water. She drank it without complaint, glad of Margaurethe's hands upon her shoulders.

She stared at the two women. Her memories held more of the Sweet Butcher's than her own, and she had long ago lost the faces of her parents to the vagaries of time. The *Ñíri Kurám* had helped her retrieve a couple of them, but that had been months ago, the visions no longer strong. These women held nothing that reminded her of her mother, try as she might to recollect something. Reaching forward with her mind, she ran into the essence of mulled wine and woodsmoke.

Glancing sharply at Margaurethe, she saw worry. *She's trying to keep me safe. Protecting me.* Whiskey placed one of her hands on Margaurethe's, only now feeling the tension in the tendons and muscle. "It's okay. I'm all right."

Margaurethe's eyes narrowed in silent examination. When Whiskey squeezed her hand, she capitulated, raising her chin in a slight movement that not many would catch without knowing her.

Whiskey again attempted to make contact with Wahca. The feel of sunshine against her skin made her smile. She inhaled the smell of fresh earth, almost seeing the reddish loam in her hands. The aroma of sage and water slipped easily into the bond, and Whiskey realized that Zica had joined the link. The sensations and odors relaxed her, and her heart slowed to a more manageable rhythm. She had been a child when they had last met, unable to feel other Sanguire until she grew up and followed the Strange Path. She had to wonder if perhaps something of an adult's essence could reach their children. How else could she know that these two women were family? *I have a family.*

A dozen years of yearning weighed heavily upon her. She had been an orphan, alone in the world as she battled sexual predators, violent offenders and mental patients released onto the streets on which she had lived. The idyllic childhood she had held close to her heart had all but faded in the reality of keeping herself fed and clothed and alive. She had learned early that love was a fantasy, that the adults who proclaimed to have her best interests at heart were usually too busy or too greedy to bother and had their own agenda. This connection, the sunshine and water and green growing things she felt in her soul, fueled that long desiccated kernel of joy. It burst from its protective cover, a seedling finally allowed to grow and thrive as it strove toward the sunlight.

Time passed, but she was uncertain how long. When she finally became aware of her surroundings again, there were fewer people. Nupa, Castillo and the *We Wacipi Wakan* had left. Wahca and Zica now sat in chairs themselves, though the physical contact between them had not been lost. Their hands were locked together, the evidence of tears on their faces. In a chair nearby Margaurethe quietly drank her tea.

Whiskey sniffled, belatedly realizing she too had been crying. She released Zica's hand, wiping at her tearstained face. After a moment, she found her voice, though it grated rough in her throat. "Where'd everyone go?"

"We decided to reconvene later, maybe tomorrow or the day

after." Margaurethe rose, a smile on her face. "It was thought best to allow you three the chance to reacquaint yourselves." A box of tissues sat on the table, and she pushed it closer to the three women. "Would you like something to drink?"

Availing herself of the chance to blow her nose, Zica held up a hand as she finished the job. "That would be wonderful, thank you. Your tea smells delightful." She handed the box to Wahca, whose stare hadn't left Whiskey's face.

"For both of you?" Margaurethe cocked her head.

Wahca reached out, and cupped Whiskey's face before answering. "Yes. That will be fine."

Whiskey wondered if asking for a stiff drink would be untoward. Deciding it wouldn't make a good impression to get roaring drunk in front of her mother's family, she instead took the time to clean herself up from the emotional maelstrom.

Margaurethe played hostess, and the four women sat at one end of the table with steaming cups of tea and a plate of Whiskey's favorite brownies.

"When Lega came to us, I couldn't believe it." Zica stirred her tea with idle restlessness. "We'd long given up hope that you or your parents were alive."

"What happened to my daughter? Can you tell us?"

Whiskey looked at Wahca. "There was a car accident—a few miles from here, actually. We'd gone to see Multnomah Falls, and when Daddy pulled out onto the highway, a semi truck hit the car."

Tears moistened the older woman's eyes, not quite spilling over.

Zica gasped. "That's horrible! How did you survive?"

There's the million-dollar question. Whiskey shrugged, the creak of leather reminding her she hadn't taken off her jacket. "I don't know. When I went through the *Ñíri Kurám*, I saw it happen again. One minute I was in the car, and the next I was on the street."

"The—" Zica glanced back and forth between Whiskey and Margaurethe.

"*Ñíri Kurám*," Margaurethe supplied. "The Strange Path. It's how the European Sanguire achieve full maturity."

"Ah."

Wahca nodded, taking up Whiskey's hand again. "We use sweats and ceremonies with a shaman for that among our people."

The words piqued Whiskey's curiosity. It hadn't occurred to her that other nations would do things differently, and she felt a stab of chagrin at her naivete. "Can you tell me about your people? And my parents…can you tell me more about them?"

"I would love to, *takoja*." Wahca patted Whiskey's hand. "When your mother was born—"

Whiskey listened carefully to the voice filling her ears, a voice that filled her heart with much more than a dry history of a part of herself.

CHAPTER THIRTY-THREE

The phone rang for the seventh time, dragging him forcibly from slumber. With a groan and a curse, he rolled over and grabbed the irritating thing from his nightstand. "Yeah?" Still not awake, he rubbed sleep from his eyes.

"Report."

It took a moment for his sleep-fogged brain to realize who was on the other end. "Sir?" Squinting at the luminous numbers of his digital alarm clock, he realized it was not quite four in the morning; mid-afternoon at the *sañar*'s office if he had his location right.

"Report! I need to know where we are in the scheme of things before this evening's session." As usual, the voice held an irritable tone as if nothing the world did was ever fast enough to suit him.

"Yes, sir. Sorry, sir." His mind scrambled to make connections. "I've set plans in motion. If all goes well, you'll be free of her by the end of the week." He vaguely wondered what his employer looked like, having never seen him in the flesh. He was probably a scowling, irascible man with floppy jowls, screaming at servants over the slightest provocation.

"This week? So soon?"

"Yes, sir. Unless you'd rather wait?" He muffled a yawn, privately hoping that would be the case. It was a waste to kill her before she'd had a chance to live. A deal was a deal, though; those were the stakes of the job for which he had signed up.

"No. This week will be fine. I'll want a full report as soon as it's finished, understood?"

"Of course, sir."

"Once you've completed your task, it'll be a few weeks before my plan will fully take effect. Your reward will be paid then."

He smiled in the dark, a lion's lazy grin. "Thank you, *Nam Lugal* Lionel. You'll find me quite patient."

"Good." The man disconnected.

He sighed, slumping on the edge of the bed. His mind had already kicked into gear, though his eyes remained grainy and dry. A bone-cracking yawn and stretch later, he decided to get up. He would take a nap in the late morning.

It was going to be a very busy and promising week.

***

Sitting behind his desk, he smiled.

Everything was coming together well. *Ki'an Gasan* Margaurethe would be certain the *Agrun Nam* had had a hand in Elisibet's second assassination. Of course, only one member of the council was involved, but she would be right in any case.

Using Lionel's name had been a stroke of genius. Once the information leaked to the right ears, the leader of the *Agrun Nam* would be punished for his treasonous activities, perhaps even killed, which would leave the ruling council of the European Sanguire leaderless.

He rubbed the arms of his new desk chair lightly, the

contented smile remaining on his lips. It was just a matter of time before he would be in charge of it all.

***

Margaurethe sat in the dark with a group of technicians, listening to a logistics presentation by one of the R&D techs. She found it impossible to follow the LCD display at the front of the room. Her strength wasn't in knowing the specific ins and outs of the technical empire she had created; it was in pushing resources in the correct direction, and seeding and watering the proper people to grow bigger, better. Her mind insisted on running through the last three days since Zica and Wahca had arrived.

She missed Whiskey. Whiskey's newly discovered relatives took up the majority of her free time, making it impossible for Margaurethe to enjoy a moment alone with her. Margaurethe could place no blame. She knew from recent experience what a shock it was to discover somebody one thought had died was actually alive and breathing years after the fact. "Stunned" hardly put a dent in the emotions. She was still recuperating from her own challenge in that arena.

The display changed as the presentation moved on to another topic. Margaurethe made a vain attempt to focus. Instead, she remembered Whiskey in the residential lounge this morning, eating breakfast with her aunt. Something in Whiskey had changed, something fundamental that Margaurethe couldn't pin down. The hard-edged teenager remained—still uncomfortable in social situations, still carrying an aura of uncertainty about her—but she was less tense, not as restive as she had been in the past. Something had released within her.

Margaurethe lightly tapped a pen on her notepad. Many people had assumed that Elisibet's callousness was one of immaturity, that her preadolescent walk along the Strange Path had ingrained that nature too deeply within her psyche. Those people never argued the necessity of her death, but offered their opinions that had she been allowed to grow into adulthood before the *Ñíri Kurám* then things may have been much different. Margaurethe couldn't say. She had been the recipient of grace, mercy and adoration by Elisibet their entire relationship, and had not wanted to see the darker side of the Sweet Butcher. She hadn't wanted to ruin her image of the woman she loved, or force herself to take responsibility for Elisibet's brutal ways. There had been many nights over the last four centuries that Margaurethe had castigated herself for not becoming more involved in the ruling of the realm, for not saving her people from the Sweet Butcher even as she saved Elisibet from herself. Such an outcome was never going to happen again.

The screen flickered, bringing her back to the present long enough to see that it would be a while before the presentation was finished.

Whiskey's new demeanor could only be explained by the presence of Zica and Wahca. It occurred to Margaurethe that this was probably the first time that Whiskey had felt like she belonged anywhere. Until now, she'd had no family, no true friends, no home. Elisibet had been an orphan, also. Despite Whiskey being Elisibet reborn, the role of *Ninsumgal* was not something to which Margaurethe's people looked forward with pleasure. Many preferred Whiskey dead for no other reason than a prophecy that half of them wouldn't confess to believing. Now Whiskey had blood relatives, ones who loved and missed her for her, not for what she could do for the Sanguire as a race.

Am I losing her?

A flash of light pulled her from her thoughts. Someone had opened a door. She craned her neck to see one of her personal guards approaching in silence. Others at the table glanced around, though one or two of the technicians remained firmly attentive to the screen.

Her guard leaned down, whispering low into her ear. "We have a situation, a visitor on the front apron."

Margaurethe frowned. "Who is it?"

"*Sublugal Sañar* Valmont."

Fire flashed along Margaurethe's veins. She jumped to her feet. "My apologies, Jimmy, something's come up." Before the man conducting the presentation could speak, she left the room. "Where's Whiskey?"

The guard trotted beside her toward the elevator. "The

executive dining room with her family, and a couple of the Indian ambassadors."

She was happy to see an additional guard in the foyer, holding an elevator for them. Stepping inside, she punched the button for the lobby with some viciousness. "That's too close to the front drive. Increase security there, notify her personal guard."

"They've already been notified, and her captain is taking care of it."

"Good. Has Valmont said anything?"

The doors opened onto the lobby. "Only that he wants to meet with the *Ninsumgal*."

Margaurethe snorted. "Like I'd let him within fifty feet of her."

Her guards wisely did not respond.

She came around the corner, seeing an unfamiliar vehicle parked in front of the revolving doors. Leaning against it, arms casually crossed over his chest, Valmont lounged, looking up at what he could see of the building. The lobby was abuzz with Humans coming and going on their lunch breaks and with a number of security at their posts. She counted at least ten officers outside as she made her way to the main doors. Valmont had picked a fine time to come calling, knowing the number of witnesses precluded her making a scene.

Valmont saw her, pushing away from the car with a smile on his face, and waved as she exited the building. "Margaurethe! How nice to see you again."

"I can't say the same." She planted herself inches away from him, hands on her hips. "Now get back into your car, and leave."

"Whatever for?" Valmont waved magnanimously. "This is a wonderful place you have here. Certainly we can sit down and enjoy a cup of tea together. There's a little coffee place right there." He gestured to the kiosk just inside and to the left of the main doors.

"You're not welcome. Leave before I have you arrested."

He feigned shock. "Arrested? By Humans? Goodness! Whatever shall I do?"

"Would you prefer to meet with me instead, *Sublugal Sañar* Valmont?"

Dorst's musical tones brought a flash of real fear to Valmont's deportment, and Margaurethe smiled. She saw that Dorst had come up the parking ramp from the bowels of the building.

Valmont gave Margaurethe an accusatory look. "Reynhard? I'm surprised to see you here."

The smile on Dorst's gaunt face did nothing to ease Valmont's anxiety. "I don't know why. I've always made it a policy to be wherever my *Gasan* wishes me to be."

Margaurethe's smile widened. Dorst had all but confessed he had sworn fealty which made him much more dangerous. Dorst was no longer just an assassin underfoot; he was one who had promised to protect his mistress to the death. "Good of you to drop by, Valmont. So sorry you must leave this soon."

Valmont looked shrewdly from one to the other. "If I must, I must." Slowly, so as not to upset the multitude of security officers monitoring the scene, he reached into the breast pocket of his long jacket. Pulling out a business card, he held it aloft so all could see it was not a weapon as he stepped around Margaurethe toward Dorst. "Will you give this to Ms. Davis?"

A scowl replacing her smile, Margaurethe moved to intercept.

Chuckling, Valmont snatched it out of her reach, keeping his focus on Dorst. "I'd like your word."

Dorst raised a hairless brow, a sardonic smirk to his lips. "You have my word. I'll see she receives your card."

Margaurethe growled, helpless to do anything but watch the transfer. "Get out."

Valmont backed toward his car, hands up in supplication, a happy grin on his face. Within moments he was in his vehicle, and pulling out into traffic.

Watching until he passed the stoplight and continued on, Margaurethe spun around to take Dorst to task only to find he had already disappeared.

"Damn it!"

In a fine foul mood, she turned and marched inside.

CHAPTER THIRTY-FOUR

Whiskey laughed in delight as Zica regaled her with another story of Nahimana's childhood. She sat at a table in the executive dining room with her aunt, grandmother, Lega and Chano. Nupa would have been there, but Chano had shooed him away, stating he didn't need a nursemaid. On the table before them was the remainder of a good meal, and they loitered over their dessert and coffee.

Wistfulness had been Whiskey's companion for several days. She had spent as much time as possible with Zica and Wahca, listening to tales of her mother's people and childhood, seeing the larger picture develop. It was difficult to overcome her Human sense of time as they discussed centuries as mere decades. She had learned her parents had met in the late 1700s when Gareth Davis had stumbled into a Lakota village in the middle of winter. The idea that her parents had met almost twenty years before the mass pioneer exodus had crossed the continent was unsettling. To this day, no one knew how Gareth had gotten to that village; the only one he had ever told of this experience was Nahimana. He became a frequent visitor over the years, eventually using his English influence to relocate the Sanguire clan before they were consigned to the reservation. The family had settled in North Carolina where Whiskey had been born.

"You'll have to come see the compound." Zica's fork stirred the remains of an apple pie. "We still have all your parents' things."

Whiskey's heart fluttered. To actually have something of her parents!

"What happened to your teddy bear?" Wahca patted Whiskey's forearm. "You carried it with you everywhere as a child. Whatever was its name again?"

"Upsy Downsy." Whiskey smiled, remembering her favorite toy.

"Your grandfather gave you that bear when you were three."

Whiskey's mouth dropped open as she suddenly recalled a craggy older Indian with a graying crewcut. He held out a white bear to her, and she hugged it close. "I remember him!" She grinned.

Conversation continued around the table. During a lull, Whiskey looked about the room. When they had arrived, there had been the standard complement of two guards at the doorway. Four now stood there.

Frowning, she scanned the room, noting the presence of two security in the fire exit stairwell nearby, and another pair in the kitchen beyond. All of them were her personal guard.

Lega leaned forward. "What is it?"

"Something's wrong." Whiskey stood, as did the others. Wahca helped Chano to his feet. Whiskey walked toward the entrance, only to be blocked by her captain.

"I'm sorry, *Ninsumgal*. *Ki'an Gasan* Margaurethe would like you to remain here for the time being."

"What's going on?"

"She's dealing with a security issue."

Whiskey found the news lacking. "Spill it, Anthony. You work for me, not her."

Anthony sighed in resignation. "*Sublugal Sañar* Valmont is here." His eyes slid to his right, toward the windows overlooking the front apron.

She wasted no time getting to the window, her heart beating double time as she sighted Valmont. He and Margaurethe were speaking. He seemed rather flippant compared to her tense stance and the ten alert security officers watching the proceedings.

"You should get away from the window, *Ninsumgal*."

Whiskey ignored Anthony. She was joined by the others with whom she had been having lunch.

"A powerful young man," Chano intoned. "Or a stupid one."

Dorst arrived at the scene below, and Whiskey felt a measure of happiness that Valmont appeared shaken. In the back of her mind, she made note of the fact that that particular secret was out of the bag—the *Agrun Nam* would know Dorst was alive, well, and sworn to her before the day was out. She stifled the urge to rush out to help Margaurethe when Valmont played "keep away" with her with whatever he was holding, a card apparently. Then he had delivered his message, climbed into his car, and started to drive away.

But Valmont looked up at her through the windshield. Whiskey stared back at him, feeling her canines unsheathe in her mouth. He smirked, winked and drove away.

"Who is he?"

The sound of Lega's voice reminded Whiskey to breathe. She inhaled, shaky with adrenaline. "He's the man who killed me."

***

Whiskey was ensconced in one of the lower level meeting rooms. Her family and pack had also been brought downstairs, and the *We Wacipi Wakan* notified of the potential danger.

"I want to see him."

"Impossible." Margaurethe paced. "You have no idea what he's capable of."

"You're kidding, right?" Whiskey scoffed, hands on her hips. "I'm pretty sure I've got a good idea what he can do, Margaurethe. I was there. I've felt it."

Margaurethe stopped, exhaling a breath. "Then let's not give him the opportunity to repeat past performances."

Whiskey threw her hands up into the air, and turned away.

A pair of large round tables had been hastily set up in the otherwise empty meeting room. Zica and Wahca sat at one with Daniel, discussing spiritual versus scientific methods of healing. Alphonse, Nupa and Zebediah played a mean game of Hacky Sack beside the other. Cora stood at the door with one of the Sanguire security officers, flirting.

"He seems rather adamant." Castillo kept his hands clasped before him and remained a safe distance from Margaurethe. "Perhaps allowing him into a controlled environment would—"

"No!" Margaurethe rounded on the priest. "It's not going to happen. He's a snake and a traitor. We cannot allow him entry, or he'll charm his way into someone's good graces, and use them to assassinate her again!" She looked at the others, noting Dorst had slinked into the room at some point. "Don't you understand? He's not to be trusted."

"I'm not saying trust him!" Whiskey spun back toward her advisors. "That was *her* mistake—she assumed her political power and long-term friendship would keep Valmont in line. She was wrong."

Margaurethe swallowed hard, restraining the urge to defend Elisibet.

Whiskey gave her an apologetic nod, but continued. "He's not going to stop trying until he succeeds in at least seeing me. You know he's a stubborn ass."

Snorting, Margaurethe looked away, not wanting to express the sudden tickle of humor running along the razor's edge of her anxiety.

"Invite him over for tea and crumpets?"

Margaurethe raised her eyebrow at Dorst.

"Yeah, exactly." Whiskey frowned. "What did he give you?"

Dorst produced the business card. "I gave him my word to give this to you. It has his current contact information on it."

Margaurethe clenched her fists to keep from snatching it from Dorst's fingers. She watched, helplessness washing over her as Whiskey read the information on it. The impotence stirred up her anger, and she felt a flush rise to her face.

Whiskey tapped the card into her other hand. "I think we should call him."

"Perhaps it would be best." Dorst raised his chin to Margaurethe in silent apology. "My *Gasan* is correct—Valmont is a stubborn ass. He'll not stop until he receives his audience with her."

The worst of it was that they were right. Margaurethe wished she could go back in time, and murder the treasonous bastard in his sleep when he had been young and vulnerable.

"Excuse me."

She turned to see Zica's approach.

"Not that I wish to disturb what is obviously a matter of political security, but who is this man?"

Margaurethe would not speak it, knowing to do so would open up a well of pain that she had fought hard over the centuries to bury. Whiskey turned her back on everyone as she stared at the card. Dorst was disinclined to respond without her express permission.

Castillo finally answered. "*Sublugal Sañar* Valmont was a member of *Ninsumgal* Elisibet Vasilla's court. He assassinated her in 1629."

Zica looked around at them. "You believe he means Whiskey harm because of your prophecy?"

"Yes. He's all but threatened her already."

Whiskey spun about to stare at Margaurethe. "When? Just now?"

"No." Margaurethe felt her shoulders slump. She had kept silent regarding her meetings with Valmont so Whiskey wouldn't worry. It was time to share their conversations. "I've run into him a couple of times while you were away."

"Why didn't you tell me?"

Margaurethe scowled at the look of disappointment and aggravation on Whiskey's face. "You weren't speaking to me, if you recall. You'd left the safety of the house to cavort about the city, regardless of the danger that stalked you." As soon as the words were out of her mouth, she regretted them.

Whiskey's irritation transformed into remorse.

Dorst spoke. "Outside Tribulations and then outside the coffee shop on Hawthorne."

Margaurethe shot him a surprised look, castigating herself for not realizing that the master spy would have known where Valmont was all along. Were they working together? She promptly discarded the thought. Dorst would never allow Whiskey to be harmed in his presence, nor would he set her up to be trapped.

Whiskey straightened, a slow process of inhaling deeply. The rueful look was gone, replaced by something else. "What did he say when he threatened me?"

"He said he wasn't going to allow history to repeat itself."

Dorst politely cleared his throat, and everyone looked at him.

"What?" Whiskey said.

"Not to malign *Ki'an Gasan* Margaurethe's recollection, but I believe he also mentioned something about putting you over his knee if you needed a reminder of your place."

Margaurethe stared at him, thinking back to her discussion with Valmont as they walked in the Hawthorne neighborhood. Her immediate reaction to his threat had blinded her with hatred and resentment; she barely remembered his following words, though she could recall he had said something he thought amusing. She wanted to deny Dorst's report, to argue the point. She had spent several hundred years harboring a grudge of fatal fury toward Valmont; it would be satisfying in the extreme to turn Whiskey against him now, before it was too late. But something stopped her.

Whiskey had been back for almost three weeks. In that time, she and Margaurethe had begun forging a friendship as they both dealt with their losses. She had lost Elisibet. It had occurred to her a few days ago that Whiskey had also lost something— she had apparently lost the Margaurethe she had known in her memories. To lie, to scheme a way to interfere with Whiskey's desires now would destroy the tenuous trust that had developed. As much as Margaurethe wanted to protect Whiskey from Valmont, the price was too high. "He's right. I'd forgotten that bit." Margaurethe lifted her chin to Whiskey. "I was so blinded by anger at the time, I didn't recall."

Whiskey gave a humorous scoffing sound and stepped forward. She put her hand on Margaurethe's shoulder. "I can believe that. Valmont's good at pissing people off."

Zica spoke, summarizing. "So this man may or may not mean Whiskey harm. And he's demanding an audience. Why not give him one? You've certainly got enough security in place to keep him from doing anything stupid."

"He's not to be trusted," Margaurethe repeated.

"As you've said." Zica reached up to scratch the back of her neck, the gesture startling Margaurethe in its familiarity. It was a move Whiskey made often when she was thinking, or preparing to counter someone's statement. "Do you believe this vision, this prophecy your wise woman told you?"

Margaurethe drew herself up. "Of course, I do!" She gestured to Whiskey. "There's the proof right there."

Zica held up her hands, warding off the annoyance. "I ask because Europeans have a different sense of…belief than Indians do. As we see it, the wise woman had a vision, and thus it is true. If it is true, then there is no need to argue it—it exists. Elisibet Vasillas will return and save her people even as she destroys them." She tilted her head, and smiled at Whiskey. "If she is who you claim her to be, it stands to reason that nothing can harm her until she completes her destiny."

"It's not that simple—" Margaurethe began.

"But it is!" Zica interrupted. "To take it one step further, consider our own 'prophecy,' White Crow Woman. She will rise again, and gather all the peoples together as one." She chuckled at Whiskey's surprised look. "Oh, yes, *cinca*. It's not just the Europeans who have heard of you long before your birth."

Castillo cut in before the conversation could deviate further. "What about your myth?"

"Our people have no way to prove or disprove that Whiskey is White Crow Woman. But she is here, a child of ours and of obvious European extraction blended together." Zica moved closer, a fond expression upon her face as she cupped Whiskey's cheek in one hand. "She has gathered around her Americans,

Indians, Europeans and Humans. In our mythos, she unites all the peoples—but it's never specified what 'all' means. If her destiny with us is so similar to yours, then consider the fact that she will not come to harm in ours."

Margaurethe frowned, running her mind through the discussion. "I'm not certain what you're getting at."

Castillo grinned. "By continuing on her path, Whiskey will satisfy both prophecies, without being hurt in the process?"

Zica nodded, dropping her hand to take Whiskey's in her own. "Yes. Exactly."

Her statements held nothing that Margaurethe had not already considered. One of the reasons she had abandoned her first goal of setting Whiskey on the European throne over the *Agrun Nam* was the knowledge that perhaps it was too limiting, that Whiskey's fate had a much larger scope. The Davis Group would be the corporate entity that Whiskey could use to rule a worldwide Sanguire empire. "What has this all got to do with Valmont?"

Zica grinned impishly. "He's harmless to her until she reaches the end of this path. Let him come, let him have audience with her. He'll be quite surprised to realize he's powerless."

CHAPTER THIRTY-FIVE

"You know it's better this way." Whiskey glanced over at Margaurethe as they rode the elevator to the penthouse. For a change they were nearly the same height—Margaurethe had chosen to wear a pair of low-heeled shoes, lowering the two-inch gap between them. Whiskey's boots more than made up the difference. "We'll have more control over the situation."

"Perhaps so, but what will he ask of you?"

Whiskey frowned. "What do you mean?"

The elevator opened, and Margaurethe led Whiskey into the foyer, leaving the two guards inside. Without a glance at Sasha at the desk, she marched into her apartment.

Hastily waving greeting to the on-duty officer, Whiskey

widened her step to keep up. "Come on! What do you mean, what will he ask of me?" She closed the door.

Margaurethe's pace did not falter until she reached the sitting room bar. She poured herself a glass of wine. "Do you want anything?"

Whiskey flopped onto the couch, realizing that this was the first time she had actually seen the inside of Margaurethe's apartment. She looked around at the provincial furniture. "I want an answer." She grinned at the exasperated scoff she heard coming from the bar. "Margaurethe, talk to me."

She didn't speak as she corked the wine bottle. Leaning her hands against the counter, arms spread wide, she pinned Whiskey with a stare. "What if he asks you to forgive him?"

The thought hadn't occurred to Whiskey. "You think he will?" she asked, disbelief in her voice.

"It's possible." Margaurethe collected her glass, and came out to sit beside her.

"It doesn't sound like something he'd do." Whiskey chewed the inside of her lower lip. Begging forgiveness had never been Valmont's style, but she had to admit that Margaurethe had changed from the woman Whiskey saw in *her* memories. It stood to reason that Valmont would do the same. *It has been nearly four hundred years.* "So, what if he does?"

Margaurethe tsked. Setting her glass down, she reached out to pat Whiskey's thigh. "You're in the process of setting up a corporate and political power base. We may no longer be focused on regaining control of the European Sanguire, but ultimately your word will be law with them."

Whiskey nodded, though she still found the entire idea ludicrous.

"If Valmont asks forgiveness, and you give it to him, he can use it as grounds to escape punishment for his past deeds."

"You mean…like a pardon, right? For the assassination?"

Margaurethe squeezed Whiskey's thigh, smiling. "Exactly!"

"You think he should be executed?"

A look of contempt flashed across Margaurethe's face, one that Whiskey found very unattractive. "He should be punished to the full extent of European Sanguire law."

Whiskey raised an eyebrow, recalling that *she* had started the ball rolling by punishing the leader of the *Agrun Nam* to the full extent of their laws. "If he should be punished, why hasn't he already?"

Margaurethe shot her a glance of pure malice.

"Whoa!" She scooped Margaurethe's hand from her leg, holding it in her own. "You think they had something to do with it? With the assassination?"

"Why else has he not seen the inside of a cell, or suffered the anguish of the torturer? Even had they not been involved, the *Agrun Nam* gave complicit support by not binding him by law."

Whiskey had to admit that it made sense. If *she* could attack the head of the *Agrun Nam* with impunity, they would gladly back the man who had killed her regardless of the reason. "If he asks forgiveness, and I give it to him, you think he'll never pay for his crime within his own government, right?"

"Yes. With you overseeing all Sanguire governments, your power of pardon will supersede their convictions." Margaurethe placed her free hand atop their clasped ones. "Do you see?"

Oh, yeah. I can see. Margaurethe's hatred of Valmont had twisted her, changing her from the woman that *she* had first met. And no doubt *her* influence hadn't helped over the decades and centuries, tarnishing a good heart with the constant brutality of violence. "I do, but it doesn't change anything. I want to meet him."

Margaurethe released her, pulling away from her touch. Picking up the glass of wine, she stalked back to the bar. "I'll make the arrangements. Will there be anything else?"

Whiskey sighed, almost wishing that the Margaurethe of *her* memories still existed. That one had been malleable to some degree, at least. Just when she thought she and Margaurethe were connecting, their differing points of view made once stable ground shift and crumble under her feet. "No, I think that's it."

"Well, I've work to do, a meeting to attend." Margaurethe poured most of her wine down the drain. "I'll see you at dinner."

Effectively dismissed, Whiskey agreed, and let herself out.

Once back in her own apartment, she stepped out onto the balcony. It was raining, though more of a mist than actual raindrops, and she leaned against the banister to stare out over the southeastern side of the city.

Tomorrow was Rufus's gallery opening, and she had yet to invite anyone. She had planned on inviting Margaurethe today. Valmont had put paid to that particular plan; she would never get Margaurethe to agree to an outing without a dozen security guards going along for the ride. Whiskey didn't want Rufus's opening to turn into a scene. Besides, Valmont knew her location—all he would have to do is follow the convoy of Town Cars to the gallery to find her.

There were a lot of ways for a single person to get out of the building.

***

"What do you mean she's not here?" Margaurethe demanded. The words echoed in her ears, reminding her of her first attempt at meeting Whiskey upon her arrival in Portland months ago.

Sithathor curtsied over her clasped hands, tilting her head to one side and baring her neck. "She left two hours ago, *Ki'an Gasan*, saying something about getting a bite to eat."

Margaurethe frowned. "She's not in the residential lounge, and security tell me she's here."

"But..." Alarm crossed Sithathor's face. "She's not here. You're more than welcome to look." She stepped aside, waving Margaurethe inside.

It didn't take long to see that the chambermaid spoke the truth. Nothing was disturbed, no evidence of a struggle visible. Margaurethe was at a loss. Her guards would hardly make such a glaring mistake on their own.

Striding past Sithathor, Margaurethe went to the security desk in the hall. "Get Reynhard, round up Whiskey's pack and family. I want a floor by floor search conducted immediately. The *Ninsumgal* is missing."

Sasha blanched, mouth open for a fraction of a second before she hit an alarm, and picked up the phone.

***

Whiskey peered at the building across the street, verifying the address from the invitation in her hand. She scanned the area for other Sanguire, finding none. As she watched, a handsome couple dressed entirely in black paused before a thick metal door, offering something to the insolent man leaning against the brick wall. Finding their credentials acceptable, he slid over and opened the door for them. Whiskey caught a glimpse of reddish light from inside before they disappeared, and the bouncer returned to his previous stance.

A tremor of excitement washed over her. She was here with no pack members, no security guards, no one else but her. *I haven't been truly alone since Seattle.* The thought brought a sense of giddiness to her. She forced the skateboarding butterflies back into their cage, and trotted across the street. Soon she glided past the surly doorman. She walked a long corridor of bare white walls, red overhead lights reflecting off the glossy black tile floor. Conventional lights ahead shone through a doorway to the left, giving off an ethereal glow. Deep bass thrummed as mood music played, mixing with the sounds of several conversations.

Whiskey entered the gallery proper at the head of a set of stairs wrapping along the wall. Below her, the room opened up into a large pit of the same black floors and white walls with the addition of industrial scaffolding suspended from the high ceiling. Lights spotlighted the displays. At least fifty Humans slowly meandered between paintings and sculptures, coming together in small groups and breaking apart in movement more akin to a lazy river than humanity. A buffet stood at the base of the stairs, and she saw a handful of servers in bowties passing through the crowd with trays of drinks and hors d'oeuvres.

She strolled down the stairs, attempting to appear aloof and disinterested though exhilaration raced through her. She could almost forget who she was, who she was destined to become. No one here knew, no one here cared. She was one of the faceless masses, here to attend a simple gallery opening without all the politics and power clouding negatively about her. Several people surreptitiously glanced in her direction, appraising the new arrival, and she dropped her chin. Coming here had been a great idea, even if she hadn't been able to bring Margaurethe. At the base of the stairs, a young man offered her a card. Whiskey peered at it with a whistle. *He certainly cleans up well.* The Rufus looking back at her from the likeness on the card had tamed his hair back into a ponytail. His beard was neatly trimmed and a Victorian cravat protected his throat. She slipped the card into a pocket.

Wandering the gallery, she studied the paintings. She liked his work, had from the time she had first been to his studio. Somber in feeling, each piece suggested a deep horrific difference from the norm. She stared at one—a gorgeous woman leaning against a wall, her arms stretched above her head, metal cables sprouting from her body and attaching themselves to a nearby machine.

"Whiskey!"

Turning, she grinned. "Rufus. Congratulations! This is wonderful."

He nodded, pleased. He had given up his paint-smattered khakis for black trousers, a white billowy shirt and a deep purple velvet vest. "I'm glad you came. I really hoped you would."

"You couldn't have kept me away."

Rufus gave her the once over, and nodded in appreciation. "Nice clothes. I might have to look through your closet before we do the official portrait."

She had taken his words to heart regarding the Gothic following, and had donned leather pants and jacket for the occasion. "Not a problem."

"How about tonight?" He leaned slightly forward in anticipation.

"Well, I don't know—"

"Ah, the artist." A man interrupted them, reaching forward to shake Rufus's hand. "I must say your work is positively funereal."

Rufus blinked, the coaxing smile on his face fading. His Adam's apple bobbed twice before he took his hand. "Thank you."

Whiskey raised an eyebrow, wondering what was up. She shook her head at his strangeness. She'd be pretty stressed out, too—all these people here to judge his talent couldn't be fun. The newcomer made a few comments and drifted away. "So, has it been a profitable night for you?"

"Um." He regained his balance. "Actually, it hasn't been too bad. I've already sold a couple of pieces. If I'm lucky enough, I'll sell a couple more before the evening's through."

"Where's the one you did of me? I haven't found it yet."

"It's right over here." He led her past a handful of frames.

"Wicked," was her first reaction. In the portrait, the dragon tattoo snaking up Whiskey's arm sprang from the skin of her forearm, twining about her, arcing up over her shoulder to glare at the viewer. "It turned out nice, Rufus."

He smiled. "Thank you. As I said, it's one of the better ones I've done. I hadn't contracted for it to be shown here, and had to get an amendment to have it be part of the exhibit." He nibbled his lower lip, staring at the painting. "So, no Margaurethe? No Cora?"

"No." Whiskey chuckled, glancing at him. "Old news, dude. Cora and I broke up a few days before I moved into the penthouse." She looked away. "Margaurethe was…busy."

He rubbed his beard, looking very much like Castillo at that moment. "How'd I miss that?"

She shrugged. "Dipped if I know." Something niggled at the back of her mind, a tingling sensation. She felt someone watching her.

"Clueless am I, I guess."

Whiskey's smile faded. "Why do you ask?" The feeling grew, distracting her from Rufus's protestations of innocent small talk. She turned away, scanning the crowd. Nothing out of the ordinary was in her vicinity, but her alarm bells slowly gained ascendance as the seconds ticked past. Stepping back from the painting, which was hung on one of many half walls sprinkled throughout the large gallery, Whiskey visually followed the stairs upward. Her heart sputtered to a near stop as she saw Valmont leering at her from the entry.

They stared at one another for long moments before he gave her an idle peace sign, and started down the steps.

Whiskey grabbed Rufus's arm. "Is there a back way out of here?"

"What?" He glanced around in confusion. "Why?"

"Is there or not?"

"Yes, I think so. I believe there's a fire exit over there."

"Call Margaurethe! Tell her I'm here!" Whiskey released him, and walked quickly in the direction he had indicated.

She slipped among the gallery patrons, easily making her way to the other side of the large room as she tried to put as many people between her and Valmont as possible. She hoped Rufus would deliver her message, and that Margaurethe would understand her sudden disappearance. At the far wall she glanced over her shoulder. She gritted her teeth in a flash of annoyance as she spotted Rufus following, determination on his face. Several feet behind him, Valmont lazily wandered in her direction. People parted at his advance and hardly noticed his presence, just as they did with her. He nodded at her as he approached, the amused smile still on his handsome face.

Whiskey didn't know which was worse, her recognition, or the sudden need to rip his throat out with her bare hands. Shaking at the adrenaline pumping through her, she turned back to the wall, looking past the artwork.

There. A doorway.

She ignored Rufus, and slipped into the gallery's back room. She paused to examine the wide storage area full of crates and canvases. Hurriedly, she moved to the center of the room, scanning the walls for exits, feeling an internal clock ticking her life away. An open door revealed a bathroom, and she growled, moving further into the room. Behind her, she heard the door open and close, knowing it was Rufus. She paid his approach little consideration as she paced the room. A rickety elevator stood on the right with a door beside it, a dimly lit exit sign above. Escape almost within reach, Whiskey's heart thumped double time, and she broke into a trot.

Whiskey reached the door, and pushed on it. Locked. Before she could voice a curse, a hand grabbed her shoulder and spun her around. "Rufus! Damn it, let me go!"

He pinned her shoulder against the doorjamb, brandishing a wooden stake in his other hand. His face was a mask of determination and reluctance. "I'm sorry, Whiskey. But this has to be done."

"What the...?" Whiskey struggled against his hold. "What the fuck are you doing?"

"I'm killing you before you can make a mess of things." His face pale, sweat beaded on his forehead, he adjusted his grip on the weapon. "It's nothing personal. Just a job. Once it's done, I'll be rewarded with immortality."

Before she could argue or fight her way out of his grasp, she heard the door to the gallery open once more. Valmont sauntered in, his sardonic aura fading as he took in their stances. Rufus was oblivious to the new presence, and Whiskey grabbed the arm holding her, twisting it to one side. He brought the stake down, hard, and she flinched away from the expected pain.

Nothing happened.

Whiskey stumbled as she was released, half crouched and leaning against the door. She glanced up to see Valmont holding Rufus's armed wrist, his other hand clapped over the artist's mouth. There came a loud *crack* as the wrist broke, and Rufus's muffled scream raised the hair on her neck. Staring in horror, she met Valmont's glare.

"Get out."

Needing no second urging, Whiskey whirled, and burst through the fire exit door.

CHAPTER THIRTY-SIX

Senses on full alert, Margaurethe walked through the gallery, searching for Rufus. She hadn't stretched out her mind, not wanting to tip Valmont off that she knew he was here. To one side, she caught a glimpse of Dorst bypassing a knot of art patrons. It eased her mind to know he was along. Soon Whiskey's personal guard would be in place, and they could find and remove her from danger. It had been quite fortuitous that Dorst had known Valmont's location—as soon as Margaurethe had heard it was Rufus's gallery opening, she knew that Whiskey had left the safety of The Davis Group to attend.

Margaurethe circled the large room, passing an office where two Humans negotiated the sale of a painting. Further on stood two more doors, one a public restroom for the guests. She paused, listening. She heard grunts of pain and a hissing sound from the other. On full alert, she slipped into a storeroom, careful to close the door behind her. The storeroom smelled of oil paint, dust and blood, the latter a thick, cloying odor that caused her teeth to extend.

"You really are a stubborn sort, aren't you?"

Recognizing the voice, Margaurethe didn't bother to hide her approach, bursting into the center of the room.

Valmont held a very large and very limp rag doll in one hand. The black suit shredded, Rufus's once white shirt was now a crimson tatter. His eyes rolled in a bloody face, pleading silently with Margaurethe as Valmont gently raked a knife tip across the artist's already lacerated belly.

She breathed a sigh of relief that it was Rufus and not Whiskey in Valmont's clutches. "What are you doing?" she demanded. "Where's Whiskey?"

"Ah, Margaurethe," Valmont said by way of greeting, his pleasant tone belying the viciousness of the scene. "Whiskey's gone for a walk while Van Helsing and I had a discussion. Did you know he had a wooden stake?"

Much as she wanted to immediately search for Whiskey, Valmont's words stopped her. She focused on Rufus. "A wooden stake?" She stepped closer. "Aren't you two working together?"

"Like I'd work with a deluded Human like this one," Valmont snorted. "I mean, honestly, a stake through the heart? How do Humans come up with these things?" He shook his head. "I stopped him before he could use it on her, and told her to leave." He gently shook Rufus, ignoring the whimper of pain as the man kept an obviously broken wrist clamped about his bleeding belly.

Margaurethe carefully scanned Rufus, noting Valmont's neat work. The deep slice along his abdomen revealed a mass of entrails. Only the pressure of the organs against the cut and Rufus's attempt to keep them contained had stopped him from bleeding to death before now. Despite her dislike of the man, she had to give Valmont credit. "As usual, a very nice job."

"I learned from the best."

Wrinkling her nose, she flashed on a memory of a similar

torture scene with Elisibet giving her young friend a lesson in proper technique. It was one of the few Margaurethe had ever attended before finding excuses to be elsewhere while they enjoyed what they had termed their "entertainment." "Yes, you did."

"Unfortunately, he seems to be very reticent on the subjects of why and who. I'm not certain I have the time or tools to get a proper confession from him. It was all a rather unexpected surprise."

The door opened, closed, and Dorst slid into the room. "Oh! I must say, is this party open for anyone?"

For a wonder, Valmont didn't become defensive, or attempt to flee. "No, it's not. Lock the door behind you."

Dorst paused, gauging the situation. When Margaurethe didn't argue the point, he proceeded to do as told. "Rather flimsy. A Human with a coat hanger should be able to pop it in a thrice."

Valmont smirked at his victim. "I doubt we'll be here that much longer, will we?"

Margaurethe looked around the room, finding the wooden stake near an ancient elevator door. She retrieved it and returned, holding it up to Rufus's view. He knew Whiskey as a mythical vampire. He had pestered the pack multiple times in Margaurethe's presence to be given the "final kiss." There was no reason he would turn on Whiskey now unless someone else had played upon his desire for immortality. Someone had filled him to the brim with all sorts of promises about living forever. Valmont would never have resorted to such fiction to gain assistance from Rufus. It wasn't his style.

She handed the weapon to Dorst, who tittered behind his hand in response. Returning to Valmont's side, she stared into Rufus's eyes, pouring all of her intensity into the gaze. "You know what we are, you know I can help you."

Valmont sniggered, realizing her ploy, but Rufus was hooked. He swallowed and nodded, face pale beneath smears of blood.

Margaurethe mirrored his nod. "Tell us who gave you your information on Whiskey. I'll grant you the final kiss."

Rufus glanced from her to Valmont, uncertain.

"Surely you must know that she's older than he," Dorst played along. "Valmont is her minion."

"I used him to force Whiskey back to my side." Margaurethe was not sure if she wanted to giggle or slap Rufus for believing this tripe. "You'll live forever, Mr. Barrett. Or you'll die now."

It didn't take long for Rufus to make a decision. Opening his mouth, he took several tries before the word finally came out. "Lionel."

"Most interesting." Dorst crossed an arm over his chest, and stroked his chin in thought.

Margaurethe blinked in surprise, pulling back. Beside her, Valmont cursed, and his prisoner whimpered in sudden pain as he was shaken.

"Barrett, is it?" Valmont's face was grim. "There's something you should know, Barrett. You were doomed to die the moment you accepted Lionel's offer."

Rufus struggled weakly against his grip, looking at Margaurethe for confirmation.

She shook her head. "I'm sorry, Mr. Barrett. The Sanguire who hired you lied. We have no ability to confer immortality on Humans. It's a myth."

Despair filled Rufus's countenance for a single moment before Valmont's knife found his heart.

Margaurethe turned away, barely hearing the corpse hit the floor.

"Well, that was entertaining," Dorst said after a moment. "Waste of artistic talent, though. Did you notice the painting of my *Gasan*? Exquisite!"

"We need to leave before his disappearance is discovered." Margaurethe turned to watch Valmont clean his knife on a patch of Rufus's pants that had escaped soaking. "This is his showing."

"What a pity." Valmont rose, the knife disappearing into the folds of his long jacket. "I noted some of the work. He was good."

Dorst liberated a wooden chair from behind an old metal desk, and jammed it under the doorknob to delay any entrance from the gallery proper. "That should hold them for a bit."

Margaurethe looked around the room. "Which way did she go?"

"The fire exit. Next to the elevator there." Valmont remained in place.

"Let's go." Margaurethe pushed at the metal bar, but the door remained closed. "What? Is it locked?" She applied more force, unable to make it budge. She turned to give Valmont a suspicious look, pleased to see he was equally confused. "Are you sure she went this way?"

"That's the only other exit." He pointed at the corpse on the floor. "He had her pinned against the frame when I came in."

Dorst came to check the door. "Most odd. Most odd." As Margaurethe got out of his way, he examined it closely, applying his force along one place, then another. "Perhaps she's *Dilída Ru'oníñ á Sudše*, and blindly locked it when she left."

Valmont frowned, coming closer. "You don't know what her talent is, yet? She should have manifested it by now."

Margaurethe fought the urge to hit Dorst for revealing a weakness. Instead, she turned, hands on her hips, and glared at Valmont. "Well we know that you're one, so unlock the damned door."

He acted pleased at her vexation. Coming forward, he placed his hand on the lock, closed his eyes and concentrated. The gentle *snick* of a bolt being drawn announced his success. Opening his eyes, Valmont pushed open the door, revealing concrete steps leading to street level.

Margaurethe led the way, with Dorst on her heels. "Can you lock it behind us? Give them a right puzzle to deal with."

Valmont gave her a sardonic bow, and proceeded to do so.

They had barely made it to the street when several Sanguire emerged out of the darkness. There was little time to talk as the group left the immediate area on foot.

Once at a safe distance, Valmont interrupted the silent march. "Did you give her my card?"

Dorst acted shocked, one long-fingered hand patting his chest over his heart. "But, of course, I did, *Sublugal Sañar*! Do you doubt my word after going through such trouble to get it?"

Valmont rolled his eyes. "I thought the role of the fop would have gotten old by now, Reynhard."

"It will never get that old, Valmont." Dorst's smile was all teeth.

Margaurethe interrupted their camaraderie. "How did you get here?"

"I followed Whiskey from your building. I've an auto parked just over there." He pointed toward a parking structure. "I have to say, I was surprised to see her on the streets alone after the discussions you and I have had."

Margaurethe ground her teeth. Now was not the time to argue with him. They needed to get away before Rufus was discovered, and find Whiskey before anyone else did. "We must locate Whiskey. You must go away and leave her alone."

"Well, that's hardly sporting." Valmont crossed his arms over his chest, showing confidence despite being surrounded by a half-dozen Sanguire sworn to Margaurethe. "I did just save her life. Don't I get some type of reward for my selfless act?"

Growling, Margaurethe almost told him what she would reward him with, and that it was quite similar to what Rufus Barrett had received. But Dorst answered for her.

"I believe your reward will be an audience with Whiskey." Dorst peered at Valmont. "That is what you most wanted, is it not?"

Valmont dropped his arms, his arrogance slipping slightly. "It is."

Dorst bowed. "She has expressed an interest in meeting with you. I expect she'll be even more intrigued now that you've rescued her from the clutches of certain death."

Margaurethe gave an explosive sigh. "Just go, Valmont. I'll call you and arrange an appointment." When he did not move, she put both hands on her hips. "I swear it."

Valmont studied her. He accepted her word despite her stance, and bowed ludicrously low as he backed away. "As you wish, dear lady. I am your faithful minion; my life has little joy but to obey your every whim."

A flicker of the old friendship between them flared in Margaurethe's heart. A ghost of a smile crossed her face at his teasing and she shook her head. It was with some difficulty that she forced the humor away. Valmont had killed Elisibet. She had no guarantee he wouldn't do the same with Whiskey, regardless of Zica's opinion.

Face once more stern, she turned and marched away, knowing he was already gone.

CHAPTER THIRTY-SEVEN

Blocks later, Whiskey slowed to a stop, bending at the waist and leaning her hands against her thighs as she panted. A stitch in her side throbbed intensely at the unaccustomed exertion, and her lungs felt on fire. As she caught her breath, her stormy thoughts coalesced beyond her initial panic.

Rufus tried to kill me!

It boggled her mind that she—the tough and untrusting street kid—could be suckered in so well that it endangered her life. She always knew when someone lied to her, and she had checked Rufus out on a number of occasions throughout their association. Each time, he had passed with flying colors, including his reason for inviting her to the gallery opening in the first place. *But you didn't check him tonight.*

Whiskey, breathing more evenly, began to walk. She kept her attention on her surroundings, realizing she had run down to Tom McCall Waterfront Park. Traffic on nearby Naito Parkway whizzed by, life continued on, no one the wiser to the twists and turns of her rapidly degrading world.

It made no sense. She had been alone with Rufus multiple times, especially when she had run from Valmont at the rave. Why hadn't he attempted to hurt her when she'd spent the night in his loft? What had changed? And Valmont coming to the rescue? Talk about bizarre. She pushed thoughts of her savior away. She needed to understand Rufus's actions first.

Rufus had always thought she was a vampire, and her pack hadn't done anything to dissuade him from his opinion. It had been a running joke with them about the gullibility of Humans who wanted so desperately to believe that vampires existed. Rufus had been the most eccentric of the lot in that regard, always hinting or asking to be made immortal. Even his friends thought him a little odd when he broached the subject.

Collapsing on a wet park bench, Whiskey stared at the dark river flowing past. The damp didn't penetrate her leather pants, but the cold did. She trembled more from the shock of recent revelations than the chill of late winter on the night air, hugging herself close as she watched the reflections of the eastern city lights ripple and dance upon the black surface of the water.

"It's nothing personal. Just a job." Someone had hired Rufus to kill her, and had fed him false information on her pack in order to entice him. But who? Valmont and the *Agrun Nam* topped the list, but she couldn't imagine Valmont hiring a Human to do his dirty work. He had done more than enough with *her* over the years; he was quite capable of doing the deed himself. Whiskey shivered as she remembered the sound of Rufus's wrist breaking, both morbidly interested in and terrified by her speculation on his fate. Forcing herself away from the subject, she logically ticked off what she knew.

Valmont would not have hired a Human. Despite her initial responses of anger and fear when confronted by him, he didn't seem to return those feelings toward her. The *Agrun Nam* was fully capable of ordering her assassination if they wanted it, but the current *Nam Lugal*, Lionel Bentoncourt, didn't seem the type. He had been on the council when *she* was in power, and had been level-headed and merciful. No, if anyone on the *Agrun Nam* was involved, it would be the Judiciary of the High Court, *Aga Maskim Sañar* Bertrada Nijmege. She had good reason.

Flash.

Nahib the Traitor's body had been strewn about the *Agrun Nam* public chambers in bloody strips. Witnesses, courtesans, and the remainder of the *Agrun Nam* stood in the gallery, all who required a reminder of who held power here. Their eyes wide and fearful, she reveled in their horror. This was as it should be.

Searching the room, she found one person who did not share the terror. Bertrada Nijmege's hawk-like face flushed with fury and anguish, her lip curled into a sneer, revealing murder in her heart. With a smile, Elisibet held the glower of Nahib's lover, pausing long enough to lick his blood from her fingers. Her only dismay was Valmont's absence. She had asked him to be here. Where was he?

Flash.

"Oh, yeah. More than enough reason." Whiskey looked up at the cloudy sky, city lights giving the overhead canopy a yellowish glow. Margaurethe would have been told of her absence by now, and be worried sick. Whiskey felt a hollowness in her chest, the same sensation she got when she had done something stupid. No matter how many times she told herself she would do the right thing and act like an adult, she inevitably followed the path of childishness instead. *You'd think I'd learn sometime.*

The emptiness grew within her, making her want to squirm and go to ground, find a place to hide until she could convince herself that skipping out on all the people who cared for her had been the right thing to do. Instead she sighed, forcing herself to her feet. Home was less than a mile away. She could be there in ten or fifteen minutes. Zipping up her jacket, she huddled beneath the encroaching rain.

***

A trilling broke her concentration. With a frown, she set her pencil down, and reached for the phone. "Yes?"

"It's me."

Bertrada Nijmege's muddy eyes narrowed in suspicion. "Why are you calling? What's happened?" Her caller remained silent. "Tell me!"

"There's been an attempt on her life."

"What?" Bertrada sat taller in her office chair. "Who? Why?"

"I think the why is evident, Bertrada. News of Elisibet's reappearance is no longer quite as secret as you'd hoped."

She drummed her fingers on the desktop, forcing herself not to dig in and scar the rich oak surface. "Do you know who was involved?"

"The assassin gave the name of Lionel before his death."

Bertrada froze, her body becoming rigid at the news. "Lionel?" Automatically, she glanced around her office, relieved she had not received this call in front of witnesses. "You can't be serious."

"I only know what the assassin said. I can't prove one way or the other whether it was true."

The thought of Lionel hiring a killer independent of the *Agrun Nam* was laughable. "Well, your assassin was wrong. I've worked with Lionel for centuries. He'd never do something as underhanded as this."

"I thought not. But you should know what I've discovered. Someone on the *Agrun Nam* may be trying to murder our little friend before we've had time to play. While the goal is the same in either case, one is less…entertaining than the other."

Bertrada, face sour, slumped back in her chair. She had hoped to keep the lid on Elisibet's return, but far too many people were already involved. It appeared someone had leaked the information. "I'll see what I can do here. In the meantime, I want her returned here as soon as you can get close. Is that understood?"

"Yes, Bertrada, though that might be a little difficult. She's on the run at the moment."

Her voice became as sharp as her visage. "How did you lose her?"

"To gain her trust I had to let her go while I dealt with the Human assassin. I've been unable to locate her, and Margaurethe's people are crawling everywhere."

"Find her, Valmont, else you'd do well not to return."

"Yes, Bertrada."

Was there a hint of sarcasm there? Valmont had become quite mordant over the decades. Half the time Bertrada couldn't tell if he was serious or not. She picked up her pencil and gently tapped the eraser on the pad of paper upon which she had been writing. "You cannot let Margaurethe interfere, Valmont. Our goal is almost realized."

"Trust me, Bertrada. When have I ever let Margaurethe interfere in something as gratifying as this?"

Despite her rancor, she chuckled. "Point taken. Do you have any more information for me?"

"No. I'm off in search of errant tyrants."

"I meant what I said. If you don't find her, don't return."

"I hear and obey, *Aga Maskim Sañar*."

The sarcasm in his voice was more evident, and brought up a swell of irritation. That he disconnected before her only made it stronger. *Whatever did Nahib see in him all those years ago?*

Bertrada stared into the shadows clouding the office. She had waited hundreds of years for the opportunity to avenge her lover's death. The *Agrun Nam*'s insistence that Valmont kill Elisibet had stolen that opportunity from her. When Mahar the *ensi'umma* pronounced a vision of the Sweet Butcher's return, Bertrada had actually felt a measure of relief; she would once again have her chance. She just needed to stay alive long enough to see the possibility arise anew.

She had talked to Nahib the night before his speech, begging him not to speak out against Elisibet. Surprisingly, Valmont had joined her in her attempt to thwart a good man from suicide. Neither had prevailed and Nahib had sat with the *Agrum Nam* and publicly denounced Elisibet's more recent horrors. Elisibet had taken offense and responded with overpowering and lethal force. It unfolded in Bertrada's mind, the torture, the screams. No one could stop Elisibet, not even the members of the *Agrun Nam*. Bertrada watched her lover's lingering death, unable to defend him as guards held her back. Valmont had disappeared, obviously knowing he could do nothing, refusing to be witness to his mentor's demise.

Elisibet watched as Nahib was drawn and quartered. When all was finished, she stopped at a piece of what had once been a man and ran her fingers through the blood. Standing, she licked the digits clean, staring at Bertrada with a smile. Two days later, Bertrada was assigned to Nahib's job as Judicar, and Lionel Bentoncourt given leadership of the *Agrun Nam*.

Snap!

Bertrada jumped at the sound, finding the pencil she held in two pieces. She carefully put them down, and pushed her chair away from the desk. *Control, I must keep myself in control until my revenge is complete.*

Standing, she switched the desk lamp off, moving easily in the shadows to the door. Tonight she'd go to her rooms and meditate, calm herself. Then she would sleep, her dreams filled with the bloody screams of Elisibet as she personally skinned her alive.

CHAPTER THIRTY-EIGHT

Margaurethe snapped up her cell phone when it rang. "Yes?"

"She's back, *Ki'an Gasan*. She just walked in the front door."

Breathing a shaky sigh of relief, Margaurethe lowered her head, fighting the tears.

"*Ki'an Gasan?*"

She lifted her head. "Get her to the penthouse immediately. Call off the search. I'll be there soon." She tapped on the window that divided her from Phineas. When it dropped, she said, "Let's go home. She's been found."

"Oi, that eases the heart, doesn't it, cuz?"

She could find no words, and couldn't dredge up the typical annoyance at his familiarity. Instead, she used the controls to put the smoky glass divider back up, separating herself from him, and her pain from public consumption.

Margaurethe considered her options. She entertained visions of throttling Whiskey, or spanking her in an attempt to impart upon the errant youngling that her actions had serious repercussions. Whiskey was so stubborn, willful, opinionated and irrational that Margaurethe could not imagine her surviving beyond her twentieth birthday. Had Elisibet been like this as a child? She had heard stories at court that had certainly indicated such. Coupled with the frustration was the desire to kiss Whiskey senseless, to remind her that people cared for her—not just who she could be, or what she could do for them in the future, but cared for *her*, for Whiskey the street kid. She wanted to hold Whiskey close, let her know through gentle touch and intimacy that she, Margaurethe, cared deeply.

***

A thump. A crash. The blood smell faded with distance, and then grew stronger. She sprinted for the ornate door that marked Elisbet's personal audience chamber, cursing that it was closed. The sounds of a fight echoed and reverberated from behind the heavy wood, creating sharp pain in her ears and head. It seemed hours before she finally reached the door, and burst into the room to confront her worst nightmare.

Valmont weaved on his feet, the black devil still holding his weapon. His back to the door, he didn't see her arrival. He towered over Elisibet's prone, crawling form, sword raised in two hands.

"Get away from her!" Her headlong motion, so slow for so long, abruptly sped up. She crashed into him as he turned. They fell to the ground with a crash, his sword skittering away on the marble.

With the immediate threat stopped, she wasted no time on the enemy. She scrambled to her lover to see the vast amount of blood smearing the floor as Elisibet crept away from her attacker. It is too much! It is everywhere! *She reached Elisbet, turned her over, calmed her, cradled her. Tears stung her.* I cannot stop this. What can I do?

Behind her, Valmont spoke. "What is done is done."

She leaned protectively over her lover, turning to hiss and bare her teeth at him. He wiped the blood from his blade, and sheathed it. For a long moment, he stared at Elisibet, revulsion and longing on his face. He spun around.

As he strode away, she turned back to Elisbet. "Stay with me, m'cara! We will get you to a healer and soon you will be fine." It was a lie. They both knew it, though she still tried to convince herself of its truth.

Ice blue eyes regarded her, and Elisibet had enough strength left to laugh. "Nay, Margaurethe. It is beyond that, and we both know it." It was hard for her to speak, her breath coming in gasps. She coughed, tried to hang on for just a little while longer.

"No! You cannot die, Elisibet." I cannot live without you! *How could she fix this? Where was the healer? Why did no one follow her as she ran past them? Certainly someone had to have witnessed her indecorous gallop through the palace corridors.*

"Apparently so, minn'ast. Will you forgive me?"

She focused on Elisibet. "There is nothing to forgive." Not to me.

"It's cold, Margaurethe. Hold me."

She gathered Elisibet into her arms, hugging her close. The panting slowed, paused, tortured and rattling as Elisibet struggled to breathe. A lethal quietness followed. The hand holding Margaurethe's arm relaxed, and fell away. The body lightly twitched in her grasp until it came to its mortal rest. The silence did not last long, soon broken by a keening, escorting her Elisibet, her heart, her life beyond the veil separating this life from the next.

The world went dark as she realized the lamenting wail came from her.

***

Margaurethe shook her head, dispelling the memory that continued to cling to her soul. It occurred to her that perhaps there was a reason it still held her in its powerful sway. As she had told her dying lover, there had been nothing to forgive in being attacked and murdered in her drawing room. But Margaurethe had never really forgiven Elisibet for leaving her, irrational as that sounded. Elisibet had held no control over her death, yet Margaurethe still blamed her for the desertion.

Maybe it was time to really forgive.

She glanced outside the car, seeing the familiar buildings that indicated they were closing in on The Davis Group. Soon she would be inside, riding the elevator to the sixteenth floor, knocking on Whiskey's door, perhaps truly seeing her for the first time.

***

As the penthouse door opened, Margaurethe stood on the precipice, still not certain which way her seesawing emotions would fall. Whiskey stared at her, ashen-faced, a hint of a cringe in her features. Margaurethe's urge to slap Whiskey washed away in a wave of emotion that she didn't yet want to examine. She kept her hands clasped, more to hide their trembling than the original reason—to keep from assaulting the hesitant youngling before her. "May I come in?"

Whiskey didn't speak. She swallowed, nodded and stepped back, allowing Margaurethe inside.

Looking around the penthouse sitting room, Margaurethe realized they were alone. "Where's Sithathor?"

"I sent her away for the night." Whiskey closed the door.

Margaurethe nodded. She turned to study Whiskey. "Are you all right?"

The aristocratic bearing cracked a little. "Yeah, I'm okay." Whiskey searched the room as if looking for words. "You weren't here when I got back. Sasha said you went out looking for me."

"Yes, I was." Margaurethe slipped past her, going to the bar. She needed something to wet her suddenly dry mouth. "Reynhard has had Valmont under constant surveillance. We followed him to you. We arrived only a few minutes after you left."

Whiskey ran a hand through her hair, watching Margaurethe pour two glasses of juice. "Did you...see what happened to Rufus?"

Margaurethe raised an eyebrow, capped the pitcher, and returned it to the small refrigerator under the counter. "I did. It wasn't pretty."

Chewing her upper lip, Whiskey nodded, then turned away. She slid open a glass door, and stepped onto the balcony.

Margaurethe trailed behind her, pausing to lean against the doorframe. A gentle breeze off the Willamette blew through Whiskey's hair as she stared over the river. The gods were both cruel and kind, allowing her to see this mirror image of her long dead lover, pensive in thought.

Whiskey turned from the view, brow furrowed. "He's dead, isn't he?"

Margaurethe pushed away from the doorframe, holding out a glass. "Yes."

"Thank you." Whiskey took the glass, and stared into it. "Valmont?"

"Took care of things." Leaning her elbows upon the balcony railing, Margaurethe let the quiet grow between them. Sometimes silence was as necessary to a conversation as speech itself.

"He tried to kill me."

"I know." Margaurethe regarded the youngling beside her. "He said that Lionel put him up to it, promising to give him immortality for your death."

A flash of confusion crossed Whiskey's profile. It whisked away as she nodded, not looking up. "We shouldn't have teased him. I should have told him the truth about us. He wouldn't have fallen for such a stupid trap."

Margaurethe studied her. "It's not your fault, you know. You didn't force him to make his choices. Some Humans can be noble."

"Only some?" Whiskey finally looked up from her glass, a faint smile curling the corners of her lips. The expression did nothing to hide the underlying pain and betrayal.

"Only some," Margaurethe echoed.

Whiskey sighed and turned away, the smile fading as she took in the view. "It's beautiful up here."

Margaurethe smiled at the non sequitur. "Yes, it is. It reminds me of…better times." A memory flashed through her, of Elisibet's balcony overlooking the garden, feeling her lover's arms wrap around her from behind as they listened to musicians playing in the dark. She closed her eyes, almost smelling the roses growing there in the past.

"Me, too."

The low voice drifted across Margaurethe's memories, drawing her back to the present. She opened her eyes to glance at Whiskey, noting a trace of longing on her face. It struck a chord within her for she had seen a similar look upon Elisibet's countenance many times as the *Ninsumgal* pined for what she could not seem to have—the love and adoration of her people. Margaurethe knew that the similarity ended there. Whatever Elisibet's desires had been, they were not echoed within Whiskey. The more Margaurethe got to know Whiskey, the more she saw that Whiskey's and Elisibet's desires, ethics and morals were diametrically opposed to one another. Whiskey was the embodiment of the Elisibet that Margaurethe had always dreamed existed.

Whiskey spoke softly, barely loud enough to be heard. "Thank you. For caring, for going out to find me."

Margaurethe smiled. "That's what friends are for."

Turning away from the river, Whiskey studied Margaurethe with somber intensity. The smell of roses grew stronger, mixing with a hint of blood and water as Whiskey reached out to cradle Margaurethe's essence. This was not the tentative touch that Whiskey had evoked between them before; this was a solid connection, one that tightly bound them together though they stood physically apart, an intimate bonding of their souls.

Margaurethe bathed languorously in the sensation, her distant youth lapping at the currents surrounding them, starved for what had been denied her for centuries. The older, more experienced part of her forcibly reminded her of Whiskey's identity, that despite the familiar feelings this was not the lover of the past. It was odd, this agitated surface that was Whiskey hiding the slow murky depths of what was Elisibet. Margaurethe couldn't decide whether to laugh in joy at the rediscovery of her lover, or weep anew at her loss. With reluctance, she lessened the mental contact, easing away from the whirlwind of Whiskey's soul. She held their connection lightly, staring at her.

"Is that what we are? Friends?"

A thrill of anticipation caused Margaurethe's heart to flutter. Her emotions were too raw from the connection between them for her to heed common sense. "Perhaps…more."

Whiskey closed the slight distance between them and cupped Margaurethe's face, concerned. "You did forgive her, yes?"

A tightly held sob escaped Margaurethe's lips. Her recent revelations on the return trip hadn't had time to scab over, leaving her emotions too tender. "I thought I had."

Whiskey's thumb caressed her cheek. "I'm so sorry, Margaurethe. The last thing I've ever wanted to do was to hurt you, and that's all I seem to be able do. Can you forgive me, too?"

Margaurethe held Whiskey's hand to her, tears filling her eyes. "Of course, *m' cara*. I forgive you. Truly, I do." She gasped, horrified as Whiskey began to cry.

If any prior comportment or opinion had made the difference between Elisibet and Whiskey more glaringly evident, Margaurethe hadn't seen it. Elisibet had never shown such emotion in her presence no matter how fraught things had become. Margaurethe had come to the conclusion early in their relationship that she simply needed more than Elisibet did, and proceeded to subconsciously protect herself from the strength of that need. Yet here was Whiskey, who needed just as much as she, who willingly showed weakness, willingly trusted those close to her despite an emotionally crippling childhood.

Margaurethe gathered Whiskey into her arms, glasses of juice forgotten as she cradled Whiskey's essence within hers. *I think I love you.*

CHAPTER THIRTY-NINE

Margaurethe scowled at Valmont across the conference table. They and Castillo waited for Whiskey. She had requested that all her advisors join her for Valmont's "audience."

The night had passed uneventfully. This morning, the local newspaper splashed a lurid photo of Rufus Barrett on the front page. His grisly murder on the eve of his dawning popularity in the art world had sparked the journalist's imagination. Being discovered in a locked room enhanced the mystery of his death. Local television had picked up the story, dissecting his childhood and talent. After a few calls, Margaurethe saw the inclusion of a police officer's televised statement that drugs may have been involved. *Saginna* Bescoe had assured her that Whiskey's presence at the gallery would be "overlooked" by investigators. She had then set her security team on digging up dirt on Bescoe to ensure the connection between Whiskey and Rufus would remain swept under the political carpet.

Attempting to make small talk, Valmont leaned across his coffee and spoke to Castillo. "I'm surprised there aren't a dozen guards in here."

Castillo opened his mouth to speak, but was interrupted by Margaurethe.

"It was a thought, to be sure."

Valmont grinned, not looking at her.

Castillo cleared his throat uncertainly. "I think Whiskey doesn't want them. She doesn't believe you're a threat."

"Hardly sounds like Elisibet, does it?" Valmont pursed his lips in thought. "She was ever the paranoid."

"She's not Elisibet. How many times do I have to tell you that?"

He turned to look at Margaurethe. "As you've made it clear, my dear *Ki'an Gasan*, I'm not to come close to her without you as chaperone. I certainly don't have the depth of your experience in this matter." He smiled brightly. "Of course, I'll defer to your infinite wisdom."

She snorted, not finding his behavior as charming as he might have hoped.

Unable to goad her, Valmont took another tack. "Considering Elisibet's nature, three quarters of our people will want to kill Whiskey. It would be best to have her in a place where she can be well protected. Have you considered taking her to Europe? There are still a number of spectacularly well-defended buildings there."

"That's not necessary. She's in a place of safety now, regardless of recent events." Margaurethe lowered her chin as she glared at him. "And three quarters of our people don't know she's returned. Beyond this company, only the *Agrun Nam* and their trusted aides are privy." She paused. "Only the *Agrun Nam* and their trusted aides are sending assassins."

Valmont laughed. "Lionel Bentoncourt? I realize you haven't been to court in centuries, Margaurethe, but he hasn't changed quite that much. He hasn't a bloodthirsty bone in his body. He used *kizarusi* for feeding long before they came into style."

"Bertrada," Margaurethe murmured.

He shook his head as he looked away. "Doubtful."

She rounded on him. "In case you've forgotten, she had as much reason to see Elisibet dead as you. No doubt she was behind the *Agrun Nam's* push to remove Elisibet in the first place." From her peripheral vision, she saw Castillo's mouth drop open as he watched them bicker like old women.

Valmont ignored their spectator. "Perhaps so; small wonder that, eh? But if Bertrada was still harboring a desire for blood, she'd want to do it herself, don't you think? She's quite the vindictive bitch when she wants to be, as I'm sure you've noticed."

"You were working on orders from the *Agrun Nam*?"

Everyone turned toward the door where Whiskey stood with Dorst. She remained focused on Valmont and no one else.

Slipping into his devil-may-care persona, Valmont stood and approached. He smirked as he bent a knee to her. "*Ninsumgal*, we've not been properly introduced. I am *Sublugal Sañar* Valmont, at your service." He stepped forward, reaching out a hand.

"Don't touch me." Whiskey made no move to avoid him, but her voice held the hard edge of control.

Valmont froze where he was, dropping his hand and blinking owlishly. He flushed at Dorst's chortle.

"You haven't answered my question."

Margaurethe smiled, fears easing as the aura of command crackled around Whiskey. She almost saw the connection Whiskey forced upon Valmont, the pair of them locked together by her will alone. Castillo still sat mouth agape, ogling both of them.

Margaurethe rose, circling around to stand beside Whiskey. As much as she wanted to interfere, to throw in with her abilities, she knew that this was a task for Whiskey alone. Valmont would never respect her if she didn't tame him in her own way. Regardless of the outcome, she would find Margaurethe at her side to support her. A rustle of leather told her that Dorst had taken up position on Whiskey's left.

Several minutes passed before Valmont's shoulders sagged

but straightened, standing confident. "Yes. The *Agrun Nam* ordered me to kill you, kill Elisibet. And I was proud to be the one selected."

"Are you proud now?"

The question perplexed him. He frowned. "What?"

"Why did you stop Rufus from killing me at the gallery?"

Valmont's face cleared. "Because I'm not here to kill you, Whiskey. You're not Elisibet."

"Really?" Whiskey cocked her head, studying him. "What was it you said when you were first presented to Elisibet at court? A willingness to follow her to the ends of the earth and beyond?" She chuckled. "I've been beyond, but you didn't follow."

Margaurethe felt a smile grow upon her face.

Valmont was taken aback, unable to do more than work his mouth as he tried to respond. "Elisibet…?" he finally asked, voice thin.

"No. Elisibet is dead by your sword. I remember the wound, the chill of death coming over her, Margaurethe holding me as I bled to death." Whiskey's hand found Margaurethe's though her view remained fixed upon Valmont. "You said it had to be done. Do you still believe that?"

Valmont swallowed, a recalcitrant child, skin blushing. "Yes, I do. I'll never change my mind on that."

"You were always one to stand by your convictions, stupid as they may have been."

Margaurethe felt a lessening of the tense atmosphere in the room, though remained worried. Whiskey's mixing of viewpoints in her speech disconcerted her.

Whiskey deflated, though not from weakness. It looked like she had simply relinquished control over her prey. "Do you believe it needs to be done now?"

Again, Valmont drew himself up. He met Whiskey's hostility without flinching. "No. You seem to have Elisibet's memories, but you're not her. You would already have ripped my throat out if you were."

Whiskey released Margaurethe's hand and moved closer, circling Valmont, who stood motionless. "Don't think it didn't occur to me," she said in a voice so low it barely registered. "You piss me off by your mere existence. You betrayed your sworn ruler and best friend." She stopped before him. "The second I think you're holding back or are a danger to me and mine, I'll gut you quicker than anything."

Margaurethe's eyebrows rose at the threat. The conviction with which Whiskey spoke was strong, an aching reminder of Elisibet ringing in her voice.

Glaring at Valmont, Whiskey still bristled.

Several minutes passed before Valmont hesitantly raised his chin in supplication, accepting Whiskey's superiority. "You have nothing to fear from me. I'll not harm you again."

Whiskey kept her stance a shade longer. "Maybe not, but trusting you isn't an option, is it?" She stood down, turning her back on Valmont as if daring him to try anything. Taking Margaurethe's hand, she kissed the knuckles.

Margaurethe smiled, feeling the caress of roses, and squeezed Whiskey's fingers.

"Sorry, everybody. That probably wasn't fun to watch." Whiskey led Margaurethe to her seat at the head of the table, taking the time to chivalrously seat her.

A rueful smile grew on Castillo's face. "On the contrary. I'm quite glad to have been here."

Valmont's countenance soured. He snorted, throwing himself into a chair.

Dorst idly leaned his hip on the edge of the conference table. "Book fodder?"

"It'll be a best seller." Castillo grinned widely as he looked at Whiskey. "I'll be most happy to write your memoirs when you're ready."

Whiskey groaned.

Margaurethe watched multiple emotions cross Valmont's face as Whiskey ran a hand through her hair in adolescent exasperation. Some expressions she recognized from long association with him, distant though those years were—surprise, preoccupation, and calculation. Others she had not seen before, having no way of identifying them. On another person, she would have described them as fear and worry. She felt a warm wave of pleasure at the idea.

"Now that we've met, Valmont, what do you want?"

He seemed startled to be called upon. "Excuse me?"

Whiskey leaned forward on the table, arms crossed. "What do you want? What are you after?" She raised a hand, half shrugging. "You've been tailing me for months now, hired a private investigator to catch me, and overpowered two of my people." Her hand dropped to the table. "Speaking of which, you owe Father Castillo and Zebediah an apology."

Margaurethe smirked, biting her lip to keep from laughing aloud.

Valmont sat up straight in his chair to glare at Whiskey, not seeing the humor. "Apology? For what? I didn't even hurt them!"

"Much." Dorst smiled. He received a sharp look from Valmont, and chuckled in response.

"Since Father Castillo is here now, you can apologize to him. I'll have Zebediah come down later." Whiskey raised an eyebrow, staring at Valmont.

Long seconds ticked past. Valmont's jaw twitched and moved as he ground his teeth. He finally turned to glare at Castillo. "My utmost apologies, sir, for attacking you without warning. Next time I'll issue a challenge so that we may duel." His head swiveled back to Whiskey. "Will that do?"

She studied him, then looked at Castillo. "What do you say, Padre? Will that do for you, or do you want something a little more appropriate?"

Castillo looked like he wanted to be anywhere else. "It's fine, Whiskey. Thank you, *Sublugal Sañar* Valmont. No harm done."

Whiskey snorted, but did not counter his statement. "That still doesn't answer my question, Valmont."

Margaurethe watched him squirm, almost wanting to fidget in sympathy. Whiskey had no experience with courtly ways, and her boardroom manner resembled a bulldozer. *She'll need extended lessons with Reynhard and myself, studying court intrigue.*

"I was sent by the *Agrun Nam* to find out if you are who you claimed to be. I couldn't very well do that from a distance."

"Are you sworn to the *Agrun Nam*?"

"What?" Valmont blinked. "No."

Warning bells went off in Margaurethe's head, pulling her

from her thoughts. She lightly touched Whiskey's mind, and was just as gently rebuffed. The alarms grew louder as she tensed in apprehension.

"You were sworn to Elisibet specifically, were you not?"

Margaurethe's scrutiny flickered around the table. It was the first time Whiskey had uttered her predecessor's name in her presence. Dorst stared at Whiskey, his intent focus indicating he noted the same. Castillo was too happy to be ignored to realize the difference.

"Yes. But you know that." Valmont placed his hands upon the table, aggressive as he leaned sharply forward. "What's that got to do with anything?"

Whiskey cocked her head. "Who are you sworn to these days, Valmont? Anyone? Did your honor-bound oath die with your honor when you killed your best friend?"

Valmont shot to his feet, face ugly. "What do you know about honor, you *unu narra?*" He thumped his chest. "I had honor before you lured me to my disgrace!"

Margaurethe sat poised, prepared to defend Whiskey from physical assault. Valmont panted, fists at his side, fangs bared in fury. Dorst had not moved, but Margaurethe had no doubt he was ready should the need arise; his proximity to Valmont meant he would reach his target before her. A whisper cut through the boiling madness.

"I'm not Elisibet."

Valmont stared.

Whiskey stood. "I'm Jenna Davis. I was born eighteen and a half years ago in North Carolina. My mother is full Lakota Sioux, my father is American. Six months ago, I didn't even know the Sanguire existed."

Margaurethe scrambled to her feet as Whiskey passed behind her chair toward Valmont. She wanted to stand in front of her, but held herself back. Noting movement to one side, she realized that Castillo had risen this time, coming around the table on the other side.

Valmont looked confused.

"Honor isn't a one-time thing. You can have it, lose it then, but still regain it at some point."

Swallowing, Valmont retracted his teeth as he glanced at the others surrounding him.

Whiskey smiled. "I think you were in a pretty tough spot. You'd sworn allegiance to Elisibet, but she'd changed over the years. She forced you to choose between your word and what was right."

"What of it?"

"Your honor is your own. You've always had it. You chose to take vengeance for the death of a man who was a father to you, knowing your actions might sentence you to a horrible fate. You decided that it was better in the long run for the twisted person Elisibet had become to be put to rest before the remainder of your people were destroyed."

Tears stung Margaurethe's eyes. She no longer guarded against Valmont, too caught up in Whiskey's words. It had been so easy to vilify Valmont. Even centuries afterward, she would be overcome with violent urges at the mere mention of his name.

"I forgive you."

Valmont's jaw dropped to his chest as he stared at Whiskey.

Margaurethe felt a loosening in her chest. The dread that Whiskey would do just this thing broke as the words spilled from Whiskey's mouth. Along with the expected resignation, Margaurethe felt a little forgiveness for him as well. She knew what Elisibet had been like, and had done nothing to stop her atrocities. Only Valmont had been pushed to the limit, and taken matters into his own hands. Perhaps the members of the *Agrun Nam* had put him into such a position, but it no longer mattered. Elisibet had been just as responsible for her own assassination as Valmont. The epiphany took Margaurethe's breath away.

"If you have no other oaths binding you, I want you to swear fealty to me."

Valmont made an attempt at closing his mouth, resembling a fish drowning on dry land before he succeeded. "You...want what?"

Whiskey raised an eyebrow. "Your oath, your *zi lugal*." She waved at the others gathered around them. "Everyone else has sworn fealty already. It's time you did the same. I can't have you as an advisor otherwise."

Margaurethe gasped. Before she could speak, she felt Whiskey's essence caress hers. It took effort, but Margaurethe gave a slight raise of her chin in concession.

"You'd have me as your advisor?" Valmont stood dumbfounded, one hand to his chest. "After what I did?"

"You did what was necessary." Whiskey acknowledged his discomfort with a faint smile. "Yeah, this is weird, huh? But if anyone knows what *she* was like, it's me. God knows what else she would have done if she'd remained alive much longer."

The sudden switch back into a youngling made the meeting surreal. Margaurethe had spent the last twenty minutes doing nothing but trying to catch up, and still wasn't certain she had made it to the finish line. She was disheartened to see that only young Castillo shared her befuddlement. Dorst grinned from ear to ear. Margaurethe's annoyance faded to wonder as Valmont slowly sank to his knees.

"I, Valmont Strauss, *Sublugal Sañar* of the European Sanguire, recognize *Ninsumgal* Jenna Davis as my liege and ruler. My dagger, my blood, my heart are yours, my *Gasan*, to do with as you will."

CHAPTER FORTY

Margaurethe stayed on the front apron long enough to bid Valmont farewell. His dazed expression would have been humorous but for the knowledge that she shared it. She paused to give a few words of instruction to one of the guards before going inside. Dorst had already disappeared to his basement lair, Castillo had returned to his apartment upstairs, and Whiskey had rejoined her pack on the lower levels.

At odds with herself, not sure what to do, Margaurethe rode the escalator down. The level of industry on this floor had increased dramatically from normal day-to-day operations. It was movie night, and the events division had provided plenty of things to keep them occupied. People, predominantly Humans, bustled to and fro with stacks of chairs, tables and assorted audiovisual equipment. She followed a group of black-clad technicians into the ballroom.

A giant screen had been erected at one end of the huge room. A scissor lift raised a pair of men to hang the projection unit from the ceiling. Others strung cables from a multitude of speakers, snaking them to a table at the back of the room. Alphonse and Zebediah were there, trying not to make nuisances of themselves as they watched the professionals hook up the sound board and video controls.

Others from the set-up department of the events division placed rows of chairs in theater style before the screen. Though the ballroom could seat two thousand, there weren't that many employees included; perhaps six hundred would actually show up. Margaurethe had acquired several newly released movies, and the viewings were scheduled to go on until the wee hours of the morning. The banquet staff set up buffet tables at the back of the room. The wonderful aromas coming from the kitchen indicated her chef was quite pleased with the accommodations for his culinary inventions.

Margaurethe scanned the area with her mind, finding the telltale smell of roses and blood coming from the service aisle. Curious, she walked across the ballroom, barely dodging an energetic young man with a stack of chairs. She ignored his abject apologies as she opened the exit doors, and stepped through.

"Hey! Lend a hand?"

She spun around to see Whiskey juggling an armful of drinks and a small ice bin. Rushing forward, she liberated the bin before it fell. "What are you doing?" She glanced up and down the aisle, seeing any number of employees preparing for the festivities. Stepping to one side, she set the bin on a counter, and helped Whiskey unload.

"Getting the crew something to drink." Whiskey blew out a breath as the last of her burden was laid to rest. "They've been working all afternoon for this. I thought they'd like a quick break."

Margaurethe smiled. Unable to help herself, she ran her fingers through Whiskey's hair, brushing back the disheveled locks. "You could have used one of those." She cocked her head to one side, indicating a banquet server hustling by with a wheeled cart full of silverware.

Whiskey blushed. "Yeah, I know." She shrugged, looking so much like a teenager that Margaurethe found it difficult not to laugh. "But I didn't want to get in anybody's way."

"Come on." Margaurethe lightly tugged on Whiskey's earlobe before releasing her. "Let's get ice into this thing. What have you found for them to eat?"

They left the soft drinks on the counter. With both holding one side of the ice bin, they managed to fill it with ice. Working in tandem on such a mundane chore, Margaurethe relished the easy laughter and camaraderie between them. It had never felt this way with Elisibet, and the longer Margaurethe compared the two women, the more she felt she had known only half a person before.

The crew was happy to be given a break. That it came from the president and CEO of the company made it quite the treat. Margaurethe admired that Whiskey knew exactly how to present herself to gain loyalty. Her easygoing manner and readiness to do the plebeian chores worked so much better than the fear Elisibet had utilized.

Now sitting in the first row with Whiskey, Margaurethe nibbled a pretzel.

"Did I do the right thing?"

She looked up at Whiskey's question. "What do you mean?"

"I know you didn't want me forgiving Valmont." Whiskey found the inside of her potato chip bag enthralling. "Do you think I made a mistake?"

"I think I had a valid fear at the time." Margaurethe considered a moment. "But with the *Agrun Nam* responsible for setting Valmont on his path, then forgiveness hardly matters. He wouldn't be punished for his deed whether you did it or not."

Whiskey nodded. "That's what I thought too."

"But swearing him in as your advisor?" Margaurethe shook her head, clicking her tongue. "I haven't decided if that was a stroke of genius or..." She trailed off.

"Or stupidity?"

Margaurethe grinned. "I didn't say that."

"No, but you thought it." Whiskey chuckled. "I didn't know what I was doing, really. It just seemed to be the thing to do at the time."

"Seat of the pants politics?"

"Yeah, something like that."

Shaking her head, Margaurethe laughed. "I don't know if the world is quite ready for you, Jenna Davis."

"Probably not."

Margaurethe took Whiskey's hand in hers. "Then we'll make it so."

***

Valmont stared out the window of his hotel as the sky darkened on the horizon.

He had stayed at The Davis Group until Whiskey had dismissed him less than an hour ago. Their all-day discussion had ranged from what she could expect during the next meeting with the *We Wacipi Wakan* to a more complete picture of the *Agrun Nam* and the politics involved. For most of it, he had remained silent.

When the hell did he lose control of the conversation? How had she known what he had said to Elisibet when he was first presented at court? She spoke with unnerving familiarity about Lionel, Aiden and Ernst Rosenberg, and her face showed actual distress when discussing Bertrada. Perhaps Castillo or Margaurethe had coached her, given her the necessary information to confuse him. Nothing else made sense.

But to what end?

Margaurethe wanted his blood, had craved for it since the moment of Elisibet's death. Mind games were not her forte, though. Those amusements had never appealed to her as they had he and Elisibet. His mouth twitched into an unconscious grin as he recalled several times he and his liege had put their heads together to baffle the sycophants at court. Margaurethe had always walked away from their fun, a disapproving mother unable to pound sense into her bumpkin offsprings' heads.

And, honestly…priest? The neuter was no doubt in hog heaven, new advisor to the *Ninsumgal*. Not a bad day's work for a youngling. *How old is he?* Only three or four hundred, if Valmont guessed correctly. It had been over three hundred eighty years since Elisibet had died. The priest possibly hadn't even been born. Certainly, Whiskey would be drawn to him, just as Elisibet had been drawn to the younger Sanguire during her reign. Valmont was not yet a hundred when she had taken him in, and Margaurethe barely Turned when she had been presented at court. Elisibet had always surrounded herself with younglings, craving the youth she had been denied.

Castillo would soon learn the meaning of "truth" when it came to politics. The concept rarely existed outside the lofty ideals of the scholar. Rather it remained in the gritty shadows, pulled out as evidence to support one's view and stuffed back into its hole afterward. Elisibet had taught Valmont long ago how easily truth could be manipulated. His eyes glittered with memory.

Whoever hired Rufus Barrett, however; that was a stroke of genius. Blame the assassination on the *Nam Lugal* and watch the Euro government tumble. Nothing like a power vacuum to create a new regime. Valmont wanted to know who it was simply so he could offer congratulations before he or she died. And die that person would, for Bertrada would never allow someone else to supplant her desire for revenge, so deep was her thirst for Elisibet's blood.

Perusing his knowledge of the *Agrun Nam*, Valmont scowled. He never would have thought any of them had the imagination to pull off a takeover. Discrediting Lionel would leave the way open for Aiden, but that one was so sympathetic—even during trials—it was a wonder any defendant received a guilty verdict. Besides, he had had centuries to throw off the *Nam Lugal* and attain his goals. Why wait until now?

Ernst was Lionel's man, through and through, had been from the beginning. Bertrada—Valmont knew her well. She had no designs on leading the Sanguire; her only goal was to have a hand in Elisibet's death after being denied so long ago. He recalled she had slipped and mentioned a co-conspirator. He frowned at the recollection.

That only left Samuel McCall, the newest member. Valmont knew little about him. Lionel had assigned McCall a couple of hundred years ago. Even younger than Castillo, McCall had no experience with regard to Elisibet. While ambition might have been a deciding factor in his placement, the youngling had a long way to go before he had enough of a power base to remove all those preceding him.

Valmont's mind returned to the day's meeting as he worried his lower lip. For a brief moment, he could have sworn he faced Elisibet herself. Even extensive instructions couldn't have given her Elisibet's mental flavor or strength when she took control of him. But it wasn't her exactly. There was a difference in the connection, as if Elisibet and Whiskey had been blended together in some fashion.

Whether that was good or bad remained debatable.

Valmont had assumed Mahar's prophecy was a sham to scare the Euro Sanguire into behaving with no monarch backing the *Agrun Nam*. It had afforded a respite from a potential war of succession. Bertrada had been incensed, wanting her shot as revenge for her lover's death. With nothing to lose, Valmont had agreed to help should the prophecy come to fruition. He wouldn't lose sleep over the possibility. Whoever appeared in the unlucky position would be no different than the thousands of innocents he had tortured and murdered at Elisibet's side. Nothing new.

But Whiskey *was* Elisibet. He felt her. That complicated matters.

Not knowing what to tell Bertrada, Valmont watched as the sun edged closer to the horizon.

Glossary

Aga Maskim Sañar - Judiciary of the High Court of the *Agrun Nam*; currently held by Bertrada Nijmege.

aga ninna - fearsome crown, ["the crown" and "fearsome lady"].

Agrun Nam - council ["inner sanctuary" and "fate, lot, responsibility"]; the ruling body of the European Sanguire.

Baruñal - midwife to the *Ñíri Kurám* process.

cinca - Lakota; child.

cunksi - Lakota; daughter, girl.

Dilída Ru'oníñ á Sudŝe - telekinetic, a talent, able to move objects with the mind.

ensi'umma, ensi'ummai - oracle, oracles.

gasan - lady, mistress, queen.

Gidimam Kissane Lá - ghost walker, a talent, able to move through solid objects.

Gúnnumu Bargún - shape shifter, a talent, able to change appearance.

Im Rigu Libi - family line, genetic clan.

ina - Lakota; mother.

Ki'an Gasan – beloved lady mistress, ["beloved" and "lady, mistress, queen"]; title of Margaurethe O'Toole.

kizarus, kizarusi - vessel ["large vessel" and "to tap" and "blood"], vessels; the Human chattal that feed the Sanguire.

lamma - female spirit of good fortune.

lúkal - dear one

m'cara - beloved (Gaelic derivative); an affectation of Marguarthe O'Toole for Elisibet Vasilla.

Maskim Sañar - Judiciary of the Low Court of the *Agrun*.

minn'ast - beloved (Indo-European derivative); an affectation of Elisibet Vasilla for Margaurethe O'Toole.

ñalga súp - nitwit

Nam Lugal - chief counselor of the *Agrun Nam*.

Ninsumgal - lady of all, sovereign, dragon, monster of composite power; official title of Elisibet Vasilla.

Ñíri Kurám - the change, the turning, ["path" and "strange"and "to take/to traverse"]; the final step a youngling Sanguire takes to adulthood. It occurs naturally over decades, or can be hastened via chants and trances.

puru um - idiot, hillbilly.

Rúmun Unkin - tribe or clan, based on talents. One is always a member of a family line, but only the talent indicates which *Rúmun Unkin* they belong to. Fraternal organization.

Saggina - local magistrate of the European Sanguire; a political office that answers to the nearest embassy.

sañar/sanari - councilor of the *Agrun Nam*.

san kurra - a foreign slave ["slave" + "foreign land" + genitive].

Sañur Gasum - eunuch assassin ["eunuch" and "i will" and "to slaughter"]; Reynhard Dorst's title.

Sublugal Sañar - military equivalent of the *Nam Lugal*, military leader; Valmont's title.

takoja - Lakota; grandchild.

Tăl dile Imramun Tu - storm singer, a talent, able to control weather.

Tăl Izisíg - trembling fire, a talent, able to start and control fire.

u-nu-nar-ra - fraud [pronominal prefix + "not" + "established"+ nominative].

We Wacipi Wakan - Lakota, ["blood" and "dancing" and "sacred"]; the leading council of the American Indian Sanguire.

zi lugal - oath ["breath"; "soul" + "king"].